DELINQUENT

ACADEMY OF MISFITS BOOK ONE

BEA PAIGE

CONTENTS

BLURB

I'm the kid your parents warned you about...

Eighteen months in prison or doing time at Oceanside
Academy.

Reform school has met its match in me, even if it is full of
young offenders. Thieves, graffiti writers, drug runners and
other petty criminals reside within the walls, and I'm just like
them.

But what they didn't tell me was that I'd be one of only a
handful of girls in a horde full of boys. It'll take more than just
street smarts to keep my wits about me.

Everyone here has a chip on their shoulders, and I'm no
different. Mine's one of the biggest, that's why they call me
Asia because mine is as large as a continent.

Rules or not, these bad boys are about to discover that I've earned my label for reason...

I'm the biggest misfit of them all.

Delinquent is book one of this new gritty, contemporary reverse harem academy trilogy and deals with adult themes and subjects you may find upsetting

BEA PAIGE'S BOOKS

Academy of Misfits (Academy reverse harem romance)

#1 Delinquent https://books2read.com/AcademyMisfits1

#2 Rejecthttps://books2read.com/AcademyMisfits2

Finding Their Muse (dark contemporary romance / reverse harem)

#1 Stepshttps://books2read.com/Steps

#2 Strokeshttps://books2read.com/Strokes

#3 Stringshttps://books2read.com/StringsFTM

#4 Symphonyhttps://books2read.com/FTM4

The Brothers Freed Series (contemporary romance / reverse harem)

#1 Avalanche of Desire https://books2read.com/AvalancheOfDesire

#2 Storm of Seduction https://books2read.com/StormSeduction

#3 Dawn of Love https://books2read.com/DawnOfLove

#4 Brothers Freed boxset https://books2read.com/BrothersFreed

The Sisters of Hex series (paranormal romance / reverse harem)

Prequel to The Sisters of Hex series:

Five Gold Rings: https://books2read.com/FiveGoldRings

Sisters of Hex: Accacia

Out Now:

#1 Accacia's Curse https://books2read.com/AccaciasCurse

#2 Accacia's Blood https://books2read.com/AccaciasBlood

#3 Accacia's Bite https://books2read.com/AccaciasBite

Sisters of Hex: Fern

Out Now:

#1 Fern's Decision https://books2read.com/FernsDecision

#2 Fern's Wings https://books2read.com/FernsWings

#3 Fern's Flight https://books2read.com/FernsFlight

The Infernal Descent trilogy (co-written with Skye MacKinnon)

Out Now:

#1 Hell's Callinghttps://books2read.com/HellsCalling

#2 Hell's Weepinghttps://books2read.com/HellsWeeping

#3 Hell's Burninghttps://books2read.com/HellsBurning

Links to Bea Paige's social media:

Facebook: https://www.facebook.com/groups/BeaPaige/

Instagram:https://www.instagram.com/beapaigeauthor/

Twitter: https://twitter.com/BeaPaigeAuthor

Pinterest:https://www.pinterest.co.uk/beapaigeauthor

Bookbub: https://www.bookbub.com/authors/bea-paige

Web:https://www.beapaige.co.uk

ACADEMY OF MISFITS PLAYLIST

It's no secret that I listen to music whilst I write. Some authors like to write in utter silence, I'm not one of them. Music is my muse. I have been known to write, listen to music and sing all at the same time! Oftentimes music will inspire an idea, just like the case with Delinquent. The idea for this story was very much influenced by "Bad Guy" by Billie Eilish and cemented an idea that had already begun to form.

Below are my favourite songs from the playlist.

Listen to the full playlist on Spotify HERE

"Peer Pressure" by James Bay featuring Julia Michaels
"Bad Guy" by Billie Eilish
"I Don't Care" by Ed Sheeran featuring Justin Bieber
"Chains" by Stormzy remix with Nick Jonas
"Snow White" by Dennis Lloyd

"Run Run" by Ray Blk
"Shut Up" Stormzy
"Into You" Julia Michaels

To all the kids out there who had a tough start in life, who may still have to fight every day to survive, this one's for you.

"My dear young lady, crime, like death, is not confined to the old and withered alone. The youngest and fairest are too often its chosen victims"

~ Oliver Twist, Charles Dickens

PROLOGUE

A licia Loi Chen which loosely means *Great Noble Thunder*... or some such crap like that.

That's me. That's *my* name. Pretty fucking great, yeah? At least my mum thought so given the amount of times she tried to convince me it was.

In her more lucid moments over the years, when she wasn't messed up on some drug or other, she'd loved to weave magical tales about far away countries filled with dragons and other mythical creatures. For a long time, she had me convinced that she'd been a concubine to the Emperor of China, and I was their lovechild spirited off to England for safekeeping, my name chosen because I was born to some great Chinese dynasty.

Of course, I realised pretty soon that she was full of shit.

My empty stomach, threadbare clothes and dirty, flea-ridden flat we called home had proven that. Our true story, the one she tried to hide from, has only ever been a tale of woe... and it's about to get a whole lot worse.

Born on December 26, 1998 during one of the worst hurricanes to hit the UK for years, my fucked-up, drugged-up, heroin addict mother actually named me after the storm that raged beyond the single glazed windows of our shitty rundown council flat in Hackney. Her wails of pain from pushing me out of her ravaged, undernourished body matched those of the hurricane that wound its way through the feeble mould-ridden walls of our home. Tracy Carter, mum's best friend and my surrogate mum growing up, had cradled my head as I slipped into the world wailing, my lungs bursting with rage at being born, my tiny little body already addicted to heroin. An angry baby junky, courtesy of my messed-up junky mum. Born with thunder inside me, thunder rolling outside, my name was fitting back then, I suppose. Except now I've shredded that name like a dirty threadbare jumper. I don't live a fairy tale life and I'm not some emperor's daughter, real or imagined.

I'm just *Asia*. A name *I* chose for myself, not because of my heritage. And certainly not because of my mother's addiction for the opium produced in the Golden Triangle of Southeast Asia that finally killed her on my fourteenth birthday.

Nope.

I'm called Asia because the chip on my shoulder is as large as a fucking continent, and with good reason. I started my life fighting to live, and I've spent every day since doing the same damn thing… Fighting to survive.

Every. Fucking. Day.

I live in a permanent state of fight or flight, except I'm not a bird and I *never* run. I've got claws as sharp as the best of them, and a left hook to match. Truth is, this state of living is as unhealthy as the addiction I was born with. I've bounced from one foster home to another, interspersed with a few months in my mum's care when she'd 'got herself clean', only to fall back into bad habits the second shit got hard. Heroin is a dirty drug that strips a human of their ability to function let alone bring up a kid. My mum was the worst kind of addict; weak, selfish and unable to fight for her children, herself even. I've pretty much brought myself up, and along the way have tried to get my younger brothers through this screwed up life we live. I've had to grow up fast.

Now that I'm sixteen going on twenty-six, I've taken life by the proverbial balls and *I'm* deciding how to live it. I'd be a liar if I said I wasn't tempted to pick up a needle and shoot up just to get away from my crappy existence for a few short moments. But I refuse to be a junky like my mum. *I refuse.* She'd forced that on me as a newborn but I sure as fuck won't make the same mistakes she made. I'm grateful that I don't remember those long months being weaned off the drug, no more than a pitiful howling creature full of pain and anger.

Years later, Tracy had told me that I screamed blue bloody murder those first few months of my life. My tiny little fists bunched up, ready to hit anyone who got too close. That was the first time my mum tried to give up heroin. She'd seen how I'd fought from the second I was born, and she did the same. Alongside me she got clean and for three years my mum managed to steer clear of the drug.

But it didn't last.

The day after my third birthday mum left me in the care of Tracy with one goal in mind, to get well and truly off her face. She didn't return for a month. When she did, she was unrecognisable.

That was the first time I was taken into care.

But unlike her, I will not allow myself to be weak. I won't give in to the lingering need that still plagues me even though I don't remember the feeling of being an addict, a state that was forced onto me without any choice or say in the matter.

Growing up hasn't been easy, I can assure you.

These days the only source of joy in an endless line of disappointment and disillusion is my art, because not only is Asia my name now, it's also my *tag*. You can see it spray painted in bright colours across the whole of Hackney. A piece of me brightening the stark and dirty streets of this inner-city London borough where I live.

But like everything else in my life, that too has been taken away from me because some asshats deem it a crime to make something ugly into something beautiful.

Truth be known, there's never going to be a happily ever after for me. I was born during a storm after all, and we all know that storms only ever leave devastation in their wake.

1

"This is a fucking joke," I mumble, just loud enough for my arsehole of a lawyer to hear.

"Can it, Chen. Sit up, take note and don't say a damn thing," my lawyer hisses at me.

Sitting here now in the magistrates' court with my lawyer, who I'm pretty sure is ready to hang me so he can get back home to his two point five kids and perfect middle class wife, I wait for the verdict.

A clock ticks loudly, the sound of a pen tapping against the table and the constant low hum of my blood pulsing in my ears makes it impossible to concentrate.

"Sit up, Alicia, pay *attention*," my lawyer snaps, repeating the demand under his breath once more.

I huff, feigning boredom and make a point at staring at a spot just beyond the ancient judge as he waffles on about my 'crimes' and my poor choices in life like his shit don't stink. *Dickhead.*

Well he, like all the other adults I've ever come across in

life, can go fuck themselves. I was doing the shopkeeper a favour by brightening his ugly back wall with my graffiti art. I'm pretty sure he gets way more customers now because of it anyway. He should be *thanking* me. Instead, here I am waiting on this fat balding twat of a judge to make a decision about my life, just like all the other bastards I've had to endure these past sixteen years. I wish I was turning eighteen this year instead of next, maybe then I could claw back some of the control I crave. As it is, I've got to wait another fifteen months until that happens. I'm just another kid who's the property of the state right now.

"Breaking and entering, criminal damage, graffitiing, possession of marijuana, anti-social behaviour. The list goes on and on, Alicia…" the judge drones on. His words mingle with the memory of all the other disappointed tirades I've had to listen to over the years from social workers, teachers, lawyers and the endless list of control freaks that seem to want to plague my life with rules and fucking restrictions.

It's not like I need reminding of my petty crimes. I know what I've done and frankly, I'd do it again given half the chance. I didn't hurt anyone. I didn't even break into the store really, given Mr Patel stupidly left the back entrance open. And yeah, so I smoked some weed. What teenager doesn't these days? I'm betting this arsehole next to me drinks himself into a coma most nights on some thousand pound bottle of brandy to blot out some shit or other that he wants to forget. So, what's the difference? I smoke a little weed, big deal. At least I don't shoot up to get a kick.

"You're on a dangerous path, young lady, one that will lead to a life of crime and imprisonment if you continue on as you are. Do you want that for yourself?" the judge asks me, his bushy eyebrows like great big caterpillars kissing as he frowns.

Talk about condescending. I shrug and look away to avoid further eye-contact, making a non-committal sound.

"You *want* this life for yourself?" he accuses, trying to get a reaction.

Folding my arms across my chest, I shift in my seat, refusing to engage.

Yep, that's exactly what I want, arsehole. In fact, being a criminal was the first job of choice on my list of things I wanted to be when I grew up. Actually, being a princess was top of that stupid list my mother had made me write. All because of her crazy stories and my need to please her. I'd have done anything to stop her from picking up a needle and shooting up.

"There's nothing you'd like to say?" he persists.

"No." I manage to bite out.

Both he and my lawyer make a distasteful noise at my lack of understanding or care. Their opinion of me is plain for all to see. I'm just another one of those kids who's a drain on the system. Drug-addict mother, absent father, benefit generation, uneducated, lazy, foolhardy. I'm the shit on their shoe. I'm worthless. *Yeah, I get it.*

"This is your last chance," the judge says, and I'm not sure whether he's now referring to my opportunity to speak or my proverbial last chance in life.

My lawyer, Fitzpatrick or something equally as fucking posh, nudges me in the side. "Alicia, now's the time to get your point across. Don't mess this up."

I turn to face him, sucking on my lip ring and giving him my best *'I don't give a fuck'* stare. I clear my throat, finally making eye-contact with the judge.

"Fuck you," I murmur.

Fitzpatrick stiffens. I can feel the annoyance and judgement rolling off him, battering against me as I resolutely ignore his incredulous look. Once he gets over the shock, I'm betting he's going to love telling his perfect family about the messed-up kid who gave the judge a big fat *"fuck you."* I know what he thinks when he looks at me; I'm the warning to his children. I'm the horror story of a life gone tits-up. You smoke weed, you'll end up like her. You wear those clothes, you're asking to be treated a certain way. You live on a council estate; you're bound to grow up a junky or a fucking criminal. I see it in his eyes, in the eyes of all the adults who make a snap judgement about the person I am based on the way I look.

Fuckwads.

"That's all you have to say?" the judge responds.

But instead of slapping my arse with another punishment, he just sighs heavily as though he's just as jaded with the world as I am. I watch as he clasps his hands together and regards me for a long time before speaking.

"Your crime holds a minimum sentence of eighteen months in juvenile prison, but both your social worker and lawyer have petitioned for a lesser sentence. For some reason they seem to think you're salvageable. Despite your appearance and lack of any remorse for your actions, I'm going to believe them."

I snort, folding my arms across my chest ignoring the pounding beat of my heart and the anger bubbling inside, the hurricane of rage I was born with is never very far away. I know for a fact my lawyer doesn't give a crap about me, and my social worker? Ha! Don't make me laugh. That bitch will be glad to see the back of me. I'm pretty sure she'd rather see me locked up, my case file neatly filed away in some cabinet in her office never to be looked at again.

"You come to my court dressed like that," he says wrinkling his nose at my ripped jeans, Doc Martens and see through mesh top.

"At least I wore a bra," I snarl under my breath, glancing at Fitzpatrick whose jaw tightens in anger.

"You've not even bothered to make an effort to present yourself in a suitable manor..." the judge continues, his words lost behind a growing haze of rage that I can't seem to dampen right now.

What the fuck has my appearance got to do with it? I have blue hair, a nose stud, lip ring and tattoos and that immediately makes me a leper to society, does it? All these thoughts make acid of my blood as he blithers on, but I don't show how I feel. On the outside I'm cold, disinterested, maintaining a sense of aloofness. It's my 'don't give a shit' attitude that I've perfected over the years. Besides, I'm not really worried about me, I can take a stint in juvie. At least I'll get a place to sleep every night and food in my belly. I'm told they even have video games. Sounds like heaven to me. The only thing I don't like about a prison sentence is that I worry for my little brothers and how they'll survive without my visits. They might be living in a different foster care home than me (not that I stay in my own very often), but I still get to visit them regularly. Eighteen months in prison is a long time to go without seeing them both. That thought makes my mouth go dry and my hands turn clammy.

"Despite all of that," he continues, whilst a buzzing fills my ears making it hard for me to actually hear what he's saying, "I'm giving you one final chance to change your ways. You will attend Oceanside Academy in Hastings."

My gaze snaps up to meet his. Oceanside Academy in *Hastings*? How is that any better than a prison sentence? I've heard about that place, a reform school for fucked-up kids just like me, but that's not even the worst part. It's a residential school, miles away from my little brothers. Is this prick insane?

Sitting forward in my chair, my mouth pops open, ready to bombard this shit-stain of a man with my response. But Fitzpatrick grabs my arm and squeezes.

"Don't be foolish," he hisses.

I'm about to tell him to get lost too when my brain finally catches up with the rest of what the judge is saying. His words somehow penetrating the anger I feel.

"You'll be able to return home during the term breaks to ensure you're still able to maintain a relationship with your siblings. I'm told that they're your one saving grace…"

The judge lets that statement hang in the air, and it successfully shuts me up. We make eye contact, and he narrows his eyes at me. But of course, I should've known it comes with a caveat, the motherfucker isn't stupid.

"This is a suspended sentence, Alicia. If you mess up, or you don't meet your obligations at the academy then I can and *will* enforce the full sentence and you'll find yourself in prison as soon as you can whip out your spray can and tag your name on a wall. There will be no visitation rights then. None. Do I make myself clear?"

Clenching my jaw and trying my best not to tell the judge what I really think of him, I simply nod my head. "I understand."

And just like that my life is upended once more.

Outside the courtroom, Fitzpatrick turns to me and rests his hand on my arm. I look at his fingers pressing into my skin, then him with distaste, a scowl drawing my lips up in a sneer. His eyes widen as though he truly thinks I'm about to bite. He releases his hold. Finally, the twat understands me.

"You start the new term in one week. I suggest you spend the time making your goodbyes and thinking about what you want out of life, Alicia. Whether you choose to believe it or not, this is an opportunity, not a sentence. Make the most of it, and whatever you do, *don't run*."

With that he turns on his heel and walks away from me. I watch him leave with dispassion. "Save your pep talks for someone who actually gives a shit," I call out after him, drawing more snotty glares from the staff milling about.

On the other side of the reception area, someone barks out a laugh. A boy around my age looks at me from beneath his black hoody jumper. I can barely see his features beneath the shade of his hood, but I see enough to get my measure of him. Besides, the attitude he gives off ensures everyone milling around gives him a wide berth. I'm pretty sure he's a misunderstood *'arsehole'* just like me. Or given the shit-eating grin that's rapidly widening across his face, just an arsehole. Folding my arms across my chest defensively and cocking my hip and eyebrow, I wait. He raises his hand, his fingers curled into his palm.

"Wanker," he mouths, moving his fist from side to side imitating a wank. His gaze slides to the retreating back of my lawyer before he smirks at me then pulls back his hood so I can get a better look at his face.

It's a good face. Handsome in a kind of 'lock up your daughters and your family jewels' way. Dark blonde hair falls over his baby blue eyes that are a little too all-knowing to be innocent. I already know from that one glance, as our eyes meet, that he's seen and done shit that would rival any adult in this building. Face of an angel, mind of a sinner, and the type of person I avoid at all costs.

Swiping his hair back off his forehead, he gives me a wink which I resolutely ignore in my calculated perusal of him. He has a light tan, as though he spends a lot of time out in the sun, and he's tall, fit, with wide shoulders and a slim waist.

Honestly, he'd be better served on a beach with a surfboard, than in a magistrates' court in Hackney, but life sucks so here we are.

Two dimples appear in his cheeks as he smiles languidly with a lazy kind of self-assurance. He totally thinks I'm checking him out, and I am, just not in the way he thinks. I'm cataloguing his face and filing it in my memory in case I need to refer to it at a later date. I've learnt to be smart, making sure when I meet a new person, I take my measure of them because you never know when you might need that kind of information.

Here's what I know in the few minutes of checking him out: he's approximately my age, seventeen max because although he's tall, broad, he still has the remnants of youth in the smooth skin of his face. There's not a single facial hair in sight. He's clearly in trouble with the law and given the way his gaze keeps flicking to the Rolex watch sitting on his lawyer's wrist, I'm thinking theft is his crime of choice. He fancies himself as a bit of a ladies' man. Those dimples in his cheek might work wonders on other girls, and probably women, but it won't work on me. Beauty is used to hide a multitude of sins, and I'm not as impressed by it as other chicks my age appear to be. He's scared. That tell is harder to decipher and he's doing a good job at trying to hide it beneath the cockiness, but the way he taps his foot is a big giveaway.

"You here for me, beautiful? Want my number?" he shouts across the room the second my gaze lands on his tap-tapping foot.

Hmm, bravado, another interesting tell. He doesn't like anyone thinking he's weak. Make everyone think you're brave, confident, and they'll believe it even when you aren't. A tool I use often enough myself.

I don't answer him, but I give him a knowing smile as I regard him.

Next to him, the good looking lawyer who has concern written across his face, looks over at me. He gives me an assessing look, his dark eyes narrowing as he regards me. I raise an eyebrow at him as he smooths a hand over his beard. The cocky, dimpled shithead, who's almost as tall as the lawyer, looks between us.

"Bit young for you, Bryce," he says with a smirk.

Bryce? On first names with his lawyer then. Bryce shakes his head and clips the boy lightly around the ear.

"Don't piss me off. You're pushing your luck already, son."

Ah, not a lawyer. Pretty sure they'd get the sack for whacking their clients. So, who is this man? My interest piqued, I watch and wait.

The boy laughs. "*Son?* You might be looking after me, but you ain't my dad, so stop pretending you are. I don't need you here, arsehole. I've been looking after myself long enough before you lot came along."

There we have it, the fit bloke is his foster parent. Pretty sure I've never come across a foster parent dressed in Armani, looking like he's just stepped out of the pages of GQ Magazine. Well, shit just got interesting.

"Wrong, you need me, and Louisa would never forgive me if I let you come here alone today. So suck it up, concentrate on the matter at hand, and stop giving that pretty little thing over there *fuck-me* eyes. I'm pretty sure she'd chew you up and spit you out," the man called Bryce says, turning to give me a wink.

I can't help but smirk, which only seems to piss *Dimples* off even more.

"Pretty sure I'd let her," the boy bites back before giving me a smile that absolutely shows me that he would, and that he'd enjoy it. "Name's Sonny," he says as an afterthought, before being frogmarched into the courtroom on the other side of the hall.

The moment the door slams shut, the world filters back in and I notice that everyone seems to be staring, making a judgement about the boy who was just dragged into the courtroom and the girl with a scowl on her face.

"Should learn some manners. This is a court of law and not some playground for a bunch of delinquents," some snotty-nosed woman says as she walks past me.

"Whatever," I mutter, leaning against the wall, all of the wind knocked out of me suddenly.

What the hell do any of these arseholes know anyway? Apart from that dude Sonny, who's clearly looking for a distraction from his shit day, I'm the dregs of society. I'm a delinquent just like the woman said, and this delinquent is about to join the notorious Oceanside Academy, otherwise known on the streets as the *Academy of Misfits*.

Fuck my life.

2

A few days later, whilst I'm minding my own business hiding from the world on the top of a garage roof behind the flats where I live, a firm hand clamps down on my shoulder. I don't bother to look up and see who it is. The only person who knows where to find me is my best friend, and partner in crime, Eastern.

"What's up, Alicia?" he asks me as he takes a seat next to me, spreading out his long, muscular legs next to mine. I try not to take too much notice of how his jeans are stretched across the firm muscle of his thigh. I'm pretty sure he's been working out.

"You been avoiding me?"

"It's *Asia*, dickwad," I respond, shaking my head as he attempts to pass me a joint. I'm not in the mood to get high. I've got too much shit going on. Besides I'm seeing my little brothers in an hour. I'm not foolish enough to visit my kid brothers high on marijuana. That'd be a sure-fire way of never getting to see them again, and I won't risk that.

"Sorry, *Asia*," he retorts, rolling his eyes.

"Well, at least I'm not named after a direction on a map," I bite back, feeling prickly. He might be my only friend, one I've known since forever, but he doesn't get to call me Alicia. No one does.

"Should I come back after you've finished your period?" he laughs.

"Piss-off."

"Alright, alright. We all know my mum can't spell and she meant *Easton*, but I'm stuck with this name. Besides, I kind of like it. You're Asia and I'm Eastern, it fits. Like we were always meant to be friends."

"Hmm," I respond, picking at the frayed hole in my jeans, my mind straying elsewhere.

"You still worrying about Oceanside? I say you got off lightly," he adds nonchalantly.

"Taking the rap for you, jerk," I bite out.

"Hey, *you* did the breaking and entering, the artwork. I just came along for the ride," he shrugs, but I see the guilt flash across his brown eyes.

"Maybe so, but you totally owe me one for not snitching on you."

He scowls, wrapping his arm around my shoulder and pulling me in for a hug. A waft of his familiar masculine scent of soap and apples unnerves me, like he's spent the day in an orchard stealing basket loads of fruit rather than smoking joints and getting up to no good. I stiffen in his arms, I never used to feel this way when he hugged me before but ever since that kiss...

"Fuck man, if I could take the rap I would. It's just..." he says, interrupting my thoughts and squeezing me tighter against his side.

"...Tracy needs you. I get it. Besides, you're right, you didn't do anything wrong... *this time.*"

I let him hold onto me tightly, ignoring the warm pit in my stomach at his closeness. We've been best friends since we were babies and always had a non-romantic relationship. Of late, things have become awkward between us. Especially since he kissed me at Mr fucking Patel's shop. That night I'd acted rashly in more ways than one. *Stupid.*

"Mum's having trouble holding things together right now," he continues, taking a long toke on the joint before blowing it out. I do my best not to breathe in too deeply. This stuff will get you high even when you're not the one actually smoking it.

"Braydon?" I question, knowing that the only thing Tracy struggles with is her youngest son who's got every disability under the sun; deaf, mute, with Multiple Sclerosis thrown in the mix. He's a sweet kid, eight years old and full of sunshine despite all his problems. Tracy adores him, we all do, and she works round the clock to care for him. Eastern does his best to be the man of the house given their own father did a runner as soon as Braydon was born. But as much as Eastern would like to ease his mum's money worries, what hope is there for a sixteen-year-old kid who spends as little time at school as I do? We both pretty much sacked school off the second we turned sixteen. They've stopped trying to get us to go in. Besides, we caused too much trouble, it was easier to permanently exclude us both. Fuck them anyway.

"Yes, Braydon..." he confirms with a heavy sigh.

His younger brother is a constant source of joy *and* worry for him. Recently, the only way he can help his mum out is by delivering Mary J. I hate that he does it, but what other choice does he have? Tracy needs the money, and even though he lies and tells her he's working cash in hand at a legit job, I think she knows deep down he doesn't. That cuts him deep. She's that desperate to help one son, that she'll allow the other to lead a life of crime. Life sure does suck.

"Bray's needed a lot of medical care lately and mum has had to skip work a few times to look after him. She thinks she's going to get the sack."

"Doesn't she get like special leave or something because he's disabled?"

"She's on zero contract hours, Asia, earning the minimum wage. Those fucktards who employ her don't give a shit. As long as the offices they send her to clean are kept spotless, that's all that matters to them."

He drops his arm from my shoulder and scrapes a hand through his hair, the warm afternoon light catching the strands of auburn within the brown curtains that flops in front of his eyes. The evenings are still mild, which is no surprise really, September is always a better month for good weather than August is. The second kids go back to school after the summer holidays the rain stops, and the sun comes out. Fucking typical really.

"She's behind on the rent and the bills. That's why I've..." he continues, bringing his knees up to his chest and wrapping his arms around them. He sucks on the last dregs of the joint then throws it over the side of the garage, blowing the blue-grey smoke out slowly. The pungent smell is acrid and lingers around us like a dense fog.

"Why *what*?" I ask, narrowing my eyes at him.

"Why I've got a run for Nash this Sunday. It's a big job, will earn me a couple ton," he responds side-eying me.

"Eastern! Delivering weed is one thing, but that kind of money means only one thing... please don't tell me you're delivering speed for that arsehole."

He doesn't answer and my heart sinks like a rock. Of course he is.

"For fuck's sake. If you get caught, they'll put you away and then what will your mum do?!" I suck on my lip ring, worry coursing through me. Tracy has been a surrogate mum to me, and I love her and Braydon like they're my own family. I hate to see them struggling but I care about Eastern too… he's like a brother to me.

You do not kiss a brother like you kissed Eastern.

My cheeks flush at the memory, which I rapidly push aside. Fuck sake, I need to get a grip. He's a *friend*. Nothing more.

"Hey, don't do that," he says, plastering on a fake smile for me and flicking my lip ring with his finger.

"Do what?" I respond, slapping his hand away, my cheeks colouring. I hope he can't read my mind, though most days he seems to be able to. That's what happens when you spend your life growing up together.

"Worry about me getting caught, of course…" he pauses, his gaze raking over my face. "That *was* what you were thinking, wasn't it, or can't best friends give a shit about each other anymore?"

"Shut up, arsehole," I retort, willing the colour to leave my cheeks. "Of course I worry about you. You're like a brother to me."

A flash of annoyance ripples across his face before he nods tightly. "Brother, sure."

"Eastern…" I begin, but he waves his hand, shutting me up. He's not mentioned the kiss since it happened either. I'm pretty sure he'd rather forget it too.

"Seriously, Asia, you've got enough shit on your plate as it is. I'll be fine. Aren't I always?" he says with a cocksureness that neither of us really believe.

I breathe out slowly, glad that he isn't a mind reader and can't tell how twisted up I am over that hot as hell kiss we shared. The truth is, I care about Eastern a hell of a lot. He *has* been like a brother to me. He *is* family. I spent more time in his house than I did my own growing up. Every time my mum fucked up, I'd run to Tracy, and Eastern would be there to cheer me up. Even when I was dumped in the care of some random foster parent, I'd always end up back at their house, his mum a better mother than mine ever was. Eastern has become someone I rely on, but of late our relationship has shifted from being just friends to something more. Maybe it's a good thing I'm going away to Oceanside. It'll put some distance between us.

"Just be careful, okay?" I say, knowing that he'll go ahead and do it regardless of what I say.

"Careful is my middle name," he retorts, jumping up on his feet and brushing little specks of ash off his jeans. "You coming back for some grub? Mum's made tuna pasta bake."

I look up at him, shading my eyes from the sun that's still bright despite it being almost six o'clock in the evening. "I love your mum, but I hate her pasta bake. Hard pass."

Eastern laughs. "Yeah, it's pretty disgusting. Want me to walk you to the bus stop?" he asks, holding out his hand. I take it, trying not to think too much about the way it feels grasped in mine as he pulls me to my feet.

"Nah. I can manage," I retort, pulling my hand out of his grasp and folding my arms against my chest. He frowns but doesn't push it. Eastern understands my need to be independent. Besides, I don't need anyone to look out for me. I'm a big girl with quite a reputation around our estate. Messing with me is a serious no-no. The last person who did got a cracked rib and a shattered cheekbone.

"Fine. Suit yourself," he shrugs. "At least come with me to Sasha's party Saturday night. I could do with some back-up should she start getting needy."

I burst out laughing. "No way, man. You got yourself into that shit with her, you can get yourself out of it. I warned you she was clingy."

"Okay, fine. Don't come as back-up, just come along. You're leaving me Monday. Figured we could have one last blowout before you go," he says, scuffing the toe of his shoe on the rooftop. Pretty sure his voice cracked a little with that statement.

"You make it sound like I've a choice in the matter. I'm not leaving you, Eastern. I *have* to go." My own voice is a little wobbly and I fucking hate it. I refuse to be weak. Sucking in a breath, I give him a light punch on the arm. "Fine. One last blowout. You bring the weed; I'll bring the booze. Yeah?"

He looks up at me, a wide grin cracking his face. "You're on."

"Okay, piss off and go eat that tuna pasta bake. I'll swing by your place at nine Saturday night."

"See you then, Alicia," he responds, dodging my punch and running towards the edge of the roof.

"*Asia*, dickhead," I shout out after him, laughter bubbling up my throat.

Half a minute later he's lowered himself off the side of the garage roof. When he gets halfway down the alleyway, he stops, turning to face me.

"Tell the little carpet demons I'll be visiting them whilst you're gone," he shouts, then without waiting for me to respond, jogs away.

My throat constricts, Eastern always has my back. Visiting my baby brothers for me whilst I'm away and looking out for them is just about the nicest thing anyone has ever done for me. I get this sudden tight feeling in my chest at his thoughtfulness. It makes me feel out of sorts, so I shove the feeling aside. Boundaries are being blurred and I know now more than ever that kissing Eastern had been a mistake. Getting close like that only ever fucks things up. I'm not one of those chicks who'd shag and run, that just isn't me. Besides, I won't lose him as a friend for a one-night stand. From this moment on, I make a promise to myself to put Eastern well and truly in the friendzone. At least then I know he'll always take care of my baby brothers when I'm not around to do the same.

Another ten minutes pass before I climb down off the roof, enough time for me to steel myself for my final visit with my brothers before heading off to Oceanside. It'll be another three months until I see them again at Christmas break, providing I even get through the first term, that is. I'd better make the most of this weekend, because it's highly unlikely I'll be doing any partying whilst at the academy. We all know it's more like a prison than they let on.

3

Saturday night comes around sooner than I expected. In fact, the whole week since my hearing has rushed past in a blur like old father time is having a laugh and speeding up the hours just to screw with me. My little brothers, Sebastian and George, six and four respectively, were their usual adorable selves when I visited them the other evening and weren't in the least bit worried about not seeing me for three months. The little buggers thought Oceanside sounded like some boarding school for magic kids in one of those books their foster mum likes to read them. I didn't want to burst their bubble, so I just went along with it. They'll have plenty of years to find out that life isn't some great big fairytale.

Now, as I hold my finger against Eastern's doorbell, I decide that tonight I'm gonna go all out and get shitfaced just like we'd planned. Might be the last time for a while.

"Alright, alright, hold your fucking horses," Eastern shouts from the other side of his front door. Half a second later, he yanks it open and for a moment I allow myself to appreciate his sexiness before cussing him out like I usually do.

"Where do you think you're going, dressed like some Eastend gangster born fifty years too late?" I ask him, cocking a brow and ignoring the low thrum of attraction that seems to want to screw with me these days. He's wearing smart black trousers and a black shirt rolled up to the elbows with a white tie and a Crombie hat tilted jauntily on his head. Teamed with a pair of expensive white trainers that he nicked from the Nike store, he's the perfect mash up of old versus new. Sasha's not going to be able to keep her hands off him. I grit my teeth, bracing myself for the night ahead. He's my friend. We might've shared a kiss but that's it.

Friendzone, Asia. Fucking Friendzone, I remind myself.

Eastern grins, showing off his perfectly imperfect crooked teeth. I love the little chip in his front tooth, got when we played *Knock Down Ginger.* The irony is, *he* was actually knocked down when Mr Roberts of number fifty-eight sprinted after us and gave him a wallop that had him sprawling face first onto the pavement. We stopped playing the game after that. Tracy ripped us both a new one for annoying the neighbours and banging on their doors all day.

"Tom Hardy, eat your heart out," he smirks.

"You been shopping at the charity shops again?" I laugh, ribbing him further.

He leans against the doorframe, making a point of looking me up and down. "Don't talk to me about style, Asia, at least I don't look like someone who's had a fight with a rainbow and lost."

His eyes rove over my outfit as he steps closer, a little too close for comfort if I'm honest. Grabbing the hem of my bright blue belly top, his finger skimming against the bare skin of my stomach, Eastern's smile turns salacious.

"Love being different, don't you?" he murmurs.

"Pot, kettle, black," I retort.

I've never been one to follow the crowd. I wear what I want, not adhering to any kind of style. Mostly I like bright colours, just like the spray paint I use in my art. Every month I change my hair colour. Last month my dark brown bob was dyed green at the ends, this month blue. But I've pretty much had my hair all colours of the rainbow at one point or another. Right now, I'm glad that I matched my top with my newly dyed hair. Blue suits me even if I do say so myself. Paired with a short black denim skirt that shows off my wrap around tattoo that sits high on my thigh, I'm feeling pretty sexy.

"You do realise that looking this hot can get you into all sorts of trouble with the wrong kind of people," he warns, a look I can't quite interpret drawing his eyebrows together in a frown.

I grin to hide my sudden nerves at his closeness. "Did you just say I'm hot?"

"You've always been hot, Asia."

I'm not sure how to respond to that, so I don't.

"Seriously, that skirt barely covers your arse..."

"Maybe I'm looking for trouble?" I respond, shrugging.

"That so?" he questions, his fingers still feathering against my bare skin.

Suddenly the space between us has closed dramatically and that same chest-tightening feeling I've been getting around him lately snatches my breath. Eastern leans forward as though he's about to kiss me, his mouth a few inches from mine. His dark eyes flick to my mouth as I suck in my lip ring. For long moments we stare at each other, neither one of us moving. The

25

air is fraught with tension and I feel a sudden tingling warmth over my skin as his tongue runs over his bottom lip.

"What the hell are you doing, Eastern? Let Lissy come in and give me a hug, you great big oaf!"

Eastern pulls back sharply as I draw in a ragged breath, the rest of the universe rushing back into focus. *Damn, that was close.*

"Hey, Tracy," I manage to say as Eastern stands aside, drawing a pack of cigarettes out of his jacket pocket and sticking one in his mouth. He lights up in front of his mum, not in the least bit bothered.

"Eastern, go smoke that cancer stick outside. I don't want Braydon breathing in that muck," she says, tapping him on the shoulder then wagging her finger at him.

"Sure, Mum," he responds leaning in to give her a peck on the cheek before casting his gaze back at me. "See you in a second?"

"Give me sixty, need to say goodbye," I murmur.

"Done," he nods, the moment between us well and truly over. He strides off down the corridor, disappearing through the door outside.

"Lissy," Tracy coos, opening her arms to me. "Give us a hug." Her nickname for me has remained the same since I was a baby. She calls me Lissy, and I let her. So long as it's not Alicia, I'm good. Stepping into her embrace, I allow her to pull me close. She smells of bleach and baby wipes, of hard work and love, a combination that should be gross but is somehow comforting to me.

"I'm going to miss you," she murmurs, stroking my hair.

"I'll miss you guys too," I respond, willing myself not to get emotional. This isn't goodbye, just a see you later. I will not cry like some baby. "You'll make sure Eastern doesn't get into too much trouble without me, won't you?"

She laughs into my hair, giving me one last tight squeeze before letting me go. "He's a good boy, he looks after the ones he loves," she says, and we both know that she can't promise he won't get into any trouble, only that he'll do anything to take care of them both. Including drug running it would seem.

"Give Braydon a kiss for me, okay?" I say, avoiding the sadness in her eyes. Instead, I run my finger over my barb wire tattoo that sits just beneath the hem of my skirt. I had it done when I turned fifteen. It represents my need for everyone to stay the fuck away. I only have room for a handful of people in my life and even then, I'm careful. I loved my mother and she fucked off and left me for drugs. Since then, I've found it hard to let anyone in. Eastern, Tracy, Braydon and my little brothers are literally all I have room for and that's only because I'd already opened my heart to them before my mother died. I don't think I have it in me to let another person in so that they can just disappoint me.

"Why don't you come in and give him a kiss yourself?" Tracy suggests, cocking her head to the side as she looks at me.

I shake my head. "I'd rather not."

She pats me on the arm gently, her warm smile filled with understanding. "That's okay. I'm guessing too many goodbyes in one night is a bit much, yeah?"

"Maybe," I mumble.

"Go on, go enjoy yourself, and make sure that son of mine lets Sasha down gently. He can be a bit of an arse with the ladies... excluding you, of course. Where you're concerned, he's the perfect gentleman," Tracy says, her eyes flicking to the entrance door of the flats and the street beyond where Eastern is patiently waiting for me.

My cheeks colour as I sneak a look at her. Thankfully she

doesn't seem to have any clue about how our friendship has moved into uncertain territory. Eastern's kiss wasn't gentlemanly at all. In fact, it was downright sinful, but I'm not about to tell her that.

"I'll make sure to tell him. Bye, Tracy," I say, striding off before the tears welling in her eyes begin to fall.

"Bye, love. Take care," she chokes out before I hear the door clicking shut.

Outside, leaning against the wall with one foot propped against the brick, Eastern waits for me. He turns when I stride through the door, the dark scowl on his face replaced with a sudden grin the moment he spots me. I'm pretty sure he's plastering on the fake smile for my sake. Usually I'd ask what's up, but we both know he hates the fact I'm going away to Oceanside as much as I do.

"Ready to party, Asia?" he asks, offering me a pre-rolled joint as he pushes off the wall.

"Too fucking right," I respond, taking the joint and lighting it. "Let's get out of here."

Eastern smirks. "Last blowout for a while, eh?"

"Yeah, so let's make it count."

"I'm down with that."

Taking his proffered arm, we stride towards the bus stop with purpose, knowing that in a couple of days I'll be seventy miles away from the only home I've ever known and the only family I've ever loved. It may as well be the other side of the world.

4

We arrive at Sasha's house just as the party's getting underway. The place is heaving with people, and I'm already buzzing from the two joints we smoked on the way here and the two bottles of beer I've downed. I'm feeling reckless. A little voice in the back of my head is warning me to slow down, but I ignore it.

"Damn, look at all the people," Eastern exclaims, salivating at the fun ahead. He loves to party, it's his favourite pastime. Living with a disabled brother comes with a shitload of responsibilities that build up and crush him most days. Letting off steam is the only way to deal with the stress.

Sasha's house is practically a mansion compared to the dingy flat I grew up in. Her dad owns a building firm and has a lot of cash to throw around. This party won't be lasting all that long given the twitching curtains from the neighbours on either side and the very loud grime music blasting out of the house. A couple of guys I know from around my estate are having a fight in the front garden, no doubt over the girl who's trying to break them up and failing miserably. Pretty sure the police will be rocking up soon. I make a mental note not to do anything too stupid, or at least not get caught.

"Her parents are away on a cruise apparently. The girl's fucking crazy posting an open invite on Facebook. She's asking for trouble," Eastern says, as we stroll towards the front door. That explains it then. No one in their right mind would post an invite to a house party on social media, but this chick has. Her house is going to get trashed.

Adrenaline courses through my veins as I take a swig of the beer I'm holding. I've been to parties like this before. It ends in one of two ways. Either the police break it up, arresting those in possession of drugs or the parents return home and their kid gets beaten black and blue for holding the party. Sometimes both. I'm not sure if Eastern senses it too, but this night is going to get wild, and fast. I can feel it in my blood.

"How long do you think we have until the police turn up and shut it down?" I muse.

"Hmm, I would've said about an hour, *but* Sasha's dad is a mean bastard and gives his neighbours shit, so they might be too scared to rat her out."

"Best get inside then and make the most of it," I respond with a grin.

Eastern taps his bottle of beer against my own then winks, tipping his Crombie hat at me. "Come on, girl. Let's do this."

Inside, the house is already trashed. Pictures hang off the walls, the place stinks of weed and spilt alcohol, and people are getting down to the music playing in the front room. I glance briefly inside and just see a mass of indistinguishable bodies grinding to the music beneath the fog of blue-grey smoke lingering in the air.

"Watch out," Eastern says, pointing to a kid spread-eagled on the hallway floor, too drunk to stand. We step over him, and after a quick glance to see if he's still breathing, I follow Eastern down the hallway. The house is even bigger inside than I first thought and there are couples getting it on in every available space. One particular guy is grinding against a girl, their noises of lust make my cheeks blush even as I feign disgust. He's tall, broad, and I can barely see the girl caught beneath his chest and the wall, apart from her bare leg which is a stark white against the mocha skin of his large hand.

"Get a fucking room," I snipe as we walk past them.

The guy raises his hand and flicks me the middle finger without even removing his mouth from the girl's lips, then he proceeds to reach between them. Her responding moans tell me he's put his hand somewhere wholly inappropriate given they're in a hallway and everyone can see. I'm not a prude but I really don't want to witness *that*.

"You want to get me into a fight, Asia?" Eastern laughs, dragging me away before I tap the bloke on the shoulder and tell him what I really think.

"I'm capable of fighting my own battles," I retort, allowing Eastern to pull me along whilst chugging back the rest of my beer as we head into the kitchen.

"I *know* that. Doesn't mean I won't jump in to save your arse though."

Depositing the bottle on the kitchen table, I punch his arm lightly. "Ah, my knight in shining armour," I respond with a heavy dose of sarcasm.

Eastern just shakes his head, dumping his empty bottle on the table too, cluttering it up even more than it already is. This room is just as trashed as the rest of the house. Empty bottles of booze are stacked up on every available surface. Most of the kitchen table is stained dark with spilt drink, and some douchebag wannabe gangster and his gaggle of bitches are huddled around the end of the table cutting up coke and snorting it up their noses.

"Nice," I mutter, my back tensing. I might smoke weed but I've never, and will never, touch anything harder. No way.

Eastern takes my arm and steers me out of the back door and into the garden. He knows how I feel about hard drugs. I hate them and I hate that tomorrow he's going to deliver speed for Nash. I know why he must take the job, I get that, but I don't have to like it.

"You alright?" he questions.

"It's their lives. I don't really care what they choose to shove up their noses so long as I don't have to watch."

"Fair enough."

We find a spot in the back garden on a low wall and watch the crowd, taking our measure of the place. There are at least another thirty people hanging around outside. Most of them are our age, a handful are a few years older, but I don't think there's anyone here over the age of twenty. For a while we sit in silence, enjoying each other's company and sharing yet another joint. It's always been easy like this with Eastern, sometimes words just aren't necessary. I'm going to miss him. A lot. I won't tell him that though, don't want him getting any funny ideas.

Eastern points to the back fence and an open gate. "Our quick exit, should we need to run," he says, knowing as well as I that at some point tonight the police will arrive, and we'll need to get the hell out of dodge.

"Clocked it," I respond, reaching into the plastic bag I brought with me and pulling out two more beers. Eastern places the lip of the bottle on the edge of the low brick wall, angling it slightly before slamming his palm against the bottle top. It pops off with ease. He does the same to the second bottle then hands it to me.

"Cheers," he says.

"Cheers," I respond, swallowing a mouthful even though I know that the third bottle of beer I drunk should've been my last.

"Seen Sasha yet?" I ask.

Eastern points to a spot opposite us where Sasha is sitting on the lap of some kid who looks like a poorer version of Eastern. The chick's got it bad if she's hooking up with lookalikes now. Her arms are draped around the boy's neck, her long brown hair tumbling over them both as she leans in for a kiss, but not before she pointedly looks in Eastern's direction.

"See she's moved on," I remark, lifting my bottle of beer in her direction. She responds with a dirty look. Whatever.

Eastern grins. "Thank fuck for that. I was getting tired of her begging text messages. We hooked up once *months* ago and suddenly she thinks we're a couple. The whole fucking world knows the only girl I have eyes for is you…"

I jerk my head around waiting for the familiar laugh to tell me he's joking, but it doesn't come. Instead he just looks at me, daring me to say something. For the first time in my life, the words won't come, and I'm left speechless. I'm so shocked that I don't even notice another girl come pelting towards us both before it's too late. My drink flies out of my hand and crashes to the concrete, beer splashing against my skin as she throws herself into Eastern's arms.

"*Eastern!!*" she screeches. The blonde bombshell whirlwind that the voice belongs to lands in his lap, practically knocking him into the flowerbed behind us as she plants a kiss on his cheek.

"What the fuck?!" I exclaim, ready to grab her by her fake extensions and yank her to the floor. Bitch.

"Oh, shit. Sorry!" the girl singsongs, smiling widely, her cute button nose crinkling up as she takes a good look at me. It's not a mean look, just a curious one. Either way I hate her already, especially since she's sitting in my best friend's lap and he's looking as guilty as fuck. Urgh, this is typical Eastern. Why in the ever-loving fuck did I kiss him and mess up my feelings towards him? Before we smacked our lips together this kind of thing wouldn't have bothered me. Now, now it does, and it pisses me off.

"And who the hell are *you*?" I growl, narrowing my eyes at the supermodel whilst absentmindedly wiping at the spilt beer on my bare leg. Great, now I smell like the grotty pub on the corner of our estate.

"I'm Opal, and you must be Eastern's bestie, Asia, right?" she retorts, thrusting her hand out for me to shake. The fact she knows who I am, but I don't know who she is pisses me off even more. Eastern tells me everything, or at least he did. Looks like I don't know him as much as I thought. Raising an eyebrow, I ignore the pretty blonde with her pert tits and long legs and glare at Eastern instead.

"Only have eyes for me, eh?!" I snort, rolling my eyes before standing and striding away from them both.

"Asia, wait. I can explain," he retorts, swearing under his breath at the same time he stands lifting the girl up and placing her on her feet.

"Don't fucking bother." I glare at him over my shoulder. She's *still* hanging onto him like a limpet and he's not even bothering to unravel her arms from around his waist. That tells me all I need to know. He's such a goddamn lothario.

"Alicia, wait!"

But I continue to walk away, lifting my hand up and giving him the finger as I do. He doesn't follow me, knowing me better than that. In this frame of mind, I'm likely to lash out before thinking and even though he's hurt me, I don't want to hurt him like that. I draw the line at knocking out my best friend.

Inside the kitchen, the same arseholes who were snorting coke are now buzzing, talking ten to the dozen. The guy who was acting like a kingpin earlier, sidles up to me as I pour myself a generous measure of rum with a splash of cola.

"What?!" I snap, chugging back half the glass before slamming it back on the counter.

"You looking to hook up, pretty lady?" he asks me, his gaze fixed firmly on my chest and not on my face.

"Do I look like I'm wanting to hook up?" I growl, my anger bubbling over.

He has the audacity to lift his hand to my face and press his finger against my lip ring. It reminds me of Eastern, and that reminds me of the leggy bitch who he's talking with right now in the back garden. *I see red*.

Pulling my fist back I punch the dickhead straight on the nose. He might be bigger than me, and probably a whole lot stronger, but he's also high and wasn't expecting me to hit him. I watch him sprawl backwards, then land another blow in his gut for good measure. He goes down with a thud, knocked out cold. His gaggle of girls scream and fawn over him.

"Next time ask before you fucking touch," I snarl, grabbing my drink and downing the rest before striding from the room and walking headfirst into a hard chest. "Fuck sake!" I spit, pushing against the wall of muscle in my way. The wall of muscle doesn't move.

Looking up, I find myself toe to toe with the guy I saw making out with the faceless girl in the hallway not so long ago. Even though I didn't see his face, I know it's him from the clothes he's wearing and the cockiness that oozes from him. He smirks at me, his blue eyes startling bright; two topaz gems contrasting beautifully with his dark skin. Despite myself, I'm a little floored by them, and the boy they belong too. He's hot and he knows it. Dangerous too, that much I sense beneath my anger and drunkenness.

"*Next time* you decide to knock one of my boys out, ask my permission first, yeah?" he states, folding his arms across his chest as I take a step back.

"He's one of *your boys*?" I smirk, ignoring my sixth sense and the sudden warning bells that tell me not to mess with this guy. Trouble is I'm too damn angry at Eastern and that prick who just tried to chat me up to pay any attention. Plus, I'm high, and drunk. *Stupid*.

"That's right, and I'm a little possessive about the things that belong to me."

"Is she one of your possessions too?" I ask, glaring at the girl he was practically fucking in the hallway a few minutes earlier. She's standing beside him now blocking the gap in the doorway I was just about to dodge through. She's as blonde as the bimbo who just threw herself into Eastern's arms a minute ago. In fact, she looks eerily like her. Twin maybe? She smiles at me, but it's not a friendly smile in the slightest. She's looking at me like I'm some kind of threat. As if! I wouldn't touch this bloke with a ten-foot pole.

"Everything alright, Camden?" she purrs, her voice practically dripping with fuck-me vibes. She can't be much older than I am, but her all-knowing sexual vibe has me feeling inferior all of a sudden.

"Don't worry, *love*. I've no interest in your *man*," I say, prickles of anger running across my skin. My eyes rove over Camden as he takes his measure of me, and whilst he's good looking with incredible eyes, he also has an intensity that screams danger. Something about his confidence and calmness has my heart stuttering with warning. But tonight, it would seem I'm looking for trouble, so rather than backing down I stand my ground and fold my arms across my chest readying myself for a fight. If this bimbo says one word out of turn, I'm not going to be able to stop myself from launching at her. Fuck the consequences. Let's see if Eastern will be my knight in shining armour then?

"I'm not *her* man. I don't belong to anyone," the guy says, smarting. Next to him the girl flinches, hurt flashing across her face.

"Well, that makes two of us. So why don't you tell your *boy* that too," I snarl, pointing over my shoulder at the kid still laid out cold on the floor. "And any others who think they can touch me without permission," I add, glaring at him.

"I'll think about it," he retorts, moving aside as I shove past him and his bit of fluff and head for the front door. "I'm surprised you're running," I hear Camden say, a challenge in his voice. "Seems like you're the kind of chick who does what the fuck she wants and damn the consequences."

I pull up sharp at his words. For whatever reason this guy is laying down the gauntlet. Normally, I wouldn't bite, but tonight I'm way past reckless.

"Actually, I came to party. So, I'm going to party," I growl, twisting on my feet and ignoring the sudden wave of giddiness from smoking too much weed and drinking too much alcohol.

Fuck Eastern, fuck the leggy blonde, fuck that dickwad in the kitchen and the punk who's staring at me now thinking he's some tough nut gang leader. Fuck the judge sending me to Oceanside, but most of all; fuck my life.

I'm here to party, so I'm going to party.

5

For ten minutes I dance, moving to the angry Grime music, my body crushed within the crowd of other drunk and pissed-off youths. There's something about this music that gets your blood pumping and the anger flowing. It suits my mood right now. I'm angry at the world.

"Alicia!"

I hear his voice over the din, but I choose to ignore it. I don't want to talk to Eastern right now.

"Alicia, for fuck sake, look at me," he bites out, his voice filled with an anger of its own.

"What do you want, Eastern? Can't you see I'm dancing here?" I snap, as he pushes his way through the crowd.

"I've given you time to calm down. Now will you let me explain?"

"No, now fuck off back to perky-tits."

Turning my back on him, I raise my arms in the air and allow my body to move to the beat of the music, fully aware that in doing so I'm flashing the black lace of my bra. I hear

Eastern mutter something under his breath then feel his hands land on my hips, his fingers digging into the material of my skirt. He presses up against my back, his body flush with mine before he leans down and presses his lips against my ear.

"You've got it all wrong, Alicia," he murmurs, the tenor of his voice dropping as his fingers slide across my stomach. For all of two point five seconds I lean into his hold, before common sense snaps me out of it.

Friendzone, Asia. Fucking friendzone. Plus, you're angry with him, remember that too.

Turning in his hold, I push away from him, bumping into the person behind me who's far too high to open their mouth with some smart remark, let alone react physically.

"You're my friend, Eastern. I really don't give a shit who you fool around with. I'm more pissed that perky-tits knew my name and I don't have a clue who she is. And stop calling me Alicia, you know I hate it!"

"You really are full of shit, you know that, *Alicia?*" he bites back, grabbing my arm and pulling me back towards him. "You're jealous. Admit it. You want me, just as much as I want you." His eyes darken, daring me to deny it.

"We're friends," I insist, doing exactly that.

"We're more than just friends, and you damn well know it."

I attempt at pulling my arm away, but he refuses to let me go. "Get your hands off me, or so help me, Eastern, I will knock you out." But Eastern doesn't let me go, if anything he squeezes tighter. Pain, anger and something else I don't want to admit to flashes across his face. My chest tightens because despite everything I've said and my determination to keep him in the friendzone, I *want* him this close to me. This push and pull within me is driving me insane.

"Let *go*," I repeat.

"You heard her. Unwrap your hand from her arm, and let her go," a familiar, commanding voice says from behind me.

I tense. What the fuck does *he* want? To my surprise, Eastern immediately drops my arm, his gaze flicking between me and Camden who is standing so close behind me that I feel the heat of his skin through the thin material of my t-shirt. What the hell is going on here?

Turning around slowly, I face Camden. "What do *you* think you're doing?" I ask, narrowing my eyes at him. In my intoxicated, rage-filled mind I don't take into account the dangerous way he's looking at me, or the fact that his command has made Eastern back off. Alarm bells should be ringing right about now, but instead I'm letting that internal hurricane of mine take over.

"Well?" I insist, prodding his chest with my finger. I have to look up at him, given he stands a good foot taller than me and a few inches taller than Eastern.

"Asia, don't," Eastern warns me. His fingers curl around my wrist, but for some stupid reason I ignore him and dig my nail deeper into Camden's rock-hard chest. Since when does Eastern take orders from anyone, anyway? What the fuck is going on here? Come to think of it, the surrounding people that were once dancing close a few seconds ago have suddenly backed off, giving us all a wide berth.

"I said, don't fucking touch her," Camden growls, his topaz eyes flashing dangerously. Eastern's hand slips away and I can hear him mumble an apology.

"What the hell is this? And who do you think you're talking to like that?" I shout, not able or willing to hold back my anger. I might be able to give Eastern a piece of my mind, but this arsehole is pushing it if he thinks he can do the same.

"I'm just doing what you asked... *Asia*, is it?" he asks,

41

looking at me with narrowed, calculated eyes, much like a predator would its prey.

"What are you talking about? I didn't ask you shit," I respond, ignoring the fact we're now on first name terms. My finger is still pressed into his chest, and despite the tension I feel rolling off Eastern, I dig my nail in a little harder, adding another couple of fingers for good measure.

Camden cocks his brow, looking between my hand and my face. He's as cool as a cucumber, not giving anything away whereas I'm all over the place. My head's spinning, my heart's racing and my rage is bubbling all because Eastern had some pretty girl fall in his lap.

"Eastern is one of my *boys*, one of my *crew*, but I'm guessing he hasn't told you that."

I feel the colour literally drain from my face at his words and accompanying smirk. I'm pretty sure most of my blood is now pooling in my feet. His *boy*, one of his *crew*? *What*?!

"Asia," I hear Eastern begin, but I hold my hand up. He growls in anger at my reaction. Screw him.

"Don't!" I snarl.

Camden lowers my hand, his touch surprisingly gentle given he's giving off a very clear *don't mess with me* vibe. But I ignore that fact and force myself to take my measure of him. He's around my age, even though he looks at least five years older. He works out to maintain his physique, yes, but also to curb the rage I see bubbling just beneath the surface. That rage is schooled for now, and even though I don't understand why that might be given the way I've acted, it is. He owns his shit, whether it's the women he fucks-and I'm pretty sure he fucks and not makes love-or his *boys*. Camden is a leader. You follow him, and you obey. That much I do know. Except for me, I don't obey anyone.

"Eastern works for me now. In actual fact, he has his first job tomorrow. If he pulls it off, then I'm open to him bringing you in," Camden says, assessing me, waiting for my response.

Ignoring him completely, I spin on my heel to face Eastern. "I thought you were doing a run for Nash. That's what you told me, Eastern. What else have you been lying to me about? Can I trust *anything* you say?" I'm referring to his confession in the garden not more than half an hour earlier and he knows it.

"Of course you can trust me. I've got your back, remember? I wanted to tell you before, but shit happened with the court case…" He runs his hand through his hair, and I wonder for a moment where his Crombie hat is. Not that it matters. "I brought you here tonight so you could meet everyone… Opal is part of Camden's crew. She's sorry if she pissed you off, but if you let me introduce you to her, she'll tell you that herself. Jade is her twin sister, so you've met both now. And this, of course, is Camden."

"I've also met one of his other *boys*, the same prick who was snorting coke in the kitchen earlier and is now laid out flat because I punched him for making a move on me *uninvited*."

Eastern's eyes darken. "He did *what*?"

"Asia dealt with him. AJ is going to have a sore head tomorrow," Camden says from behind me. His voice is level, neither annoyed nor impressed by the fact I knocked out one of his crew.

"So, let me get this straight, you're not running drugs for Nash…?" I question, only just noticing that the room has cleared apart from a dozen or so people, the music has turned down too and I can actually hear myself think. The rest of the partygoers are heading out into the garden but despite all the space now surrounding us, neither Eastern nor Camden have backed off. That should worry me, but tonight it would seem I'm off my game.

"Nash is a cover, Asia. The figurehead of my crew so to speak. His age gives him respect my youth doesn't yet command with the big players. But rest assured, I am this crew's leader and I hold all the fucking strings."

There's a warning in that statement that isn't lost on me. Camden is telling me he's the puppet master and he *owns* Eastern. It pisses me off more than I can say.

"Eastern is one of *my boys* now. Question is, Asia, do you want to be one of my *girls*?" Camden asks, stepping around me and standing beside Eastern. Shoulder to shoulder they're a fine-looking pair even though they're complete opposites in every way. Where Eastern is approachable, warm, good looking in a boy next door kind of way with a slight edge, Camden is aloof, confident, exotic and *dangerous*. Not that it matters in the slightest because there's no way in hell I'm going to be a part of his crew. No way.

"I'm not into sharing," I respond, making sure to look him up and down. "Besides this is the twenty-first century, why should I be one of your girls when I can have *boys* of my own?"

If Camden is annoyed by what I've just said he doesn't show it. If anything, he looks impressed. Next to him Eastern looks like he's about to have a stroke.

"The offer will be extended only once," Camden warns, crossing his arms over his chest as he waits for my answer. His thick forearms are corded with muscle and I can see the edges of an intricate tattoo beneath his t-shirt. This guy has no right to be so built at such a young age. It's indecent. Dragging my gaze away from him and settling on Eastern, I refuse to respond to his offer. I'm nobody's possession, and I don't do gangs. End of discussion.

"I can't believe you're in a gang, are you *insane*? What have we always said to each other, Eastern?" I ask.

"I was going to tell you tonight, Asia. You know why I have to do this," he pleads with me.

"Tell him you've changed your mind. There are other ways you can help Braydon."

"Once in, you can't get out. They're the rules, Asia," Camden says coolly.

"Fuck the rules," I shout, narrowing my eyes at him. "Give the job to some other fool."

"No can do," he snaps back, those beautiful topaz eyes flashing with anger.

"This is bullshit. Who the hell do you think you are, taking advantage of someone who's desperate?" Around us I hear the murmurs of the remaining group of people who I'm guessing are the rest of Camden's crew. They're standing round the edges of the room, giving us space but clearly interested to see where this is going. Beneath the fog of booze and weed, I feel a low level danger rolling off them. One word from Camden and we're fucked, or rather I am, given Eastern is part of Camden's crew now.

"You're feisty, ain't ya?" Camden laughs, showing off a golden molar I hadn't noticed before now. But his laugh isn't warm, it's full of warning.

"I protect *my* own," I retort, not backing down. I know I'm pushing my luck, that I'm facing off with someone who has the power to make my life a living hell should he choose to, but I can't seem to stop. I'm leaving for Oceanside the day after tomorrow and I won't be here to protect Eastern or his family. I need to get him out of this mess now. Desperate times call for desperate measures and all that.

"Give the job to someone else and let Eastern go," I press.

"No."

My fingers ball into fists, all common sense well and truly evaporating beneath the storm brewing in my chest. It's never very far away and I'm going to show this arsehole who he's messing with. Eastern's my family and I will do *anything* to protect him.

Camden's eyes flash with a darkness that matches my own when he sees the intent in my eyes. "Careful, Asia. You really don't want to make an enemy of me," he growls in warning. That low level danger I feel ratchets up a notch.

"Too fucking late," I snap, pulling my fist back ready to knock Camden out, but it doesn't smash against his face as I intended. Nope. The next thing I know I'm being thrown over his shoulders, the rest of his crew catcalling and jeering as he carries me out of the house. His grip on me tightens as I struggle against his hold.

"Get out of the fucking way!" he roars at some bystanders milling in the hallway.

"PUT ME DOWN!" I shout, lashing out at Camden and losing all sense of self-preservation. I manage to get some jabs into his ribs and stomach, but he's so built that it's like a child swatting at a giant.

"You're pushing it, Asia," he growls.

Through my own rage, I'm vaguely aware of Eastern running to catch up with us.

"Camden, man. Put her down," he shouts.

There's a wobble in his voice as though he knows he shouldn't be ordering Camden to do anything but that he'll risk his own neck to save mine. Halfway down the street and away from prying eyes, Camden does exactly that, dropping me unceremoniously to the ground. I stumble backwards grabbing hold of a low wall to stop me from falling on my arse. Camden stands before me, whilst Eastern reaches for me and hauls me upright, holding me against his side.

"Jesus, Asia, why can't you leave well enough alone?" he grinds out, a muscle tensing in his jaw.

Camden looks at me with distaste, his gaze lingering far longer than is comfortable. His topaz eyes are like shards of ice, sharp enough to do irrevocable damage.

"Take her home, Eastern. Next time she disrespects me in front of my crew there'll be consequences, and you know I follow through on all my threats."

"Fuck you," I retort, unable to help myself. Eastern stiffens, his fingers digging painfully into my side.

Camden barks out a laugh. "I like your grit, but you've drawn a line in the sand, Asia. We're enemies now. Be prepared." And with that he strides off, not giving either of us a backward glance.

"Shit!" Eastern exclaims. "Shit, shit, shit!"

But I can barely hear him as the world closes in and bile rises up my throat. The last thing I remember is puking up on the pavement before the ground tips away and I pass out.

6

It takes just under two hours to get to Oceanside, and the whole time I've spent it nursing a hangover from the party Saturday night. Normally I'd be over a hangover in a few hours, but this one has lingered for a hell of a lot longer, and I can't seem to clear my head. I spent all of Sunday in bed, avoiding Eastern's texts and pretty much hiding from the world. He'd come to my house asking to see me, but I'd refused, ordering Libby, my foster carer, to send him away. In the end he gave up, no doubt running off to Camden and the *Hackney Hackers Crew* he's replaced me with. I still can't believe he would be stupid enough to join a gang. The one thing we've always promised each other is to never, *ever*, get mixed up in a gang. I feel betrayed. Then I remember how, despite the dangerous situation I put us both in standing up to Camden the way I did, he still stuck up for me. He still got me home safe. I was out of my head, and he made sure I was okay. Despite my anger at him still, guilt lacerates my chest.

"Shit," I curse, feeling like the worst person in the world. I should've at least said goodbye. I decide to respond to his texts the moment I get time alone.

"You alright, Alicia?" my social worker, Annie, asks me as she pulls into a long winding drive. At the end of it, I can just about make out my new home for the next three goddamn years. A white brick building that looks more like a mini Buckingham Palace than a school for kids who are one step away from prison. Other people might be impressed by its grandness, but I know appearances are deceiving. Just because the outside looks pretty, doesn't mean to say what goes on inside reflects that. My gut tells me that my time at this place isn't going to be a breeze. More like a bloody storm.

"Alicia, I asked you a question," Annie states, the tone of her voice irritating me.

Pressing my eyes shut, I bite back my usual sarcastic retort and just nod my head. Even that movement has my stomach roiling.

"Car sick," I lie. Heartsick more like. I don't actually think I'm going to puke; I just feel nauseous and have a banging headache.

"We're here now anyway. No need to throw up in my car," she responds, eyeing me warily. I've half a mind to shove my finger down my throat to make myself sick just to piss her off and ruin the perfect black leather seats. Then again, I'll probably get most of it on myself and I really don't want to turn up on my first day smelling of sick. I do have some self-respect.

"You should've said earlier. I would've got you a bag or something," she continues, reprimanding me before rolling down my window from the control on her side of the car. A flush of fresh air hits my face, and I breath in deeply, cracking one eye open.

"Well, here we are, Alicia," she singsongs, slamming her foot on the break and throwing me forward before my seatbelt saves me. I'm pretty sure she did that on purpose, and I have a very sudden need to punch her in the face.

"Time for a fresh start," she smiles, grinning inanely. She looks as pleased as punch with herself. I'm pretty sure she thinks she's done me a solid getting the judge to send me here rather than juvie.

"Fresh start?" I spit, unable to hide the sarcasm from my voice.

"That's right, Alicia. You have a chance to set things straight."

Is she actually okay in the head? The *only* reason I'm doing this is so I don't get thrown in jail for eighteen months and miss out on seeing my kid brothers for all that time. At least this way I'll get to visit them regularly, even if it is every three months or so.

"Come on, let's get you checked in," she says.

The minute she unlocks the car door, I fling it open and stride to the trunk to grab my bag. That's all I have, one threadbare rucksack filled with all my earthly possessions; a few clothes, a couple of photos, my sketchpad and pencils, and my mobile phone. Not much for almost seventeen years of life. My phone vibrates in my pocket and I briefly flick my phone on and can see another load of messages from Eastern. Without reading any of them, I send him a quick message.

Will respond L8R.

"Let's get you inside. Mr Carmichael, the principal, is waiting to meet you in his office," Annie says.

I shove my phone in my pocket, grunting in response as I

follow her reluctantly up the front steps and past some girl who glares at me from beneath a pair of Ray Ban's. Her long red hair falls over her shoulders in pretty waves and matches the colour of her lips, which are pulled up in an ugly snarl. I might not be able to see her eyes, but her resting bitch face tells me all I need to know about the kind of person *she* is.

"Eww," she says, wafting her hand under her nose, confirming my thoughts.

Bitch. Class bully. One to watch. That pretty much sums her up.

"Watch it," I snarl, stepping towards her.

Annie grabs me by the arm, pushing me none too gently through the door. "Let's not get yourself expelled on the first day now, Alicia," she reprimands me.

The girl just laughs.

***

"WELL, that pretty much sums this term up. Any questions, Alicia?" Mr Carmichael, my new principal, asks me.

I look up from the wad of papers he's handed to me and narrow my eyes at him.

"Yeah, where's my room? I need to fucking lie down. I've got a banging headache."

He smirks, looking at me from over the rim of his glasses, a flop of salt and pepper hair falling into his eyes. Pretty sure he's trying to figure me out, just like I'm doing the same to him. Either that or he's a perv.

Thing is, he might think he knows who I am because of the way I choose to present myself, but he'll never get to know the real me. That privilege is reserved for those closest to me.

But I've already worked him out. He's so easy to read.

Mid-forties, fit for a silver fox, though way too old for me. Psychology degree, I suspect. Probably some doctorate in fucked-up kids like me. Thinks he knows his shit but really, he hasn't got a fucking clue. All his knowledge comes from the pages of a book and not from personal experience. He's a pencil pusher, the handsome Cambridge University student with a doctorate in juvenile delinquents. Made it to principal of this academy before the age of forty. But this dude hasn't lived a life on the streets, he hasn't lost a mother to heroin or his best friend to some street gang and he certainly hasn't lived a life in care. He reeks of middle class privilege and it fucking stinks.

He steeples his fingers, pressing them beneath his chin and just looks at me. Even Annie is getting twitchy sitting next to me, so I must be on the money. Need to watch this one.

"Something you want to say?" I bark, sitting up in my chair as I fold my arms across my chest.

"Yes, the clothes, the make-up, the tattoos and piercings. They're… *interesting.*"

I snort out a laugh. "What were you expecting, some prissy little princess with a knee length skirt, ballet pumps and a fucking twinset? Jesus Christ, what kind of kids do you have here?"

"Alicia! Don't be rude," Annie butts in sharply.

"No, it's a perfectly reasonable question," Mr Carmichael says, his gaze flicking to Annie. He picks up a pen and writes something on a pad in front of him. "Okay, let me put this another way, Asia," he says, referring to me by the name I've chosen for myself rather than the name I was given. "You dress this way to make a statement, that's clear for anyone to see, and yet you don't strike me as a kid who's looking for attention of any kind. I'm pretty sure you'd much rather your art do the talking. That's why your tag can be found on almost every available space in Hackney. Am I right?"

I shift uncomfortably in my seat. This dickhead doesn't know shit. "I happen to like the way I look. Why is everyone so hung up about how I choose to present myself?"

"Not a hang up. Just an observation."

"Well, I'll give you an observation or two of my own, *Mr Carmichael.*"

"Alicia," Annie warns, but my new principal just waves his hand, shutting her up instantly. Instead he looks at me intently.

"Go on..."

"You're a man who wants to change the world, but it isn't because you genuinely want to help, it's because you seek the glory that comes with it. You want to be *respected* but you don't want to dirty your hands to get the kind of respect kids like me would give," I begin, lifting an eyebrow as he sits back in his seat and looks at me like I'm a piece of bacteria under a microscope. There's a begrudging respect in his eyes, but that too is calculated.

"What else, Asia?"

"You'd happily fuck Annie here, but would never commit because you're married to your job. Even your wife knows better than to compete for your attention." Beside me Annie sucks in a surprised breath.

"Alicia!" she says sharply, but I ignore her and continue on my tirade. Now I've started I can't seem to stop. He asked for it. What's a girl supposed to do, ignore the bait?

"You want to fix things others think are unfixable and you get really fucking pissed off when you can't do that. It drives you crazy," I bark out a laugh. "You grew up in middle class suburbia. Your parents are either teachers or accountants, aka fucking boring. Oh, and you've got Daddy issues."

Mr Carmichael nods his head slowly, then folds his arms across his chest and leans back in his chair, lifting his feet onto the desk. He's wearing fucking Doc Martens just like mine and they're paired with drainpipe jeans. It's like the bottom half of his clothes don't match the top half. He waits until my gaze lifts, then he cocks his head and rolls up his pinstripe shirt. Both forearms are covered in detailed sleeve tattoos. What the actual fuck?

"I grew up in an estate in Croydon," he says holding eye contact with me. "My younger brother was murdered by a group of gay bashers in a case of mistaken identity. They were looking for *me*. I'm married to a man called Anthony. He's a therapist here at this school actually and whilst you are right about me being a workaholic, I'm not in this job just for the glory... though a little would be nice," he adds, laughing at that. "My dad was a drunk, my mother a prostitute. I spent twelve years in prison after being convicted for grievous bodily harm." My mouth pops open and he grins, shrugging. "Yep, I got the arsehole who murdered my brother and put him in a wheelchair for it."

"Really!" Annie exclaims, but I ignore her, way too fucking intrigued by this man. Not that I'd let on.

"I've done my time, Annie, get over it," he snaps at her. That makes me grin.

"I decided to get a degree in psychology in prison. I worked hard. After my release I got into youth work back on the estate I grew up in. At a charity function a few years ago, I met some men who wanted to do something for kids who grew up on the 'wrong side of the tracks' or just had a shit start in life," he explains. "They heard my story, they grilled me, and then they hired me as principal of this school. Most days I wing it. Fake it until you make it, right?"

"And your point is?" I retort, still not ready to give him my respect for throwing my observations right back at me and crushing them beneath his Doc Martens.

"My point, Asia, is that what we choose to wear can be just as calculated as our actions. People dress a certain way to fit in, to make a political or social point, to rebel, to present themselves as a professional or a *misfit*..." he says, grinning whilst I scowl. "And some people dress a certain way to hide their true nature, to put others off the scent, so to speak. You made a judgement about me based on what I'm wearing up here," he says waving to his shirt and tie. "But you failed to look deeper, to see what was hidden."

"Great analogy, well done... So, *what*?" I ask, not bothering to hide my sarcasm.

"So, *I* look deeper. I give an actual shit, not a metaphorical one. You are not a statistic, or a file in a cabinet to me," he says, glancing at Annie who winces. "And by the time you leave my school, you won't be hiding who you truly are even if you do choose to wear the same clothes. You'll be the person you need to be, and yes, I will take some of the glory for that. All my past students think I'm a decent guy, a *saint* some have said, but what they don't realise is that I'm a borderline narcissist. At least you got that part right."

He winks, then grabs a key from his desk and chucks it at me. "You're in room 104. First floor of the residential annex. Go settle in. Do what you need to do to make yourself feel better about being here, then take a look around. Dinner is at 6pm in the dining hall, after that you're free to watch tv, mix with the other pupils in the breakout area or go back to your room. We will start the full induction tomorrow morning at 9am sharp after breakfast, once all the kids have arrived. Now, if you don't mind..."

And with that he dismisses me.

"Arsehole," I mutter, but even that cuss is half-hearted. I kind of like the silver fox and I think he likes me. Shame then that over the next few months I find out the same can't be said for the rest of the fucking school.

7

I find my room easily enough. On the way, I pass several other kids lingering about the site, all boys, but I pay them no attention. Even when they jeer and catcall, I ignore them. Their sniggers and remarks about my appearance don't even penetrate the hardened exterior I've built up over the years. I'm tough enough not to let a few names hurt me.

Besides, I've got plenty of time to work everyone out over the coming days and my phone is burning a hole in my back pocket because it's filled with messages that I really need to answer. Opening the door to my new room, I take in my surroundings. It's larger than I expected. A single bed is tucked in the corner, the duvet, sheets and pillows folded up at the foot of the bed. There's a wardrobe, a desk and chair, and the room is painted white. On the opposite wall to the bed is another door, through the gap I can see a shower. Ensuite then? That's a bonus, I suppose. Otherwise the room is bland, boring. Clinical almost, and in desperate need of colour. I'm itching to fill the space with my art, the huge expanse of white wall is just begging to be painted. Then I remember why I'm here and sigh. Apart from sketching in my pad, I haven't tried to do any graffiti art lately. Toeing the line hasn't been easy, but I keep reminding myself of my little brothers so my sketchpad will have to do.

Wandering over to my bed, I dump my rucksack on top of the mattress and look out of the window. The academy building and residential annex are surrounded with fields and sits high on a hill away from Hastings' seafront and town centre. I have a great view of the town that's filled with hotels, houses and little bijou shops (or so Tracy told me). Just beyond is the seafront and an endless ocean that stretches out to meet the horizon.

This is the first time I've seen the ocean, and for a while I just stare out at the dark blue expanse, mesmerised by just how *big* it is. The closest I've got to the ocean is the dirty grey-brown water of the River Thames. Not exactly comparable.

I lean my head against the windowpane, my breath misting up the glass as I take in the view. Today, the sky is clear and the sun warm and bright, that combined with the surrounding fields gives the impression of space and freedom. In reality, I'm just as trapped here as I would be if I were behind bars. It's not as if we're going to be given permission to leave the grounds, and I know from Annie that there's a ten pm curfew. Apparently, the residential staff will do their rounds every evening at that time to ensure that we're all in our rooms. Urgh. I do remember reading about the curfew from the *welcome pack* Annie shoved at me this morning when I got in the car, but that's about it. Mainly, I just flicked through and mused over the fact whoever produced the brochure has made Oceanside out to be like some holiday park. The kids photographed on it are most definitely models handpicked to give a good impression. In fact, the whole thing had made me feel a little nauseous. I prefer honesty, not bullshit.

Pulling out my phone from my back pocket, I scroll through the texts. A couple are from Tracy wishing me good luck and asking me to stay out of trouble… I roll my eyes at that. Trouble seems to follow me wherever I go; she knows that better than anyone. I fire off a quick response, promising to call her as soon as I've settled in.

The rest of the messages are from Eastern.

U still mad?

I'm sorry I didn't tell u sooner.

I knew u'd be pissed.

I know what we promised each other.

But u know I didn't have a choice.

I don't, Alicia…

Camden ain't that bad. Seriously.

I snort at that one. Not bad? Yeah, right. He's bad as bad can be, and that's coming from me who's on the wrong side of the line already.

Ok, maybe a little bit. But he looks after his own.

Fuck, Alicia I can't believe u tried to punch him!

I grimace. It wasn't the best decision I've ever made. In fact, in the cold light of day I know it's *the* worst decision. Pretty sure I've made an enemy for life... it's just as well I'm here then and Camden's back in Hackney.

The drop-off will go okay...

"For fuck sake, Eastern," I mutter, my throat suddenly constricting with worry. Eastern is part of the Hackney Hackers crew now. He's drug running for Camden, the actual gang leader who I insulted. Will Eastern's life be made hell just because he's friends with me? I've put Eastern in an impossible position all because I couldn't control my anger.

I promise not 2 get into any shit.

Well, not too much anyway...

Alicia... answer me.

Is your head still banging? Mine is. That shit was strong!

There are a lot of puke emojis after this message, but I refuse to smile at his change in tactics.

Are u going to ignore me 4ever?

I miss u.

My heart bleeds a little at that.

Fuck, Asia. I just want 2 talk.

Asia, I'm sorry I hurt u.

"I'm sorry too," I mutter, sitting heavily on my unmade bed. How am I going to survive without him? How is he going to survive without me to look out for him? We've done it our whole lives. My eyes scan over several emoji messages until it falls on the final text he sent me this morning. This time my heart stops beating. Actually, I'm pretty sure it's twisting in a knot just like my stomach is right about now.

If it's about the kiss…? About what I said…?

Shit.

I don't want to talk about the kiss. I don't want to talk about what he said to me at the party either. That's a conversation I don't need to have today of all days. I don't know how I feel about it. Okay, that's a lie, I *do* know how I feel about it. I feel messed up and confused. I *liked* kissing Eastern, but I *shouldn't* have done it. My reaction to Opal throwing herself at him was proof enough of that.

"*Friendzone*, Asia… Fucking friendzone." I say, reminding myself that there can never be a relationship between Eastern and me that goes beyond being best friends. Now what the hell do I say? After a minute of pacing up and down, I send a reply:

I'm not mad. I still think you're an idiot for joining Camden's crew coz he IS that bad. Guys like him don't get to where they are being good, Eastern. You're my friend, and I care about what happens to you. Let me settle in. I'll try to call in a few days. Be safe.

I hit send. After a minute I can see that the message has

been read, but after another five minutes of torture I give up waiting on a reply. Clearly, Eastern's getting his own back but I'm not going to play that game. Stuffing my phone in my back pocket, I stride from the room, locking the door behind me.

Time to check out Oceanside Academy.

THE RESIDENTIAL ANNEX has four floors. The ground floor houses the members of staff that sleep onsite, and the first, second and third floors house the students. There are fifteen rooms on the first and second floor and ten on the third, adding up to a grand total of forty. Assuming every room is a single, then that means there are just forty students. Forty students housed in this huge site. That should make me feel better, but somehow it doesn't. You can't get lost within forty students. You can't keep your head down. Everyone is going to know everything, and that makes me more than a little uncomfortable.

When I head past the last set of rooms on the second floor to make my way back downstairs, I hear muffled laughter coming from room 225. A girl's voice giggles whilst the deeper cadence of a male voice chuckles. The sound is strangely familiar. Pressing my ear up against the door, I listen. The giggles quickly turn into moans.

"Christ," I mutter, stepping back. Don't the adults who run this place realise how horny teenagers are? I'm pretty sure there's going to be a lot more room hopping going on during my time here. Except I won't be joining in. Don't get me wrong, I'm no prude. I've had my fair share of sexual experiences, but I'm not about to jump in bed with any of these arseholes. I'm not that stupid. I could do without the complications.

"What the fuck are you doing?" A voice says from behind me. I turn around and come face to face with a mean looking kid with shaved hair and a grimace that could rival my own. He's not much taller than me, but he's wide and built like a brick shithouse with brown eyes that are almost black and a nasty scar running down his left cheek. He has pimpled skin making his pasty complexion look as angry as he does.

This kid is dangerous in a hit first, ask questions later kind of way. I'm betting he'd murder his own mother and laugh about it too.

"Well?" he snarls, poking his finger into my chest and shoving me back against the door. I hit it with a thud. Inside the room I can hear the female voice swearing whilst the male voice just chuckles. If I'm not mistaken, she's just ordered him to climb out of the window.

"I'm Asia. You got a name?" I respond, evading his question entirely. I stand tall, pushing off against the door. He might be unhinged, but then again so am I if pushed too far. Besides, I'm not about to show any weakness on my first day here. I'm no fool, I get how it works. You're weak, you get picked out from the crowd and crucified. Well, fuck that.

"I'll ask once more, what are you doing listening at my girlfriend's door?"

"Not entirely sure she's your girlfriend anymore," I retort with a smirk.

"What?!" he growls, shoving me out of the way. I step backwards and wait for the fallout. This should be interesting.

"Open the fucking door, Red!" he shouts, his meaty fists pounding against the door. His face has turned puce. Any second now one of those veins on his neck is going to pop. He continues to bash his fist against the door, and when it remains stubbornly shut, he starts to throw himself against it. Whoever the guy inside is, well, let's just say he's gonna lose his balls in the next five seconds.

With one last almighty thud, he throws his full weight against the door. It flies open, crashing against the wall as he stumbles forward landing face first on the carpet. The air rushes out of his lungs with a whoosh and the same girl who was standing outside the front of the academy when I arrived runs forward, fawning over him. Her hair is wrapped up in a towel and she's wearing the same tank-top I'd seen her in earlier, paired now with just her knickers.

"Oh my god, Bram. What are you doing? I was in the shower!"

Her gaze meets mine and I roll my eyes. *Yeah, right.* I know what I heard. She was *entertaining* someone else. I bet that beautiful red hair is dry as a bone under that towel.

"What are you staring at, bitch?" she seethes as my grin widens. This should be interesting. I hope the guy in her room has found a good hiding spot.

"I was just telling Bram here how I heard some noises coming from your room. There was a lot of… moaning? Thought you might be in trouble," I respond, shrugging my shoulders.

"Moaning?!" Bram rages, getting up onto his feet. "Who the fuck do you have in here with you, Red?!" He pushes past her and Red scowls at me. Her face in full-on bitch mode.

"What?" I question innocently. "This place is full of criminals, I thought you might be in trouble."

"Bitch!" she bites out under her breath.

"Yeah, that one gets old," I retort.

Red turns on her heel and rushes after Bram who is now

tearing up her room, looking under her bed and yanking open her wardrobe. He heads into her bathroom and comes rushing out like he's just about ready to explode. Woah! This guy's unhinged.

"You lying bitch!" he roars, rushing towards Red. Only, he pushes past her and heads towards me. Behind him, Red is grinning maliciously. Great, her bit on the side must've climbed out of the window just like she'd asked him to do.

Now, I'm in trouble. Fucking perfect.

8

Bram rushes at me. Any sensible person would make a run for it, but I'm not sensible and I don't run. Ever. Readying myself for the blow I know is coming, I curl my fists and wait.

Except his fist never meets my face. Instead, I find myself wedged between the wall and some dude that smells suspiciously of perfume and sex. From my position I can only see the back of his head and the broad width of his shoulders. He seems vaguely familiar, but I don't have a chance to figure out why because before I've even had time to blink, Bram is laid out on the floor once again. I've no doubt Bram can throw a heavy punch, but only if he's quick enough. The guy in front of me got in there first.

"Motherfucker!" Bram roars, as I peer around the shoulder of the guy standing in front of me. "That bitch is mine, Sonny!"

Sonny? You've got to be fucking kidding me. I peer out from behind my wannabe saviour and am greeted with the same cocky smile I remember from the courthouse. He winks at me.

"This bitch is no one's *arsehole*," I shout back, sidestepping Sonny. I hear him chuckle and I know he's the guy who was in Red's room not more than a couple of minutes ago. Blood is pouring from Bram's nose and behind him Red is glaring at us both with wide eyes. She looks both impressed by Sonny's show of manliness and horrified by the fact he's defending me. Not that I need defending.

Her gaze flicks between us both and I glance at him again. He's grinning widely, a toothpick of all things gripped between his teeth which he spits out before speaking. It lands on the floor inches from Bram.

"Back the fuck off. She's with me," he says lazily, dropping his arm around my shoulder. For a second, I'm too shocked to move. Overfamiliar much?

"*With* you?" Red snaps, her eyes narrowing at me. Jealousy slides across her features. It's just as well she's standing behind Bram because the way she's looking at us both right now would give her feelings away in a second.

"Yep, that's right. Sonny and I go way back," I lie, leaning into his side a bit more as I look up at him and smile, playing along. I even press my hand against the firm muscles of his chest for good measure. Sonny's blue eyes flash with interest and a little bit of intrigue, but he continues with the charade anyway.

Red makes a strange growling noise, then grabs hold of Bram's arm and yanks him backwards into her room. "Come on baby, let me make you feel better, yeah?" she purrs, glaring at Sonny beside me who, it would seem, is entirely unimpressed.

"It ain't over, *Bitch*. Come near me or Red again and I'll

make sure you know who's the fucking boss around here," Bram snaps, allowing Red to pull him into her room.

"You know it, Baby," Red simpers, kissing Bram in full view of us and making a real good show of it. Eventually, Bram kicks the bedroom door shut and Sonny's arm drops from around my shoulders.

"What a tramp," I snort.

"You got that right... Fancy seeing you here," he adds, as he crosses his arms over his chest and grins at me with amusement. Ignoring him, I stride off down the hallway towards the stairs wondering how many other *delinquents* were saved from prison that day in the courthouse. Just my luck this arsehole has been sent here too.

"Hey, wait up. Why're you in such a hurry? Don't I get a kiss for saving your arse?"

"Yeah, like *never*," I grind out. This guy is trouble with a capital T. I knew it at the courthouse, and I know it now. Deciding I've had enough excitement for one afternoon, I head back to my room instead of outside. "Besides, I don't follow where skanks have been. Not my style to mess with the inmates, though I see you've made yourself at *home* already."

"Inmates?" he barks out an amused laugh at that. "I don't see the problem. I'm just getting the *feel* of the place." He grins, running to catch up with me.

I cock an eyebrow, glancing at him as he steps in stride next to me. "Is Red the kind of girl you usually go for then?" I ask, surprising myself with such a probing question, given this guy is no more than a stranger and so damn full of himself that he'll probably take it the wrong way.

"You mean beautiful, with killer tits and arse? Yep, pretty much. Why, you bothered I picked her and not you?"

"As if," I retort, wondering if he really thinks that his

knight in shining armour act will be a sure-fire way to get into my knickers. Not. Going. To. Happen. Glaring at him, I pick up my pace.

"So, looks like we both got let off with a slap on the wrist then. Oceanside is a goddamn palace!" he remarks.

"You call coming here a slap on the wrist?" I ask, pounding down the stairs two at a time.

"Are you kidding me? Of course, I do! Have you seen this place? It's got an Olympic sized swimming pool, games room and a fucking maze out the back. Plus, the dining hall is ridiculous. We get to choose from a buffet every time we eat. Can't say we'd get the same in juvie, can you? And we get to mix with the opposite sex. A fucking bonus in my opinion."

I push through the door on the first floor, not bothering to keep it open for him. "How have you managed to look around this place and hook up with that bitch all in one afternoon?" I ask, changing the subject. I really don't care about what Oceanside Academy has to offer. I won't be swimming. I certainly won't be spending time in the games room with the rest of these arseholes and I sure as hell won't be getting lost in some maze so Bram and his bitchface of a girlfriend can jump me. I've got way more street smarts than that.

"I arrived Saturday. Plenty of time to case the joint, and the residents," he says, giving me a salacious wink.

"Didn't take her long to find a guy or *two*," I smirk.

"They're both year two residents. Been going out since they started last year. Can't help it that when I arrive, she's all over me like a rash. "

"Right… and you thought you'd lay it on her?"

"What?" Sonny questions, looking like butter wouldn't melt as he follows me towards my room. "She offered herself on a platter, what was I supposed to do?"

I just give him a scathing look. "I don't *actually* give a shit."

"Fair enough," he responds, not in the least bit bothered by my rudeness. In fact, given the shit eating grin that seems to be permanently plastered on his face, I think he kind of likes my attitude. Well, there's more of that where it came from.

"So, you've probably worked it out by now, but all the first years have their rooms on this floor, second year are on the floor above and the third years get the top floor. In the past they had gatherings up on the roof away from prying eyes," he explains, still trying to make conversation even though I've made it clear I'm not interested in talking with him. Still, gatherings on the roof? Sounds interesting.

"How? Doesn't everyone have to be in bed by ten?" I laugh, rolling my eyes at that. I've had curfews before and never once stuck to them. So, unless they're going to lock me in my bedroom, I'm going to do whatever the hell I want, so long as I don't get caught.

Sonny laughs, his blue eyes sparkling with mirth. "They check once. Then pretty much leave us to our own devices. This is *not* juvie and therefore they can't *enforce* a curfew. We just get credits deducted if we're caught out of our rooms after ten pm."

"Credits?"

"Yep, gain them for good behaviour, doing well in class, being teacher's pet, that kind of thing. Lose them for bad behaviour. If you get enough credits, you can buy time out of this place. Day trip on the weekend into Hastings, that kind of thing. Catch my drift?"

"Yeah, I get it," I sigh. Looks like I'm going to be stuck in this hellhole until the term break.

"Any other questions? I'm like a walking encyclopaedia

when it comes to Oceanside and all the rules. Hazard of living with the douchebags who fund the place."

"You live with the people who own this place?" I ask, my mouth agape.

"Yep, it's both a curse and a…. No, not a blessing, actually," he says grimacing. "So, anything else you'd like to know?"

"I do have one question actually," I respond, stopping at the door of my room. "You lay Bram out with a punch and a guy like that doesn't retaliate, what gives?"

Sonny leans against the wall, crossing one foot over the other. He's wearing drainpipe black denim jeans with a loose grey t-shirt and scuffed up leather boots. He's put together in a way that implies he doesn't really care about what he wears or his appearance, but it's too contrived. Sonny most definitely cares about what he looks like. The groomed hair, neat brows and bright white teeth tell me as much.

"Nothing gets past you, does it?" he grins appreciatively, checking me out as much as I'm doing the same to him. I'm not sure if he's taking the piss or not, but either way I can feel heat creeping up my neck at his steady perusal. I will myself not to blush. I'm not used to being looked at in this way. Eastern might have started a new trend recently, but I'm not happy about anyone else stepping into his footsteps and taking the baton at making me feel uncomfortable in my own skin. Most of my life I've been left alone by the lads on my estate, partly because I'm so unapproachable, but also because Eastern has been by my side every second of every day. Apart from a few heated kisses and a couple of one night stands at parties I've attended over the last year, I've not had a boyfriend. Never really wanted one.

"Not if I can help it," I retort, narrowing my eyes at him. "So, what gives?"

Sonny swipes a hand through his hair. "You remember the dickhead I was with at the court?"

"Yep. Armani suit, silver fox, beard, sexy."

Sonny scowls. "Yeah, him. Well, he's one of the Freed brothers, rich as fuck with shedloads of properties and holiday resorts all over the world. They're the dudes that fund this place."

"I've heard of them," I say. They're legends in our neck of the woods. Three foster kids from shitty backgrounds made good. "I thought he was your foster parent?"

"He isn't my foster parent, he's my *guardian*. Bryce knew my dad when he was a kid. When my dad died, he stepped in and became my guardian. Like I said, I've been living with them for five months now."

"Them?"

"Yes, Bryce and his family. Don't ask, it's a weird as fuck setup."

"But what's that got to do with the fact that Bram didn't get into a full-on brawl with you?"

"Bram knows if he fucks with me, Bryce has the power to get him kicked out of Oceanside faster than you can say... *Ah, fuck!*"

"Ah, fuck?!" I question, frowning. But when Sonny's eyes widen at someone or something behind me, I realise he's no longer talking about Bram.

"There you are, you little sod!" a man says, approaching us both. There's a light-heartedness to his words, affection even. In two seconds flat, I know he isn't a teacher here. He's way too groomed for that. This guy, though dressed down in a pair of dark blue jeans, black jumper and suede loafers, oozes money. As far as I know, teachers aren't paid enough to wear Gucci and Ralph Lauren.

"You were supposed to meet us out front before we head off. I should've known I'd find you chatting up the most beautiful girl in the building," he says, swiping his blonde hair off his face. When I look a little closer, I can see that some of the blonde is grey, but man is he fit for an oldy. I frown as this complete stranger gives me a sincere smile that isn't at all judgemental, which is a drastic change to what I usually encounter. Most of the men on my estate vary between lecherous to completely perverted. This guy seems genuine enough.

"Max, give me a break. You guys told me to settle in. Well, that's what I'm doing," Sonny huffs.

"And I suppose settling in consists of shimmying down the bloody drainpipe, does it? What were you doing climbing out of a second story window?"

"You *actually* climbed down the drainpipe?" I snort, glancing at Sonny who just shrugs like it's no big deal. The kid's a bona fide lunatic.

"On second thought, don't tell me. I really don't want to know," he responds with a shake of his head, before turning his attention fully to me and thrusting out his hand to shake.

"Given Sonny isn't going to introduce us properly, I'm going to. My name is Max Freed and this lad here is one to avoid unless you want your heart stolen," he says, winking at Sonny who grumbles something along the lines of 'arsehole' and 'cramping his style' under his breath. My teeth find my lip ring in a gesture I always do when I feel uncomfortable and out of my depth. This guy seems nice, really nice, and I'm not used to it. His hand falls to his side when I don't take it, a frown creasing his brow.

"I don't plan on letting *anyone* steal my heart, especially not by some *kid* who has really bad taste in women," I retort, turning my back on them both and stepping inside my room before either can see the stupid arse blush rising up my neck and colouring my cheeks. When I lean against the closed door, I can hear Max cracking up with laughter and Sonny cussing him out with a few choice words. A smile plays around my lips, but I force myself to stop. I will not be drawn in by some bighead lothario who shags anything with a pulse, even if he does have really good hair and a nice smile. Nope. Nope. Nope.

9

J ust after 6pm, I head down to the dining hall. My empty, grumbling stomach forces me out of my room and into the main building. Eastern still hasn't responded to my text, and I haven't managed to get hold of Tracy either. A tiny part of me thinks that something bad has happened to Braydon, but I push that thought aside. I'm sure they'd call me if that was the case. Following the sound of chatter and the delicious smell of home cooked food, I head towards the dining room entering through a set of double doors.

Laughter erupts the moment I step into the room, a second before a cream cake comes flying towards me. I duck. The cake misses me and splats on the double doors. I watch as it slides to the floor. Anger bubbles in my stomach and I clench my fists, but instead of launching myself at the nearest person like I normally would, I cock my brow then bark out an unimpressed laugh. Besides, I'm not sure which of these arseholes threw the cake.

"Next time use someone with a better aim," I say to anyone

who's listening before striding into the room and nudging past a bunch of arseholes who are attempting to be intimidating but failing miserably. Bram and Red are sitting with them, which figures. I glare at them, baring my teeth. I don't think they realise who they're messing with. *Dickwads.*

Picking up a tray from the counter, I start grabbing items. I'm suddenly not particularly hungry, but there's absolutely no way I'm letting any of these arseholes think they've got the better of me. So, I pile my plate with curry and rice, a bowl of salad and some bread. It's self-service, and as far as I can tell on my quick sweep of the room, there aren't any adults or staff around at the moment. Figures. None of these arseholes would be ballsy enough to throw food at me were an adult in the room. At least, I don't think they would.

From the far corner of the dining hall, a group of about fifteen guys start to jeer and catcall. It's the same group I came across earlier today. They're all looking at me like I'm a nice juicy piece of meat that they want to chew up and spit out. Bunch of dicks. Actually, wait, three of them are chicks. A crew of dicks *and* chicks then.

"What?!" I sneer. If they think they're going to intimidate me, they've got another thing coming. I've dealt with bigger and badder men than these bunch of arseholes.

"Well, if it isn't the resident skank. You manage to shower yet?" Bram sneers, drawing my attention back to him and the group of fools he's sitting with. He's laughing loudly at his own weak as fuck cuss and I can't help but respond. He's walked right into this one.

"You managed to get your dick up long enough to satisfy your girlfriend or did she find *another* victim to get her off whilst you whacked out a ten second jizz party?" The room erupts with laughter and more catcalling, this time aimed at Bram and Red.

"Why you little…"

"Bitch?" I ask before Red can finish her sentence. "Ever heard the saying '*sticks and stones may break my bones, but words will never hurt me?*' Call me every damn name under the sun, *Bitch*, but know this… I. Don't. Give. A. Fuck."

Her mouth pops open as her face flushes an angry shade of red. I make a point of looking at each of them, not dropping my gaze and not backing down. "Next time one of you attempts to decorate me with cream cake you better be ready, because this *bitch* ain't a pushover."

With that I stride over to an empty table, place my food on top of it, and start to eat. I expect more backlash, but the room descends into silence. Even the jeering has quietened, and there isn't any food being thrown at me, so I guess that's a win?

"Bram was right, you have got big *balls* for a girl," a deep, almost melodic voice says from behind me. "If you wanna show me just how big, now's your chance."

"Oh for fuck sake," I mutter.

What now? Don't these dickheads have anyone else to mess with? I slam my fork down on the table making the water inside my drinking glass spill over the sides. Slowly I push my chair back then stand, turning to face whoever it is that's trying to screw with me this time, only to come face to face with a god.

A literal fucking god.

He smirks because he *knows* it too. I blink a couple of times, swallowing heavily as I realise that isn't a halo around his head but the afternoon sun shining through the window behind him, lightening his hair.

"I'm Ford," he states, and it *is* a statement, not an introduction.

He stares at me from beneath hooded eyelids, giving off the impression of someone who's both distinctly unimpressed and nonchalant, but it's all an act. Beneath the half-mast of his facade, his eyes are sharp, focused and calculating.

"And?" I retort. His grey-green eyes rove over my skin, making it prickle... with fear? I'm not sure. I guess that would be a yes if I was fearful of what this guy could do to my heart. Just as well I'm not afraid of that. No, I'm really not.

"Yeah. I like it," he states, running his assessing eyes over me. I'm not sure if he's talking about my name, or some other aspect of me. Either way, I feel weirded out by my immediate reaction to him.

"Such a tiny girl with so much *fire*," he mutters, running his knuckles over my cheek. The second they graze my skin my stomach tightens and my heart flip-flops. What is wrong with me? I need to get my shit together and fast!

He smirks, his gaze travelling from my eyes to my lips that have parted of their own accord. There's an edge of superiority in his gaze, like he really doesn't give a shit about what anyone thinks of him, least of all me. Some people will say they don't care about what others think when really, they do. But this guy he really, really doesn't. He's the type of guy to play chicken with cars on a motorway. The kind of guy who'll lead you to war without you even questioning why, then stand over the dead and the dying without so much as a shred of guilt.

If I want to survive Oceanside, *this* guy is the one I need to keep an eye on. Not Bram, not Red and not the mob of dumb arses who think throwing a cake at me will force me into submission. Least of all the other residents I haven't even had time to consider just yet.

Ford's the kingpin and so far, the most dangerous person of all. At least to me.

"So easily breakable…"

"What the fuck do you mean by that?" I retort, pushing aside my growing… desire? And drawing out the hardened me.

His tall six-foot frame crowds me beyond the point I'm comfortable with. I stiffen feeling both acutely annoyed, a little intimidated and turned on, to be honest. The whole room has fallen deadly silent telling me two things; I was right about him, and they want to see how I'm going to react next.

"I'm not breakable…" I insist.

He cocks his head to the side, sliding his tongue along his bottom lip. "The best things generally are," he mutters. I literally have no idea what he's talking about. It doesn't seem to matter though, because my body seems to be reacting to him of its own free will.

Honestly, when looking at him you wouldn't immediately assume 'danger'. He isn't an obvious threat, and if he smiled, I'm pretty certain he'd be a heartbreaker. But I reckon smiles from him are as rare as a total eclipse of the sun. This guy isn't built like Bram, he has a wiry kind of physical strength. More like a runner than a heavyweight boxer, and yet I already know he gets into more scraps than the most bloodthirsty fighters I've come across on my estate. His nose is a little crooked, and there are a few tiny white scars scattered across his face. One slices through his top lip, another his eyebrow, and the third across his cheekbone. A mop of ash blonde hair hangs over his forehead, partly covering a deep purple bruise blooming there. For some unknown reason, I have the sudden urge to sweep it off his face. *Stupid*.

"What do you want?" I growl, stepping towards him, rather

than away. I never back off. No matter what I might be feeling. No matter that my head is screaming for me to run this time.

The room sucks in a collective breath.

"Bram, Red, and those guys over there," he says, jerking his thumb over his shoulder, "Are *my* crew here at Oceanside. I want you with us," he adds, his voice lowering as he gazes at me.

"You've got to be kidding me," I mumble under my breath. What is it with me and getting into shit with gang leaders? First Camden, now Ford.

"No, I'm deadly fucking serious."

"And what if I choose not to join your motley crew of *misfits*," I sneer, glancing at them all with distaste whilst simultaneously trying not to pay any attention to the fact that I feel a strange pull towards this guy. I'm like a spaceship caught in the gravitational pull of the sun. It's not a feeling I like or want.

"Then I can't protect you from them," he says, dropping his hand away from my cheek. The spot where his knuckles once touched now burns.

"Protect me from who, your crew?" I scoff. "I've dealt with worse than that bunch of losers."

Ford shakes his head. "Not *my* crew. The rest of *them*," he says, his gaze turning towards the mean looking bunch of arseholes in the corner of the room who are now watching our every move. Included in his sweeping statement is Sonny and two lone girls not sitting with anyone. I briefly wonder why they're not in a gang, and more to the point, why they're being left alone. Sonny is staring at us both, watching the exchange with a look of both amusement and annoyance.

"The one with the scar slashed across his face is Monk," Ford says, bringing my attention back to the group of kids in the corner of the dining hall. One of them is pushing a cream cake around on his plate, smiling evilly at me. So it was *that* douchebag who threw the cake then? Duly noted. I never forget a face.

"What about him?" I ask.

"He's their leader. He oversees the newly recruited Hackers at Oceanside."

10

"Wait, *what*? Did you say Hackers? As in the Hackney Hackers?" I respond, my mouth feeling dry all of a sudden. This isn't good. This isn't good *at all*.

"The one and only. Why? You know them?"

"Shit." I mumble, this can't be happening. "What kind of set-up is this?"

"One where the reach of the most powerful gang in London can infiltrate the walls of this establishment. Mr Carmichael might've grown up in a similar environment to us all, but he sure as fuck ain't aware of Camden's power in our world or if he is, then he turns a blind eye to it. I'm not sure what's worse, ignorance or compliance."

"*You* know Camden?" I respond, ignoring Ford's remark about Mr Carmichael whom I happen to like. I'm betting he knows more than he lets on about what's happening here, and he doesn't seem the type to let it continue without having a reason for it. No, there's more to this than meets the eye.

"Everyone in London knows Camden, including you it would seem."

"Yeah, we've met," I confirm, looking over at Monk who gives me a wide grin. The dark pools of his black eyes are stark against the paleness of his skin. I don't know him, but somehow he knows all about me... Fucking Camden. I'm in big trouble now. BIG trouble.

"Look, I appreciate your concern," I say sarcastically, because this most definitely isn't about any concern Ford has for me, but more about recruiting me to his crew and building his army. There's safety in numbers, right? "But I can look after myself, I've done it for a very long time," I say, stepping backwards, not willing to take his offer.

"And you think they haven't? They'd chew you up and spit you out. You'll need my protection, *our* protection."

"You think Red and Bram are going to protect me? They hate me already."

"They'll toe the line if I tell them to."

I bark out a laugh. "Sure."

"Then trust *me*. I've got your back."

"Why? You're a stranger. We literally just met."

"Because I'm a good judge of character."

That really makes me laugh. "Are you fucking kidding me?" I ask, pointedly looking at Bram and Red who are looking more and more annoyed that their leader has deigned to talk to me.

Ford follows my gaze. "I've known Red and Bram my whole life. Trust me, they're good."

So, they grew up together. Interesting.

"*Good*? Red is a bitch and Bram a wildcard with about as much sense as a rabid dog. I'm betting the rest of them are just as volatile. Thanks, but no thanks."

"You don't know anything. Look, you might not have had the best introduction to my crew, but I can assure you we're a way better option than that lot."

"Those two girls don't seem to think so," I retort, motioning towards the two lone girls sitting away from the rest of everyone else. One of them is dressed similarly to me with a bright pink streak in her long blonde hair. The other looks like she'd be better placed at some prep school with her neat looking black hair, simple jeans and white shirt combo. I mean, really? What the fuck has she done to warrant being sent to Oceanside? That girl is about as unlawful as Marjorie Black, the resident charity worker slash religious nut who lives on my estate back home.

"Those two girls have their own agenda," he shrugs, not bothering to elaborate further. "My point is, I'm not recruiting *them*. I'm recruiting *you*."

I roll my eyes. "You do realise that you're not the British Army and I'm about as interested in joining your gang as I am copping off with Sonny, the resident manwhore over there," I say loudly, hoping Sonny can hear me. Ford's responding smirk tells me he did.

"Ford, she ain't worth the hassle, man. Leave her to the wolves," Bram says, scowling at me.

Ford turns sharply to look at Bram. His eyes narrowing. "Shut the hell up, or next time you fuck up I'll be feeding *you* to the wolves, got it?"

Bram nods his head, his eyes wide with shock. "Got it," he mumbles.

Now that was unexpected. Threatening to cast his friend aside over me, someone he doesn't even know. So much for loyalty. I watch as Red whispers something into Bram's ear, who responds with a rumbling growl and stands suddenly, forcing Red off his lap. If it wasn't for the guy standing next to her who caught her, she would've ended up on her arse. Bram's an animal. If he treats his own girlfriend like that, then God only knows what he'd do to me.

"The offer still stands," Ford says, returning his gaze to me, a flash of doubt and annoyance crossing his features. Yeah, arsehole, your mate's a dick.

"To join..." I pause for effect, cocking my head. "What *is* the name of your crew?" I ask, vaguely interested to see what this bunch of misfits have called themselves.

"No Name."

"What?!" I laugh. I can't seem to help myself. "You haven't got a name?"

"No, that isn't what I said. We're *No Name Crew*."

"This just gets better and better," I say, sighing heavily.

Seriously, one thing I wasn't expecting to find here was more of the same kind of bullshit I've had to live with my whole life. What is it about a human being's need to find a home with like-minded people? I'm a loner, always have been, always will be. I prefer my own company and that of a select few. Namely, Eastern. Though that's gone to shit now that he's joined Hackney's bloody Hackers.

"So, what's it to be, *Asia*? That is *your* chosen name, right?"

"How did you know?"

"News travels fast in a place like this. Seems fitting then that the girl who doesn't use her real name should join the *No Name Crew*."

"That makes no sense," I retort.

"Every single one of us has abandoned our real names for one reason or another. For a while we all lived without a name before we chose one for ourselves. It fits. We fit, and you could too."

"I'm not weak, I don't need to join a gang to feel safe or worth something."

"I didn't say you were weak or worthless, and I imagine you'll put up a good fight," he says, his gaze boring into mine. So much so that I feel the tension between us all the way down in my toes. "But eventually those fuckers will wear you down. If you join my crew, they'll leave you alone. I have enough sway to make sure they do."

"And if they don't leave me alone, what could you actually do about it?"

"Challenge Monk to a fight at the Tower. The winner gets you and the loser backs the fuck off. I never fucking lose. It's why I have their respect. No one has been able to beat me, not even Camden."

Whoa! That's one statement to make. So there really is history between them. Who is this guy and why don't I know about him already, given he seems to hang around in the same kind of circles as I do? "What's the Tower?" I ask, tucking that thought away for the time being.

"Exactly what it says," Ford says cryptically.

Interesting, and whilst I'm intrigued enough to want to know if this was what Sonny had been talking about earlier, I'm not about to delve any deeper with everyone watching us. Right now, I want this conversation over so that I can get out of Ford's orbit and breathe again.

"You're assuming again that I *need* you to fight for me. Listen," I say, losing my patience now, "I'm a big girl. I can look after myself and I don't need you or anyone else fighting my battles for me. Got it?"

"You're a fool. We can afford you sanctuary."

I chance another glance at Bram and Red who are looking at me with distaste. Yeah, right. I don't care what Ford says, those two will stab me in the back quicker than you can say Count Dracula. "I'll take my chances, thanks," I snap.

"Then you won't last past the term break... I can already see Sonny has his eye on you. He might not be part of the Hackney Hackers but that doesn't mean you should trust him either. Bram said you were close."

"I don't trust *anyone*." I'm not sure why I feel relieved that Sonny isn't part of that crew, but I am.

"Then that makes two of us," Ford responds, leaving me wondering why the hell he asked me to join *his* crew if that's the case. I watch him walk over to the group, taking a seat at the head of the table. He glances at me, then at the other group of boys he warned me against. I follow his gaze as it finally lands on Sonny who's glaring at Ford like they're old enemies. Sitting back down on my chair, I pick up my glass of water and take a sip. The coolness slides down my throat but fails to temper the heat inside my chest that remains alight partly from my immediate reaction to Ford, but also because my instincts about people seem to be way off. First Mr Carmichael, then Sonny and now Ford. I've got them all wrong.

Mr Carmichael has lived a life less befitting of a headteacher and more of an ex-gang member. Sonny isn't everything he seems, and Ford may be the leader of his crew, garnering the respect of all the residents because of his fighting skills, but I was wrong about him being the kingpin of Oceanside Academy. My game is off, and I need to sort it out, otherwise I'm going to find myself in deep shit before the week's out, let alone by the term break. There's more at play here than even I can figure out right now.

Cold dread sinks like a stone in my stomach and I know

that bravado and courage aren't going to help me this time. I don't know who to trust. I wish Eastern were here, but then again even if he was, what good would it do me? He's part of Camden's crew now.

11

Back in my room a few hours later, I lay on my bed studying my timetable attempting to push away thoughts of the two opposing crews and what they have planned for me. Shortly after Ford's proposal and my refusal to join the No Name Crew, Mr Carmichael had entered the dining hall to introduce himself officially. He was straight to the point giving us all a quick rundown of the teachers and staff that we'd meet over the coming days. Most of the teachers aren't starting until the morning so they weren't there to greet us in person, but we were all introduced to Bobby Rusk, the head of the residential annex. A glorified caretaker of sorts. Ex-security guard, with a big gut and thick arms. If you ask me, he looks like half the men on my estate who spend their weekly benefits on booze and cigs. I've no idea what possessed Mr Carmichael to hire him.

Not that it really matters, all I need to know is that he's the guy I'd need to give the slip if I ever want to get out of this room past curfew. Then again, that's probably the *last* thing I want to do right now given I've managed to piss off most of the students at Oceanside Academy.

Turning down Ford's offer won't have gone down well and whilst the south coast arm of the Hackney Hackers Crew is yet to bother me again, I'm wise enough to know that it won't last. Then there's the rest of the residents. So far, I've counted just nine girls, ten if you include me. Red and three more bimbos of the same ilk are in Ford's crew. Three girls in the HH crew- as they are more commonly known here- and two more in the general populous who kept to themselves in the dining hall the whole time shit was going down. Those two lone girls intrigue me more than anyone, and I'm determined to find out their story. How have they managed to avoid being recruited? Or maybe they've turned both gangs down already? Either way, I need to find out. I'm hoping to find allies in them at least. I'm not looking for besties, because that isn't really me, just people who might feel the same way I do and who want to stay out of the bullshit.

Ten girls. Thirty boys. Fuck. Whilst my maths isn't that great, I'm pretty sure that's a ratio of three guys to every girl. No wonder there are five P.E. lessons in a week, all that testosterone needs an outlet that doesn't include pussy.

"I fucking hate P.E," I mumble, huffing out a sigh. At least I have Art class to make up for it. I scan my timetable once more, memorising it. After a discussion with Annie, this timetable was put together before I arrived. She wasn't keen on me taking art as a subject but once I threatened to spray the whole school with my tag, she backtracked quicker than a husband caught with his dick in another woman's mouth.

"Better to focus on your art in the right kind of way," she'd said.

Whatever.

In addition to an Art class every day, I have an hour

therapy session with Mr Burnside who I'm assuming is Anthony, the head's husband. Once a week there's also a group therapy session which I'm not looking forward to in the slightest. Fuck that sharing crap. I draw the line at that. The rest of the time is split between Maths, English and P.E. as the mandatory lessons. There's also a two-hour class once a week for learning a new skill but for me that won't start until after Christmas so for now that free time is supposed to be used for studying… yeah, right. Anyway, I've chosen physical therapy. Out of everything available, that seemed the most relevant to my life given Braydon and his needs. At least I can help Tracy when I return home; she might appreciate the support. To be honest, as timetables go it's not that bad and a hell of a lot less rigid than what I've been used to. Not that I've been to school for months.

The day starts after breakfast at 10am and ends at 3pm. The evenings are our own so long as an hour is spent completing homework. We can spend the rest of our free time in the games room or using the gym and swimming pool. Whilst homework is mandatory it isn't enforceable. The punishment for failing to complete any homework set is a loss of credits. The more credits you gain, the more rewards you receive, and I, for one, want to get out of this place as soon as I can, even if it's for just a few hours on the weekend in exchange for a few hundred credits. I'll play the game, for now.

Chucking my timetable on the floor, I pick up my mobile phone and quickly scan for any voicemail or text messages. I've neither. Deciding that now is a good a time as any, given it's fifteen minutes before curfew, I call Tracy.

After a few rings, she picks up.

"Hey, Tracy. It's me."

"Lissy! I've just managed to top up my phone to call you.

Oh, thank God," she responds, sounding like she's got a million worries on her mind.

"What?" I snap, wincing at the sound of my voice. "Is it Braydon?"

"No, no, Lissy, it's not Braydon. He's just fine. Missing you already, but fine."

Relief floods through me at that, followed quickly by worry. That leaves only one person…

"Eastern then?" I bite out.

Tracy sighs heavily. "He's got himself into a spot of trouble…" She's whispering now, and I can't quite hear her over the sudden banging on my door. Must be Bobby, checking I'm in my room and not trying to escape the grounds. I need to wrap this conversation up. I don't need my phone being confiscated.

Bang. Bang. Bang.

"What kind of trouble?" I ask quickly, sitting up and swinging my feet onto the floor.

"The kind of trouble that involves the law and being on the run…" Her voice trails off. "I shouldn't be worrying you with this," she says eventually, since I'm suddenly incapable of speaking. This is all Camden's fault. The job yesterday must've gone wrong. I knew it! Why didn't he mention anything in his texts? *Fuck!* My thoughts run wild whilst my heart gallops in my chest.

"Do you know where he is, Tracy?"

"No, but I know he's safe. He messaged me just now."

Bang. Bang. Bang.

Why didn't he tell me what happened? All those texts and nothing about being on the run. He's probably turned to his new crew for help. That hurts. "Tell him to turn himself in. It'll only be worse if he doesn't," I say, unable to hide the mixture of anger and concern in my voice.

"I did, Lissy. I begged him to. But he *won't* listen. I was hoping you could persuade him."

"He didn't answer my last text, Tracy. I'll try again, the minute I get off the phone from you."

"Thanks, Lissy. He always listens to you."

"Not always," I mutter.

"What was that?"

"Nothing. I'll do my best, Tracy, but he can be stubborn and pig-headed, as you know."

Suddenly my bedroom door opens and in steps Bobby. He looks mad as shit.

"When I knock, you open the damn door!" he shouts, his fleshy jowl shaking.

"I gotta go, Tracy. I'll call you if I manage to get ahold of him."

"Please, Lissy. You're the only person he listens to. Try and get him to come home," she begs, her words coming out in a rush.

"I'll try," I respond. Bobby looks like he's about to pop a vein in his forehead. "Look, I gotta go."

"Bye, Lissy," Tracy responds before I whisper a quick goodbye back then scowl at Bobby who's glaring at me, holding his hand out.

"Phone, now!" he demands.

"What's the problem, *Bobby*? I was just speaking to a friend. Is that a fucking crime?" I retort, clutching my phone tightly.

"It's Mr Rusk to you and this *is* a problem. No phones. Those are the rules. In an emergency you can use the school office phone. Hand it over or find yourself in minus credits before you've even started your first day."

"This is bullshit," I growl. I really, *really* don't want to give him my phone. "No one said I couldn't have my phone."

"Well, boo for you that you didn't read the rules and regulations properly. Hand. It. Over," he growls, his meaty fingers wiggling.

"What about everyone else? Have you taken their phones too? If I'm being mistreated because I'm new here and don't know all the rules, I'll make sure Mr Carmichael knows how much of a prick you are."

"Mr Carmichael *wrote* the rules, missy. It must've slipped his mind when he had you all to himself in his office," Bobby sneers, showing nicotine stained teeth. His eyes run over me, and my skin crawls. Definitely a pervert.

"Fine, take it," I snap, throwing it at him. He doesn't know about my spare phone in my bag and I'd like to keep it that way. I've had enough phones confiscated from me to know that I always need a spare. Eastern knows I have two mobiles. The one I gave to Bobby is the one I use generally, but the other one stuffed in the bottom of my bag in the back of my wardrobe is what we call the hotline. When I ring him on that he knows something serious has gone down. Bobby catches it, shoving it into his back pocket with a grin.

"*Good girl*," he says. Those two words are filled with innuendo and make my skin crawl. "Off to bed now, and make sure you keep this door locked. You never know what kind of miscreants could end up entering the wrong room by *mistake*."

For a second it looks as though he's going to step further into my room, but then the sound of someone shouting from down the hall catches his attention and he backs out.

"You want to remain on the right side of me, darlin'," he drawls, before rushing off to see what the commotion is about.

I get up quickly and slam the door shut, locking it before

grabbing my chair and sliding it under the door handle for good measure. Sitting on my bed, I put my head in my hands. My day has just gone from bad to worse. Not only am I stuck between two warring gangs, my best friend is on the run and I'm living with a pervert who has the keys to my room. Fucking great.

12

The next morning, I head to the dining hall at 9am readying myself for another food missile to come hurtling towards me as I walk into the room. This time, however, there are canteen staff milling about and the two crews I was introduced to yesterday seem to be behaving. Good. I'm not averse to conflict, I've dealt with that for most of my life, but I could do with a bit of peace given I spent most of last night trying and failing to get hold of Eastern. I'm shattered and worry burns a hole in my stomach at the thought that he's in trouble and making it worse by not handing himself in.

Grabbing a tray and filling my plate with sausage, scrambled egg, and bacon I head over to the table where the two girls from yesterday are now sitting together. I know the rest of the people in the room are watching me, I feel the heat of their gaze but do my best to ignore it. Bram and Red are sitting with their crew chatting in hushed tones. Ford is nowhere to be seen. On the opposite side of the room, Monk and the HH crew are a little rowdier but at least their attention is on one another and not me. I don't see Sonny either. Knowing him, he probably pulled one of the other girls and is busy dealing with all that testosterone, I imagine.

"Mind if I sit here?" I ask, plonking myself down without bothering to wait for a response.

Both girls look up at me. The blonde with the pink streak gives me a wary smile before shrugging, whilst the neat freak girl with the perfect dark hair and pressed clothes raises an eyebrow.

"Why bother asking if you're going to sit down anyway?" she responds sharply.

Her accent isn't like mine, i.e. common. Her voice is clipped, her vowels pronounced. She sounds educated and from money, if you know what I mean. What is a girl like her doing here? I always thought money could buy you out of any situation.

"Last I heard it's a free country."

"You weren't invited," she snaps, meeting my gaze.

There's no fear in her eyes, just annoyance, some weariness and a defensiveness that tells me she's had her fair share of shit from people in her past and is over it. Ignoring her snappiness, I answer her previous question. "*Because* like you two, I don't belong to either of those crews," I respond, cutting up my sausage and eating a slice. Miss Prim and Proper raises a perfectly shaped eyebrow at me, as if to say that she thinks that's exactly where I belong.

"I'm Pink," the girl with the pink streak says, interrupting the awkward conversation. "My mum named me after her favourite colour, but everyone assumes it was because of the singer. Except she didn't release her first song until four years after I was born." Her voice is kind of tinkly, like a bell summoning fairies. It seems to go with the pretty, cute look she's got going on. She grins, pointing towards my hair. "Like the blue, suits you."

"Thanks," I mumble, not used to being complimented, least of all by another girl. Most interactions I've had with girls at my previous schools and around my estate have been less than friendly. "I'm Asia." Pink smiles, her gaze flicking between me and Miss Prim and Proper. She lifts her chin, looking pointedly at her friend as though to say; 'talk to her'.

"So, what's your name?" I ask eventually. Pink gives me an encouraging smile whilst the other girl just sighs heavily. Jesus, I wouldn't have bothered sitting with them if I knew it was going to be this much effort.

"Kate," she responds curtly.

"And what's a girl like you doing in a place like this?"

"Girl like me?"

"Yeah, someone who's about as street as the Queen of bloody England."

She rolls her eyes, but I see a spark of mirth in them. Pink snorts, her laughter completely different to her pretty voice. In fact, it's downright indecent; deep and throaty. She sounds like one of those sex-line women, not that I've called many sex lines... okay, so maybe once because Eastern dared me. It was a funny, if not expensive call. Eastern and I lived off that conversation for weeks.

"I'm a genius hacker. Broke into my private school's computer system and messed with the results of some fellow students' exam papers... The bitches deserved it," she shrugs.

"Nice!" Pink says, grinning.

Hmm interesting, so my instincts were right about her. She's been on the receiving end of some shit nasty enough to want revenge for it. Maybe she isn't so bad after all?

"And doing *that* got you sent *here*? Sounds like a pretty minor offense to me," I say.

"I might also have messed with the school accounts a little bit. I had a nice summer break spending the money."

"Whoa!" I exclaim, genuinely impressed now. This chick *is* a genius hacker.

"Proper little criminal, aren't you, Kate? You really can't judge a book by its cover," Pink exclaims, her smile widening. "So why here of all places?"

"My parents are on the school board of my previous school, Brompton Prep. They paid back the money and managed to get me out of juvenile prison and sent here instead. One year here, then I return to Brompton, reformed and ready to face my *real* punishment."

"What do you mean, *real* punishment?" I ask.

"Let's just say that this is just a reprieve and leave it at that." Her eyes flash with pain, but she shuts it down quickly.

"Fair enough. Not my business," I reply, turning my attention to Pink. "So, what about you? What did you do to end up at Oceanside?"

"Kleptomania. I like all the shiny things. Actually, I like *things* full stop. I guess I shoplifted one too many times. Everything I'm wearing was lifted." She pulls a face that sits between a grimace and a grin.

"You actually chose to steal that stuff and *wear* it? I thought you were colour blind or something, or a little funny up here," Kate says, tapping her head. She's genuinely miffed about Pink's choice of clothing. Pink and I burst out laughing at that.

"Nope, I'm fully compos mentis. I just happen to like things most people don't," she shrugs, stabbing her fork into a piece of bacon and eating it. She looks at us both then and smiles sweetly. Both Kate and I look away.

"Whatever floats your boat," I respond eventually, a small sign of solidarity for the girl who's shown me that not every person in the world is an arsehole. I like her individuality. She's a lot braver than me in some ways. I mean, I like colour, but I often stick to one bright shade pairing it with anything black. Pink loves to mix it up. Her silver headband and green polka dot shirt clashes with her bright orange mini skirt, not to mention her silver-toed trainers and several glittery necklaces. She's a walking Christmas tree, and she doesn't give a shit.

"So, between us we have a graffiti artist, a hacker and a klepto. Who'd have thought it," I say, finding myself grinning despite everything.

"Looks that way," Kate responds, her lips lifting a little at that.

Pink takes a gulp of her orange juice then glances over my shoulder, her cheeks reddening a little. "Ah, shit," she says.

"What?" Kate and I respond in unison.

"It's Ford… and *Sonny*," she responds, pointing. The way she says his name has me smarting a little. Is there history between them both? Her pink cheeks tell me that there might be.

"What's the deal? Has Sonny tried to cop off with you as well?" I ask, not able to help myself.

"Erm, well yes. But, he's not really my type."

"What, so you like Ford…?" I question a little too sharply, raising an eyebrow from both Pink and Kate.

"No. *Neither* are my type. I'm *gay*," she says, her cheeks flushing a darker shade of pink.

I don't know why she's blushing. I don't care that she's gay, in fact it's a relief, though I don't really want to delve too deeply as to why that's the case. "I'm guessing he propositioned you anyway?"

"Both of us, actually," Kate scoffs, rolling her eyes.

"Both of you? What, as in…"

"Yeah," Pink confirms. "He thought Kate and I might like to, you know…"

"You're gay too?" I ask.

"No, but that didn't stop him from asking us to give him a show… The guy's a walking, talking hormone. Seriously, the dude needs to get laid already," Kate remarks.

"Oh, I'm pretty sure he's managed that."

Turning, I watch as Ford and Sonny walk into the dining hall together. Not together, together, just side by side. Sonny has the same shit-eating grin plastered on his face, whilst Ford is scowling. I wonder what they've been up to. Sonny catches me looking and his grin widens, whilst Ford continues to scowl. My stomach clenches, and my heart suddenly thumps a little too loudly. What is it with those two? More to the point what's up with *me*? I don't react like this normally; that weed I smoked with Eastern must've messed with my head.

"Look at them both giving you the eye," Pink remarks, the smile in her voice evident even though I can't see her face. I whip back around willing my cheeks not to flush at their attention.

"Not interested," I blurt out. This time it's Kate who laughs.

"Yeah, right," she says. I ignore her knowing smile. She doesn't know me and therefore she doesn't know shit.

"I'm *not* interested."

"You didn't join Ford's crew then?" Pink asks, as she spears some bacon and stuffs it in her mouth.

"No fucking way. What about you two?"

"I wasn't asked. I'm probably too *posh*," Kate responds with a smirk. "Or I just don't fit in. That's kind of a problem of mine."

"And you?" I ask Pink.

She wraps her hair around her fingers and cocks her head. "I'm keeping my options open. Early days yet."

"You'd actually consider it?" I'm kind of flabbergasted by that. She doesn't seem the type to join a gang. She's too... *sparkly.*

"Nah, of course not, but they don't know that yet. I'm smart enough not to piss them off on my first day. I mean, Ford seems alright even if he is a bit broody. But Monk, he's a mean arsehole. I intend on keeping them guessing for as long as possible, then I'll figure out what to do."

"Not much of a plan," I suggest.

"Maybe, but it's the only one I've got," she responds with a smile, not in the least bit bothered. I'm wondering whether she has any street smarts at all because sooner rather than later, she's going to have to make a stand like I did and suffer the consequences, or choose a side. I wince. It won't be good either way.

"Well, if it isn't my favourite group of outliers," Sonny says, sauntering over with his breakfast tray. He plonks himself beside Pink, flashing her a grin, then resting his gaze on me. My skin immediately heats up. "How's tricks, Asia? Pissing off anyone else this morning?"

"Not yet, but there's plenty of time," I retort, before chugging back my lukewarm cup of tea and standing. "Well, I've got shit to do before class. Catch you both another time?" I blurt out.

"I'll be here waiting, willing, and very much able," Sonny says with a wink. I roll my eyes.

"I wasn't talking to you."

"I'm offended," Sonny retorts, covering his heart as though he's in pain. But I see a flash of challenge in his baby-blues.

Great, now I've managed to make myself his target. Nothing like wanting what you can't have. Urgh. He's going to be like a dog with a bone, I can feel it. Dragging my gaze from his, I look between Pink and Kate.

"Sure, we'll be around," Pink says, responding for both of them.

"Cool," I mutter, feeling more and more awkward by the moment as Sonny's gaze slides over every inch of me; my skin flushes with heat everywhere his gaze lands. "Stop gawking," I snap, before turning on my heel and striding from the room. Sonny laughs at my retreating back and I suddenly wonder why I feel the need to run, when usually I stay and fight.

Damn it.

13

It's my final lesson of my first full day at Oceanside, and only second to group therapy is my worst bloody nightmare...

P.E.

The *last* thing I want to do on a scorching hot Tuesday afternoon is workout with a bunch of arseholes. I know how this shit goes down, getting physical in some team sport equals hidden jabs and punches. I don't expect to leave this lesson without a few bruises. Then again, if anyone touches me, they're gonna get it back bruise for bruise. Striding out onto the open field that sits just beyond the back of the main school building, I do what I always do when out of my comfort zone, I suck it up and fake it. Holding my head high and ignoring the jeers of the Hackers and the scathing looks from the majority off No Name crew, I make my way over to Pink and Kate. Pink is wearing a bright orange shorts and vest combo, showing off her long legs and fit body. She's talking animatedly to Kate who's dressed head to toe in black. By the look on her face, Kate dislikes P.E as much as I do. Black joggers and a long, baggy t-shirt aren't really doing anything for her figure, but like me, I don't think she wants to draw attention to herself. I've also got on a pair of jogging pants but have teamed them with a tank top, my shoulder length hair pulled back in a rough ponytail. I'm not here to impress anyone, I'm here to get this shit over and done with.

"Well, lookie here, if it ain't the spawn of Hackney's most famous whore," Monk sneers as I walk past him. I stop dead in my tracks. My mum might've been a junky, but she was no whore.

Motherfucker.

"I heard she coughed you out then straight up fucked a man for her next dose of smack."

"What did you just say?" I seethe, taking the bait and swallowing it whole. Monk is fishing, and he's reeled me in good and proper.

"You heard," he snorts, folding his arms across his chest.

Monk's surrounded by his crew and they're all looking at me with a violent kind of hunger. Well, maybe not all. One girl looks just plain scared, though she's trying to hide it. He meets my gaze with a mocking smile, looking me up and down.

"What? Truth hurts, doesn't it?" he continues, stepping forward and getting into my personal space. He's a big guy, tall with wide shoulders. According to Kate, he's a year three student. We had quite an interesting chat in our Maths class earlier today, spending most of our time discussing the other residents of Oceanside rather than completing the mental arithmetic test we were given. Ms Collins deducted twenty credits from both of us for failing to complete the test. Fuck her anyway. I hate maths.

"Ain't got nothing to say?" he sneers.

By now the whole group has gathered around watching us both. Monk's crew is standing in a semi-circle behind him, whilst the others from No Name crew gather behind me, effectively blocking us off from anyone who might be looking our way. Mr Langdon, our P.E. teacher, is far away on the other side of the field with his back to us, talking to a couple of students that I can't quite make out. Now that the gap has closed and we're surrounded, I can't see them at all. Not that it matters really, I'm not about to wimp out and go running to the teacher for help anyway.

Squaring my shoulders, I stand my ground. If I'm quick I might be able to get a punch in first, but if he hits me, I've no doubt it's going to hurt. *A lot.* It doesn't matter though. This isn't about winning, this is about making a point. I won't take shit lying down. No way.

"Oh, I've got plenty to say, but I'm not sure you'd understand. Ever heard the saying *thick as shit?*" I retort, gritting my teeth and readying myself to fight. Monk barks out a laugh, but despite his bravado I can see that I've hit a nerve. He growls, stepping closer.

"Asia, this isn't a good idea," Pink says, suddenly beside me. She rests her hand lightly on my arm.

"I can handle it," I bite back, not taking my eyes off Monk. I can see the bloodlust in his eyes and know instantly that he's the type of guy without any kind of morals. Hitting a woman isn't something he'd think twice about. I glance at one of the girls in his crew; she looks at me aghast and I know instinctively that she's been beneath his fist more than once. Men like him make me sick and knowing that Eastern is part of this crew makes me feel even sicker.

"You can handle *this*? You're delusional. I'd snap you in two and throw your bones to the crowd," Monk says, mocking me. Behind him, his crew make barking and howling noises like a pack of wolves, and now I understand the reference Bram made yesterday. Still, I'm not afraid. Take out the pack leader and the rest will jump on each other, right?

"Tell me, Monk, is your cock so small that the only time you feel like a man is when you square up to a woman? Having a tiny dick must be hard for a tough *mutt* like you, hmm?" I retort, my gaze flashing to the girl who looked horrified a second ago. I can see her smirk briefly before she hides her mirth with a blank look.

He barks out a laugh, cupping his dick and circling his hips. "Why don't you get over here and see for yourself... fucking a *bitch* like you could be fun so long as I don't have to look at your face." Then he leans forwards and sniffs, grimacing. "On second thought, I don't dip my cock in pussy that stinks like fish!" The rest of the boys behind him start laughing and wafting their hands in front of their noses.

Arseholes.

Stepping forward, my rage simmering like a kettle about to boil over, I poke him in the chest. This time Kate grabs my arm, pulling it down. "Don't!" she begs.

But I can't back down now, I'd look weak. It'll be worse for me if I do. Besides, this dipshit deserves a good punch. It's not as if anyone from the No Name crew are going to help, otherwise they would've done so by now. In my opinion, not stepping in to prevent a fight is just as bad as starting it. They're just as dickish as this arsehole and his pack of *wolves*. I briefly wonder whether Camden knows half of what's going on at Oceanside. He might be an arsehole too, but this doesn't seem his style. Then again, he's got my best friend into trouble with the law, so maybe this is exactly what he's capable of.

"Where's your backup now?" Monk taunts me, his

sharpened gaze looking between Pink and Kate, dismissing them with a snarl.

"I don't need any backup, *prick*."

Ford and his crew can go to hell... And Sonny? So much for his knight in shining armour act yesterday. I've no idea if either are watching this because I have my back to a lot of people. And, frankly, I don't expect or *want* their help, but if they're here and they're watching to see how this plays out, then they're on my shit list good and proper. At least Pink and Kate are standing by my side.

"You're nothing but a mouthy piece of arse," Monk jeers.

"Say that again," I bite out, my fingers curling into my palms.

He grins now, his lips curling back over his teeth. "Camden was right, you *are* feisty. It would turn me the fuck on if you didn't stink so bad."

"He put you up to this?!" *Fucking prick.*

"Nah, *baby*. He might've given me the heads up, but this is all on me. *I'm* the leader here, and you, *whore*, are mine. Besides, he's got his hands full with your prick of a friend... Eastern, is it? The guy's a liability."

I see red. Without even considering the rest of his crew or the fact I am launching myself at a six-foot beast, I pull back my fist and punch him as hard as I can on his jaw. The pain I feel as my knuckles hit bone is intense and stars appear in front of my eyes for a moment. Fortunately for me, I've scrapped many times before and my adrenaline kicks in quick, forcing me to focus.

He stumbles a little. Shock lighting his dirty-brown eyes, followed quickly by aggression and fury.

"You've thrown the first punch, *whore*, all bets are off!" he yells, before pulling his fist back. I dodge his punch, ducking.

Unfortunately, Pink wasn't quick enough to move out of the way, and his fist meets her temple with a sickening thud. She falls to the ground out cold. *Shit!*

"You motherfucker!" I scream, throwing myself at him like a wildcat. I use my fists, my nails and my teeth as I attack Monk with everything I have. I might be a girl, I might be small, but I *can* fight. If he can hit a woman and not blink, then I sure as hell can fight dirty.

He takes it all with a gleeful smile, batting me off easily before a couple of his gang members grab hold of me, hauling me backwards. My chest is heaving as I struggle against their hold, but instead of hitting me, Monk steps forward and grabs my jaw roughly with his fingers.

"We'll finish this later," he spits, his eyes scanning behind us.

"What the hell is going on here?!" Mr Langdon yells as the two boys holding me let me go with a shove. I stumble forward, falling to my knees beside Pink. Kate is already there, her hand pushing back the hair from Pink's forehead. Her eyes are fluttering open and she groans.

"Shit, that *hurt*," she mumbles, tears smarting her eyes.

"Thank fuck," I say, relieved to find Pink is okay. Well, as okay as she can be with what is likely a concussion and a huge bruise forming on her face.

Looking up at Monk, I bare my teeth. "Next time, I'm going to kill you."

He just laughs.

14

"Get out of my way," Mr Langdon says as he pushes through the crowd. "What happened?" he asks, bending down beside Pink and helping her to stand.

"An accident," Monk says, glaring at me in warning.

Fuck him if he thinks I'm covering his arse. "Bullshit, this dick tried to hit me and got Pink instead. He knocked her out," I snap, getting to my feet and pulling Kate up with me.

"He did *what*?" Sonny says, pushing through the crowd, Ford following closely behind him. He looks between Monk and I, his eyes narrowing as he makes a quick assessment of what's just gone down.

"You know the score, Monk," Ford says, as he moves around me and steps in front of Monk, pushing against his chest.

"You tried to hit *my girl*?"

"*Your* girl?" My mouth drops open. Is he for real? I'm no one's girl, especially not *his*. I didn't join his stupid gang. I thought I made that fact pretty damn clear yesterday in front of the whole school. Ford ignores my remark, continuing to press his finger into Monk's chest.

"You go near Asia, or any of them again," he says, pointing at Pink and Kate, "and you'll be dealing with *me*."

"She's fair game," Monk retorts, seething.

"Prick," Sonny growls, glaring at Monk. His fingers are curled into his palm, and his body is as tense as Ford's.

"No one is *fair game* at this school," Mr Langdon snaps, supporting Pink with one arm, whilst Kate holds onto her other side. I watch as he pulls a walkie-talkie from a clip on his belt and requests assistance. "Everyone break-up or watch your arses get expelled from this school. There's plenty of space in juvie for every single one of you. Remember that when you think of starting a fight on my field. Start running. Ten laps."

The crowd don't move, some of them make cutting remarks beneath their breath. Mr Langdon loses his shit. "NOW!" he roars.

"Do what he says," Ford snaps. His crew, including Red and Bram, start jogging around the field. The HH crew follows shortly behind them once Monk gives the nod. Nice to know the teachers are in charge here...

"Move away from Monk," Mr Langdon says to Ford.

Ford leans in and says something under his breath to Monk, then gives him one last shove before stepping back. He looks at me, then at Pink who is groaning in pain.

"You've got *my* protection now, whether you want it or not," he says, standing beside me. A muscle ticks in his jaw and I can feel the repressed anger rolling off him. I've no doubt he would've set upon Monk if Mr Langdon wasn't about.

"I don't need your damn protection," I mutter under my breath. Ford makes a grumbling noise but says nothing further.

Sonny watches us both, opening his mouth before slamming it shut without saying a word.

"Take Pink to the medical room. I want her checked over," Mr Langdon says to Sonny.

"Ford can do it," Sonny says, folding his arms across his chest.

"I'm not asking Ford, I'm asking you. Medical room now, and take Asia with you."

"Fine," Sonny snaps, picking up Pink who's still groaning. I watch as he folds her against his chest. She curls into him, her fingers clutching at his t-shirt. "Come on, Asia. Let's get out of here for a bit. Looks like you could do with a break," he says, with genuine concern and minus any smart remarks this time.

"I don't need to go to medical. I'm *fine*. Take Kate, she'll look out for Pink," I say, refusing to leave her alone with this bunch of arseholes.

"Asia, just come get checked out," Sonny insists, gritting his teeth as he looks between me and Ford.

"Please, come with us," Kate adds. I know she's worried. She's also a little shaken up too, but I'm not. I'm used to this kind of bullshit. This was a weekly occurrence on my estate, or at least it was until I knocked that dickhead Mickey out when he tried to mug me on my own doorstep.

"Isn't this *lovely*?" Monk laughs, enjoying the show.

"I'm *fine*! Just *go*," I hiss. Jesus, are they purposely trying to make me look weak in front of this prick?

"Then stick with *him*, and don't start any more fights you can't finish," Sonny warns, before giving Ford a look. "Keep your hands off," he mutters before striding away from us both, Kate in tow.

Ford's nostrils flare, but he doesn't respond to Sonny's territorial statement. I wonder what the deal is between them.

Sonny isn't in his gang, but there's a kind of love-hate relationship between them both that comes from knowing each other for more than a couple of days. But more to the point, where does Sonny get off thinking that he's laid some claim on me? I'm not a piece of meat to be fought over by a bunch of predatory lions. This is *bullshit*.

"Ahh, I'm feeling all left out. Maybe your pussy is worth a go after all." Monk smirks, looking at me with a curled lip and unwelcome interest.

"Shut the fuck up, dickhead," Ford growls, glaring at him.

"That's enough, Monk. You'll be pleased to know that you're needed in the Principal's Office. Can't have you feeling *left out*," Mr Langdon retorts sarcastically, before handing Monk over to two big burly men dressed like security guards who've managed to creep up on us all. I've not seen them around before, but then again, it's not as if I've gone looking.

"See you later, Asia," Monk says, allowing the men to walk him off the field.

"Not if I see you first," I retort, letting out a long steady breath. What a dick.

"Are you sure you don't need to go to medical?" Mr Langdon asks again the moment Monk is out of earshot.

I shake my head. "I'm sure."

"Then get going. Ten laps."

Without even waiting for Ford, I start running. I might hate P.E. but that doesn't mean to say I'm unfit. Running from the police on numerous occasions means I've got stamina, and with anger still bubbling inside my chest I need to expend it somehow. Back home, on occasions like this, I'd let off steam by taking off in the middle of the night and finding a blank wall to spray. I guess running around this field a few times will have to do.

Concentrating on keeping a steady pace and schooling my emotions, I chase the group in front of me. Ford catches up and falls into step, his soft breathing the only thing I hear over the pounding of our feet on the track. I don't speak to him and he doesn't speak to me. The silence between us does all the talking. When everyone else finishes their ten laps and heads off the field, I keep going. I don't want to go inside just yet, and despite the sheen of sweat covering my body, and the thirst I've got going, I carry on. Ford sticks with me, not letting up.

Glancing at him, I notice that his dark blonde hair is stuck to his head and his white t-shirt has a circle of sweat on the front, sticking it to his chest and defining the muscles beneath the thin material. He catches me looking and I snap my head around, picking up the pace. Suddenly this has become a race that I need to win, and I pump my legs harder, focusing all that pent-up anger.

But like me, Ford has stamina and keeps up stride for stride. After another ten minutes I stop running by a copse of trees at the edge of the track. Leaning over, my hands on my knees, I breathe deeply. Sweat drips from my forehead and down my nose, falling to the floor. I see Ford's feet just in the periphery of my vision. He's stopped too, his breathing as ragged as my own.

"Are you done?"

"What do you mean, am I done? Who the hell do you think you are?" I ask, standing upright.

"Has your anger run its course or are you still looking for a fight?" he retorts, running his hand through his hair. It sticks up all over the place, but he still manages to look sexy... *sexy*? I groan loudly. I really don't need this shit right now.

"Whether you like it or not, Monk outmatches you. I can help you get the upper hand."

"I told you I don't need your kind of help or protection. I can look after myself," I snap, striding off across the grass.

"Let's see about that," I hear him say, and before I can do anything about it, Ford has me pressed beneath him on the ground, the wind knocked out of me. "Just as I thought." He smirks, but there's disappointment in his eyes too as though he'd hoped he wouldn't be able to take me down so easily. I can't believe the arsehole just jumped me. His strong thighs encase my hips whilst his hands have my arms pulled up above my head. Beneath my tank top, my nipples are embarrassingly hard.

"Get. Off. Me!" I shout the second the shock has worn off and I'm able to think about something other than the fact that he's straddling me.

"Make me." His breath tickles against my skin, as he leans over me and brushes his lips against my cheek. When he pulls back, I can see that he's just as shocked by that action as I am. Shocked *and* turned on. Or maybe that's just me?

"You fucking asked for it," I respond, bucking my hips at the same time I bring up my knee and aim for his crotch. But he's too quick. Before I can predict his next move, he's thrown himself to the side, grasped my hips and yanked me on top of him. My pelvis is crushed against his, but before I can break away, Ford wraps his legs around the back of my thighs. If I'm not mistaken, he's hard. My cheeks flush a deep shade of red. It's just as well I'm still sweaty and breathless from running, or my reaction to his hard-on would be embarrassing.

"What now?" he murmurs, watching me. His grey-green eyes flick from my mouth to my eyes and back again. I'm so shocked by the fact that I'm as turned on as he is, that I just lie there, spread out over him like some cheap blanket. He grins darkly, goading me with his plump *kissable* lips.

Kissable? *"Get a fucking grip, Asia,"* I tell myself.

"Cat got your tongue?"

"Dickhead," I mutter, pushing upwards in an attempt to get away from this boy who's fucking with my head. Except Ford has other ideas. In another ninja move I am pinned beneath him once again. He's flipped me over so many times that I'm positively dizzy. Between us his dick is pressed firmly against a part of me I wish it wasn't, given the way it's making me feel; stupid, brainless, *distracted*. Holding my breath, I wait for his cheeks to colour as deeply as my own. They don't. He knows he's hard and he owns it.

Arrogant... *cock*. I almost laugh out loud at that thought.

"If you want to survive in this place, you need to learn how to fight *properly*, Asia. You might've got a few licks in with Monk, but he would've wasted you before you could've done any real damage."

"I *can* fight," I retort angrily, twisting beneath him in a pathetic attempt to get away.

Ford laughs, keeping me pinned down with one hand holding my wrists, using his free hand to swipe the sweaty hair off his forehead. "That might be true, but you lack skill, strength and *sense*. Whether you like it or not your size puts you at a disadvantage. Sometimes rage just isn't enough."

"And I suppose if I join your gang, you'll be the one to teach me?"

He opens his mouth to respond but I cut him off. "I told you I don't do gangs, and in case you need reminding I *can* look after myself."

Ford sighs, easing up his hold. "I don't *want* you to join my crew, Asia. I *want* to teach you how to fight so that when that arsehole Monk or another member of the HH crew tries to jump you, and believe me they will, you'll be ready."

"I thought I had *your* protection?" I say sarcastically, trying not to react at the way his jaw tenses and his pupils dilate as I wriggle beneath him.

Screw him... Do I *want* to screw him? Thoughts of Ford smashing his lips against mine has my hips circling beneath him again. Ford's responding groan snaps me out of my thoughts, and I stop wriggling. He looks at me a beat too long before jumping up, holding his hand out for me to take. A rush of heat prickles my skin at the lack of contact. My eyes flash to his groin, then snatch back up when I see his dick tenting his joggers slightly. Damn him and damn my body having a mind of its own.

"Take my hand," he offers, still completely relaxed about the fact that he's got a raging hard-on.

Ignoring him, I get to my feet, my stupid legs wobbling beneath me. I know it isn't just because of the twenty laps I've run either.

"I will do what I can to look out for you..." He sighs, frowning.

"Why?" I ask, confused by his insistence.

"It doesn't matter why, I just will. But I can't be there all the time. You need to know how to fight someone who's twice your size and *win*. Like I said, rage isn't enough."

"It's saved me countless times before. I won't be beholden to you, or anyone else for that matter. I've been at the mercy of others before, believing in them when I had no business to. They let me down, so the *only* person I rely on is myself. Besides, rage is *all* I've got left," I say, before turning around and quickly jogging away from him, pushing thoughts of Eastern out of my head.

This time, he doesn't follow. I should feel relieved, only I'm not. I feel very, very alone.

15

Later that same week, I sit in the spacious art studio with my teacher Miss Moore, or Ros as she likes to be called, a thirty-something art enthusiast. The only other student is some nameless boy from the No Name crew who I've no intention of getting to know any time soon. Looks like art isn't a favourite subject of most of the residents at Oceanside Academy. Not that I care, because frankly it's bliss. I can actually relax a little without fear of some snide comments or food missiles coming my way.

For the first time since arriving here, I feel another emotion other than a constant low level pissed-off. I'm almost… *happy*. Well, as happy as I can be when I'm continuously worrying about my best friend and waiting on tenterhooks for the moment I get jumped by HH crew. I've been in a state of *fight* since I arrived here and for the first time in years, I'm getting the urge to run. Not because I'm weak or afraid, but because I'm *tired*. Tired of fighting all the damn time. A week in and I already feel worn down. How the hell am I supposed to last three years here?

Picking up my acrylic pen, I press the nib against the thickened paper and begin to colour within the pencil outline I've just laid out. It's not the same feeling that I used to get back home in Hackney when I was painting murals with my cans, always on the lookout for a copper. The excitement and adrenaline rush were addictive. This kind of feeling is nothing compared to that, but at least I can express myself, even if it that expression is confined to just a sketchpad.

"Nicely done," Miss Moore murmurs as she looks over my shoulder. I automatically hunch over, not used to anyone praising my artwork. "The shading's beautiful, Asia."

She hovers for a little bit but when she realises that I'm not about to start up a conversation with her, she leaves me be. I like that about her. She gives me space and doesn't try to force a relationship between us. All the other teachers, except for Mr Burnside the therapist, are jerks who want to enforce their rules on me. Thing is I can't be ruled, that's why I'm here after all.

For the next five minutes I'm so consumed with my artwork that I don't notice another student enter the room until said student has pulled up a chair and sits down next to me. I don't bother to look up, because I know who it is from his signature scent of coconut and sea breeze. This guy even smells like a surfer on some faraway beach. He's a walking, talking contradiction given he's nothing more than a petty thief.

"There's plenty of other tables in the class, Sonny. Take your shit and sit somewhere else," I snap, feeling both irritable that he's invaded my sanctuary, and unnerved at his closeness. This guy really can't catch a hint.

"How's this?" he asks, getting up and moving across the table from me.

"Not nearly far enough away," I retort, refusing to meet his gaze and look into those baby-blues that have somehow managed to infiltrate my dreams this past week. I *don't want* to dream about him, but somehow, I manage to.

"Is that a person?" he asks, half a beat later.

From beneath my lashes I can see him leaning over the table trying to get a look at my drawing. Instinctively, I wrap my arms around my sketchpad. Funny how I can spray a six-foot wall with my artwork and not care that the whole world will look at it, but I can't let this one guy look at my quick sketch. Don't get me wrong, it's a good drawing. Actually, it's pretty fucking great but I hadn't offered to show it to him, so he shouldn't assume it's okay to catch a glimpse.

"Are you drawing me, is that it?" he says with a smile in his voice.

This time I lift my head and meet his gaze. "Not *you*, no," I respond.

He pulls a face. "As *if* there's anyone better. I've got a pretty fucking fantastic face, Asia, no wonder you're committing it to paper."

The arrogance! Determined to swipe that smile off his face, I do something reckless and twist the sketchpad around so he can see who I'm *actually* drawing. It takes monumental effort not to laugh when his mouth pops open and his eyes widen when he sees just who it is that's caught my attention.

"*Ford*?!" he shouts, gaining a cross look from Miss Moore. "Sorry, Miss," he mutters, narrowing his eyes at me. I shrug, twisting the pad back around to face me and loving the fact he's so pissed off. That'll teach him.

"*He's* your fucking muse?"

"What can I say, he's got an interesting face," I respond, biting my lip to prevent the laughter from escaping. This is just way too much fun. And whilst, yes, Ford does have an interesting face, so too does Sonny. Even though they're similar in colouring and could even pass for brothers, they're actually polar opposites and definitely not related. Ford is broody and cross most of the time, constantly tense and on the lookout for the next fight. Whereas Sonny is effervescent, happy, light-hearted even. He always has a joke on his lips and a glint of mischief in his eyes. And yet beneath Ford's brooding countenance is a warmth waiting to escape, just like there's anger bubbling under Sonny's skin. Their outer appearance and inner secrets make for interesting subject matter, but I'm not about to tell Sonny that. Let him believe what he wants. Besides, *confidence* is attractive, arrogance is most definitely not. Maybe he'll learn something today.

"Interesting face?" he mutters, a muscle jumping in his jaw. He cocks his head and stares at me for a full minute before pulling out a dogeared sketchbook of his own.

For the rest of the lesson Sonny remains uncharacteristically quiet. He doesn't crack a joke or even try to start a conversation. I'm pretty sure I've successfully knocked the wind out of his sails. When it's time to pack up, he rips out the page he's been working on from his sketchpad and hands it to me before striding from the room without a backward glance.

When I look down at the drawing it's my turn to feel shocked. On it is a stunningly intricate drawing of a girl with bright blue hair and a lip ring... a girl that looks *exactly* like me.

AFTER LUNCH, my final two periods of the day are taken up by group therapy. It's Friday afternoon and I'm expected to sit here with a bunch of strangers and talk about my feelings.

Not. Going. To. Happen.

I don't care how nice Mr Burnside is. I'm *not* opening up in front of everyone. My one-on-one session on Wednesday might have gone okay, but this is way out of my comfort zone. Way, *way* out. Especially since my group consists of Sonny, Ford, and two dudes from the No Name crew. I'm the only girl and completely outnumbered. Mr Burnside coughs, drawing me out of my thoughts and bringing me firmly back into the present. He looks at each of us in turn, his warm hazel eyes kind and intelligent. I instantly feel threatened. Intelligence I can handle but kindness... that's a whole other ball game.

"By now, each of you have had a one-on-one session with me this week so I don't need to introduce myself again, and we don't need to go over how I'm Mr Carmichael's partner. Pretty sure we've dealt with that part of my private life already, yes?" he says, looking pointedly at the kid from the No Name crew who just shrugs in response. "Good, because the gay jokes get boring. My personal life is private, and I expect you *all* to respect that."

"Yeah, but you expect *us* to chat about *our* personal shit in front of everyone. How's that fair?" the boy he's addressing asks. I hate to admit it, but he's got a point.

"Part of the deal in gaining a placement at Oceanside was your agreement to attend therapy sessions, both one on one and in a small group setting like this. If you choose to walk out of here, then you know what the alternative is."

"Yeah, but no one actually said anything about this group shit," the same boy persists.

"It's in the brochure that each of you would've had chance

to read before arriving here. In addition, your social worker should've made you aware of the requirements."

I can't help it, I laugh at that. "My latest social worker said barely two words to me the whole time I was in her care. You honestly think she told me about this?" I say, moving to stand.

Mr Burnside holds his hand up. "Sit down, Asia."

"I signed a bit of paper that says I must *attend* the therapy sessions. At no point did it state that I must *partake*. So, if you don't mind, I'm going to make myself comfy over there and sit this shit out."

Mr Burnside gives me a look of disappointment, but he doesn't argue with me. Instead, he turns to the rest of the group. "Anyone else?"

Everyone bar Sonny stands up, finding their own spot in the room. Opposite me, Ford leans against the whiteboard, his face void of emotion. I'm not surprised he's opting out given the guy's a therapist's wet dream. Admittedly, even I'd like to know what's going on in his head. Right now, I can't even begin to decipher what he's thinking. Ford catches me staring but his expression remains neutral, and for some reason that pisses me off even more.

Across the room, Mr Burnside sighs heavily before grabbing a seat and sitting opposite Sonny. "Looks like you've got yourself two-hundred and fifty credits, Sonny," he says, flashing us all a look.

"Fuck yeah." Sonny grins, looking smug as shit.

"Yep, enough for a whole eight hours freedom from this place on any weekend of your choosing. The rest of you are deducted ten points. That will continue to happen every time you refuse to *partake*."

Sonny laughs, whilst the two guys from Ford's crew swear loudly. Ford remains tight-lipped as usual.

"That ain't fair," one of them says. I think he calls himself Dagger, but I can't be sure.

"I think it's *entirely* reasonable," Sonny responds mimicking a random posh accent. I watch as he folds his arms and smiles at Dagger who steps forward with a growl.

"Don't," Ford snaps from his spot in the corner of the room.

Sonny's smile widens as though he's the cat who got the cream and I wonder, not for the first time, what the deal is between those two.

"So, Doc. What do you want to know?" Sonny asks, stretching his legs out before him and crossing them at the ankle.

"Whatever you want to tell me. Pick a subject and start talking," Mr Burnside responds, leaning back in his chair, his pen ready and poised over his notepad. For a while Sonny just muses over what he can talk about, tapping his chin for effect.

"Any subject at all?" Sonny asks, glancing at me then back to Mr Burnside.

"Yep, absolutely anything."

"Well, if I'd known we weren't talking about ourselves I might've taken part," Dagger grumbles.

"Perhaps next week you might want to do just that. For now, you can sit this out with the rest of them," Mr Burnside responds as he starts scribbling on his pad. "Start talking, Sonny."

Over the next hour Sonny gives us a rundown of his favourite subject: Victoria Secret underwear models. I can tell he's enjoying himself immensely and is particularly smug about the fact he's managed to nab himself two hundred and fifty credits for doing so. I'm also pretty sure he thinks he's managed to swerve any kind of in-depth psychoanalysis.

Except Mr Burnside is smart, and by the end of the session has successfully turned the discussion on its head and has somehow managed to get Sonny to open up a little about his obsessive desire with all things beautiful. Concluding that perhaps Sonny's childhood lacked the kind of beauty that he seeks out so relentlessly now, both in the things he's stolen over the years and the women he's pursued.

Clever.

When the session ends, Sonny smiles widely slapping his hand on Mr Burnside's back, congratulating him on being a sneaky bastard. And whilst he appears unbothered about it, I see what lies beneath the bravado. I see the fear and the pain just as much as Mr Burnside, confirming that Sonny isn't as one dimensional as I'd first thought. Today has shown me that he's just as layered and complicated as the rest of us, and fuck if it doesn't intrigue me more.

16

The first thing I do when I wake up the next morning is call Tracy. It's almost lunchtime on Saturday and I've already missed breakfast, but that doesn't matter, Eastern does. It soon becomes apparent that she has no more news since the last time I spoke to her. Eastern is still AWOL and I can't even reach him on the hotline. Tracy had managed to get news on my brothers and I'm thankful that they at least are unaffected by all this shit. The less they know the better but I make a mental note to contact them just as soon as I get my own head straight. Though that doesn't stop me from trying to reach Eastern again the second I get off the phone from her.

Eastern, please. It will only get worse. HAND YOURSELF IN!

The message is read almost immediately, and I wait for a response. An hour later I finally give up staring at the phone and stuff it back into the hole I cut into my mattress.

"Arsehole," I mutter, picking up my rucksack and stuffing my sketchpad and pens into it.

On my desk is the drawing Sonny did of me yesterday, I run my finger over it, marvelling at his talent for a few minutes.

"There's more to you than meets the eye, isn't there, Sonny...?"

And now I'm talking to myself, about Sonny no less? Fucking great.

Pulling out my sketchpad, I slide the drawing inside before stuffing it back into my bag. I don't want to leave it here in my room because I don't trust creepy Bobby not to invade my privacy, let alone any of the other bastards in this building. Pretty sure most of them know how to pick a lock. Deciding that I need to keep my head occupied with something other than thoughts of Eastern, Ford and now Sonny, I head outside bumping into Kate on the front steps of the main building.

"Hey, Asia, we missed you at the canteen. You going to grab some lunch?" she asks.

"Nah. Not hungry. I'm heading to the library for a bit."

"The library?" she asks, surprise written across her face.

"Yes, the library. Got an issue with that?" I snap, not feeling particularly friendly right now. She winces, giving me an apologetic look. Yeah, she's not the only one with a brain. Though I'm not going to the library to study or anything, just chill, but she doesn't need to know that.

"Did I just hear you're going to the *library*?" Pink asks as she exits the building and joins us. She's munching on a cake, little flakes of pastry falling onto her bright pink top.

"Jesus fucking Christ. Yes, I'm going to the library. Why is that so hard to believe?"

"Oh, I get it! You're meeting Sonny there, aren't you?" Pink wiggles her eyebrows at me. When I don't answer she sucks in a breath, her eyes widening dramatically. "Ford! You're meeting *Ford*, you little sneak. He's got to you, hasn't he?"

I roll my eyes just as dramatically. "I'm not here for any of that shit. I haven't got time for romance…"

"Who said anything about romance? I'm pretty sure both would be happy with a quick fuck."

"Jesus, Pink. *Shut up!*" Kate says, shoving her a little before they both start laughing.

When I don't join in, they stop giggling, training their smiles behind wobbly lips.

"Well, enjoy your time in the library," Kate says eventually.

"Yeah, when you're done come swing by my room, we're gonna hang out for the rest of the day. Might even head down to the rec room after dinner for some Netflix minus the chill," Pink adds with a wink.

"Sure, maybe," I respond before heading inside.

"Oh, and make sure you avoid the gym. Monk and his crew have taken it over. It's like a testosterone bomb has gone off in there. Either that or they're all hyped up on roids. I walked in and walked straight back out again. Fortunately for me I don't have a target on my back…" Pink slams her mouth shut, realising how shitty that sounded. "Sorry… that was a crappy thing to say."

"It's not, it's the truth. Don't worry, I'll be careful to avoid the area. Catch you later, *maybe*," I say, jogging inside before they can stop me.

"NEED ANY HELP, ASIA?" the librarian, Ms Mariner, asks me.

I shake my head. "No, I'm good."

"Well, I'll be here if you need me," she responds as she settles behind her desk and starts tapping at the computer. "If you want to get ahead with the English coursework, I can help. There's plenty of Charles Dickens you can choose from."

"Sure," I mumble from my spot at a desk in the corner. I don't particularly want to get into a conversation with her, but I don't want to be rude either. Ms Mariner is nice, if not a little boring. Truth is, I dislike English as much as Maths, but I do the work I'm given so I can get enough credits to earn a day out of this place. I wasn't actually planning on doing any homework today. I came to the library to get a change of scenery and to do some art given the studio is closed over the weekend. Besides, I feel a certain kind of peace here with all the musty old books and lack of people.

The library itself takes up almost half of the first floor in the main building and sits directly next to the art studio. It's light and airy, and perfect for drawing with all the natural light pouring through the floor to ceiling windows. Not only that, none of Monk's crew would be seen dead in the library, and on the handful of occasions I've been up here, I've only ever come across one member of the No Name crew.

Today's it's just me and Ms Mariner, and that's the way I like it.

Glancing over at her as she taps away at her computer, a pencil gripped between her teeth, I wonder why the library's open on a Saturday given no one bothers to use it during the week, let alone the weekend. Not that it appears to bother Ms Mariner. I'm guessing she gets paid double time for coming in on the weekend and given she seems happy enough to be here, what do I care?

Placing my sketchpad and pencils onto the table, I open the pad up onto a clean page and begin to sketch. Like most times when I draw, I let my brain connect with my hand without too much thought as to what I'm about to draw. I kind of like it that way. On the streets back home that's exactly what I'd do when out and about with my cans. I'd find the perfect wall and just start to paint. Eventually a mural would appear, then I'd slip off into the night leaving behind a piece of art just like Banksy, but without the notoriety or the cash.

Letting my mind wander, I press the tip of the pencil onto the paper. Before long an image begins to appear. For a fraction of a second I pause, then start shading in the detail, not allowing myself to question why I'm drawing *him* of all people.

An hour or so later I've finished. Resting my pencil on the table, I lean back and look at my work. It's one of my better portraits, which is unnerving given the subject matter. In all honesty, I'm not sure what to make of it.

"Well, well, if it ain't our resident skank."

Monk.

I react instantly snapping shut my sketchbook just before he gets to my table. He pulls out a chair and sits opposite me, flanked by two of his crew. The same two who grabbed me and held me back that day on the sports field.

"What do *you* want?" I ask, sliding my sketchbook it into my rucksack. There's no way I'm keeping that within reach of this dickhead. There's too much personal stuff in there. Contrary to popular belief, I don't just do graffiti art. The sketchpad is filled with images of Braydon, Tracy and Eastern. Of late it has a few new faces too, and it's those drawings in particular that I don't want him to see, specifically not the one I've just drawn. I'll *never* live that one down.

Monk watches me, his eyes narrowing as I zip up my bag. "I have a message for you," he says, his gaze snapping to meet mine. This kid hates me. Like proper, *I want to beat the crap out of her*, kind of hate.

"More shit about my mother, I take it. Or perhaps you want to reiterate what a slut I am. Or *maybe*, you want to finish what you started on the field?" I retort sarcastically. It's risky giving him such mouth, but I can't seem to help myself. It's ingrained in me. Act first, think later. Typical Asia.

"We can get to that if you want, but first the message," he responds, sliding the phone across the desk and tapping the screen.

I look down, my chest tightening as I see an image of Eastern.

"Play it," Monk snaps.

Without hesitation, I press the play button, my throat constricting at the sight of my best friend. He looks exhausted, dark circles ring his eyes and his skin is pale. He has a black hoody pulled up over his head, but it doesn't stop me from noticing the bruise blooming on his cheek. What the fuck has happened to him?

"I'm safe, Alicia. Don't call me, it's too hot right now. I'll contact you when I can. Just don't piss him off…"

The video stops abruptly. I'm pretty sure Eastern had more to say, but whoever was videoing him cut it short. Either that, or Monk has edited the video before letting me see it. What had Eastern meant, don't piss him off? Don't piss *Monk* off? He's asking for a miracle right there.

Monk snatches the phone up. "Better listen to lover boy, *Alicia*. Don't piss *me* off."

"Where's the rest of it?" I snap, ignoring his remark and the fact he's called me Alicia. If I let on how much I hate it, he'll only use it to wind me up.

"That's it." He shrugs, giving me a look that tells me that most definitely is *not* all of it.

"Liar!" I whisper-shout, trying not to get the attention of the librarian. She glances over at us both, her eyebrows pulled together in a frown. She knows as well as I do that Monk and his sidekicks aren't here to study.

"Okay, you got me. There *is* more, but you don't get to see it... unless," he says, lowering his voice and giving me a nasty grin.

"Unless *what*?"

"Unless you pay a visit to the Tower and join in on the festivities tonight."

"What *festivities*?" I ask. I know as little about what happens at the Tower as I did the first day I arrived here.

"If you come as *my date*, you'll find out."

"Date? You've got to be fucking kidding me?" I almost puke up a little in my mouth.

"You want to see the rest of the video, that's the deal. Take it or leave it."

"And if I say no?"

"Then you'll never know what lover boy here had to say, and next time he sends a message it gets deleted."

"You're such a prick," I retort, not caring that I'm putting myself in a vulnerable position right now with three against one, not to mention lowering my chances of seeing the video at all.

"And you're a prick *tease*, just like your mother was."

I stand abruptly, my chair falling backwards, clattering on the floor behind me. The library is so quiet that the sound is deafening. Ms Mariner jumps. "Everything alright?" she asks, looking worriedly between us.

"Everything's fine, *Miss*," Monk says, curling his lips

upwards in what I think is supposed to be a smile, but comes off as something way more frightening. The guy can't even smile without looking like he's about to murder someone.

"Asia?" she asks me, as unconvinced as I am by his half-arsed attempt at being non-threatening.

"Yep, all good," I bite out, picking up the chair and sitting back down on it.

"Really?"

I *know* that she knows I'm lying. I also know that whilst kind, she's not the type of person to stick her neck out for someone who might be in danger. Self-preservation appears to win out over altruism. I smile brightly, and punch Monk lightly on the arm just like two friends might.

"Monk and I are mates, isn't that right?" I ask him, whilst a little bit of puke actually does fill my mouth.

"Yes, Alicia and I are close," he agrees. Then turns to me with a wicked glint in his eyes before sliding his snakelike tongue out over his thin lips. Yuck!

"Well, that's okay then. Just keep the noise down, please. This is a quiet space for studying," she says, before turning back to her computer and turning a *blind eye* on what's really going on. Shame, I was beginning to like Ms Mariner. But like most adults, she'd rather a quiet life than one complicated by delinquent kids like us.

"What time do the *festivities* start?" I ask Monk.

I can't believe I'm actually entertaining his proposal, and if I hadn't seen the video, I would've told him to shove the invite up his arse. But now that I've seen a glimpse, I really need to hear the rest of what Eastern has to say. Like me, Tracy hasn't heard from him since that first day he messaged her. If I can give her any information to set her mind at ease then I'm willing to go to some party with Monk to do so.

"10.30pm sharp. Entrance is via the third floor fire exit. It will remain unlocked for five minutes. Meet me there. You arrive late, you get shut out. Got it?"

"Got it," I repeat.

Monk nods, standing. He motions for his sidekicks to give us some space, then leans over the desk, placing his palms flat against the surface. "Make sure you come dressed for the occasion. I like short skirts and tight little tops, understand?"

"Perfectly," I bite out, wanting nothing more than to slam his head against the table. Instead, I nod tightly and watch him leave wondering what the fuck I've got myself into now.

17

For the rest of the afternoon I avoid everyone. Pink and Kate knock on my door at about 8pm asking whether I want to go and watch a movie in the rec room before curfew, but I decline their offer. I need to get my head straight before my *'date'* with Monk.

Fuck.

What was I thinking?

Now it's ten minutes to curfew and despite Monk's request I am *not* dressed in something short and tight. He can go fuck himself. Instead I'm wearing my trusty pair of black denim jeans, Doc Martens and a black t-shirt. I'm not feeling particularly colourful this evening. I just want to get this *'date'* over and done with so I can see the rest of the video.

Grabbing my phone, I dial Eastern again. It rings, then goes straight to voicemail. The dickhead is avoiding me. Why is he making it so difficult? I get that he's on the run and he needs to keep his head down, but doesn't he realise we're worried about him? Doesn't he understand that *I'm* worried about him? I really don't need to get messages from him via Monk. He's the last person in the world that I'd want to communicate through. I have a damn phone he can contact me on. Speaking of which, I stuff said phone back in its hiding place. Grabbing my rucksack, I pull out my sketchpad. I'm not willing to take it with me to the Tower, and I can't risk someone finding it should anyone get any funny ideas and break into my room. So, I stuff it in a sealable plastic bag and shove it into the toilet cistern. Monk might think he has me fooled, but I know there's more to this evening than a chance for me to see the rest of Eastern's video message. I'd put money on him getting one of his crew to ransack my room just for the hell of it.

Once I'm satisfied everything important to me is safely hidden, I head up to the third floor arriving exactly at 10.30pm just like Monk said. This will be the first and last time I obey any of his orders, that's for damn sure. I try to push open the fire exit door, but it's locked. I'm guessing with one minute to go I'm still too early. So, I lean against the door and wait, assuming Monk will be here any moment now.

Then the lights go out.

And the whole fucking floor is pitched into darkness.

Intuition tells me this is not a random blackout, and my stomach bottoms out as my heart thumps so loudly I can barely hear myself think. This all for me. *Fucking Monk and his gang of wolves.*

I don't hesitate, I run blind towards the stairs at the other end of the corridor, my hands held out in front of me. Laughter echoes down the hall pulling me up sharp, and all I can think is where the fuck is everyone? It's curfew, but there are no sounds coming from any of the rooms on this floor, or anywhere else for that matter. I find it hard to believe that everyone is tucked up in bed fast asleep and oblivious to the power cut.

"Skank!" a voice whisper-shouts.

"Where are youuuuuuuu…?" another voice singsongs creepily from the far end of the corridor I'm moving away from. Forcing myself to control my breathing, I try and work out if it's just me and these two arseholes, or if there are more of them.

"There's nowhere to ruuuuuuunnnnn," another voice calls, this time coming from in front of me. Motherfuckers have me surrounded. I feel blindly for the wall, then push my back against it the moment my hands find the smooth plaster. I ease myself along it, step by agonisingly slow step, trying not to breathe too heavily and give away my position. I figure these arseholes are just as blind as I am, unless they've managed to get hold of some infrared goggles that you see in the movies. If that's the case, I may as well give up now.

"Here, *pussy, pussy*," another dickhead says, followed by a round of laughter. I'm not certain, but that's at least four different people going by the voices. None of which are Monk.

"Fuck, shit!" I hear someone shout, the sound of them stumbling to the floor reverberating down the hall.

"Dickhead, give away our position, why don't you?" another guy whispers.

Another two more.

I hear the scramble of feet and I'm assuming one of the bastards is helping the other guy stand up. They're both very close by and I can only assume they've walked out of one of the bedrooms on this floor. Fucking perfect.

"Monk is gonna beat your arse if you fuck this up," the same arsehole hisses to the other.

I hold in a nervous laugh. No infrared goggles then, good.

At least that levels the playing field somewhat. Well, maybe not level it out, given there's at least six boys on this corridor with me, but if I can't see them, they can't see me. It's all I've got. I just need to get off this floor and down to my room without getting caught.

No such fucking luck.

"Come out, come out wherever you are..."

My head whips around and I stiffen like a deer caught in headlights. A flashlight turns on at the far end of the corridor highlighting a face I've quickly come to despise.

Monk.

He's standing by the door that leads to the staircase and escape with a flashlight pointing up under his chin. He looks fucking insane with his nasty grimace contorted into a scary mask because of the light and the shadows it casts across his face. It reminds me of some long forgotten scene in a horror movie. You know the ones? Where everyone *dies*. Now what am I going to do? If he points the light in my direction, I'm caught. My fingers curl into my palms... I'll just have to fight. I can do that, even if it is now seven on one. What other choice do I have?

Yet, he doesn't lower the beam of light towards me. I'm still shrouded in darkness, but I think that's the point. He wants me to know he's there and that he has the power to light up the whole corridor at any given moment but is choosing not to. He has the power to end this, but instead he flicks off the switch and throws the corridor back into darkness just to make this whole fucking episode even more fucked-up.

I hate to admit it, but I'm scared. One-on-one fist fights I can handle, maybe even seven-on-one but mind games like this? Not so much. For the second time I wonder where the fuck everyone else is.

"Time to learn who's the boss around here, *skank*," Monk sneers and I swear he's looking directly at me even though I can no longer see him, and he sure as fuck isn't able to see me.

Fuck.

"This is going to be so much fun," he continues with a sinister laugh. His bastard crew laugh with him. Thinking quickly, I sink to my hands and knees. They'll expect me to be creeping along the wall, but they won't expect me to slide along the floor, so that's what I do. Pressing myself as low as humanly possible to the ground, I move as quickly and as quietly as I can. Then I almost have a heart attack when the body heat of one of Monk's crew seeps into my skin because he's standing so close to me. After a moment, the soft tread of his feet moves away.

"This is stupid, just turn the torch on and grab her," someone whines. I think it's the guy who tripped a second ago, but I can't be sure. That comment is followed quickly by a loud thud and a moan.

"Shut the fuck up. This is *my* game, and this is how we're going to play it," Monk growls before switching the torch on again and lighting up his ugly-as-fuck face.

"Come on, Asia, just give yourself up and let's have that *date*," he sneers, breaking into laughter that makes my skin crawl before flicking off the flashlight once more. I'm not afraid of the dark, never have been, but this is something altogether different...

I'm being hunted.

That's what this feels like. But I'm no easy prey even though I *am* scared. Instead of letting my fear overwhelm me, I do what I always do, I use it to fuel my rage.

Coaxing the storm within I let it get more violent. That violence drowns out the fear. It bubbles and boils inside my chest, giving me the strength to do what I must to survive, and whilst a large part of me wants to reveal my position so I can release the rage, I must be smart. Ford was right, rage *isn't* enough. I'll get my revenge on Monk, but not today. Today, I run.

I keep moving, shimmying along the floor as quickly as possible, the sounds of my attempts to escape drowned out by the heavy footfall of Monk and his crew pounding up and down the corridor. After another minute of slowly shuffling along, I can feel a slight breeze and know that I can't be far from the door leading into the stairwell. It's always cooler in that part of the building.

"She's not fucking here, Monk," an exasperated voice says. "Must've gone into one of the rooms."

"They're all locked, I checked before," he snaps back.

"Look, man. The film finishes at eleven in the rec room, they'll be back soon," another voice adds.

"We've got time," Monk retorts.

"You think? Trying to get an extra hour out of Bobby was fucking hard enough. Took all my stash to get him to keep quiet about it. The fat bastard is a greedy cunt," one of the guys says.

So *that's* where everyone is. In the rec room watching a fucking movie whilst these bastards play out a scene all of their own. Figures.

"She's *here*, the skank couldn't have gone far. Though I have to admit, she's pretty fucking good at hide and seek. Just as well since we enjoy the hunt, ain't that right, boys?"

Laughter and jeering erupts right before the corridor begins to echo with howling and barking.

Jesus Christ. What the hell are they going to do to me? More to the point, *why*? I know I was a mouthy bitch to Camden at that party, but does that really warrant this kind of fucked up mind game? Maybe I underestimated him. Or perhaps Monk has gone lone wolf, and this is all on him.

Either way, I need to get back to my room and fast.

Listening intently, I figure I've only got one of Monk's crew between me and the door to the staircase. I *think* the rest are behind me. Making a decision, I jump up to my feet and make a run for it.

Worst. Decision. Ever.

I slam headfirst into a hard chest and we both go down with a loud, bone-cracking thud. It takes me a second to realise that I'm not the one howling in pain.

"BITCH!" the guy shouts, as I waste no time jumping to my feet and stomping on him for good measure. The air whips around us as he tries to make a grab for me. Whether it's sheer good luck or plain old stupidity on his part, I manage to dodge him. By now the flashlight is switched back on. Monk and the rest of his gang can see me in full technicolour, or at least in black given I'm dressed head to toe in it.

"Get her!" Monk shouts and I run for my fucking life.

Slamming into the door, I leap into the stairwell, hitting the steps two at a time just as the lights flick back on, small mercies and all that. Funny how, when adrenaline takes over, fear evaporates. My thoughts are filled with one word and one word only.

Run.

And that's what I do. Despite the rage and the anger, I run.

Pretty soon I'm on the first floor pelting it towards my bedroom. All those years spent running from the police has given me an edge, and I make a mental note not to bitch anymore about P.E. If Mr Langdon wants to start making me run five kilometres a day, I'm going to do it. Fuck, I'll even run ten if it means I can stay ahead of this bunch of bastards. Reaching my door, I whip out my key, slide it in the lock and open the door in one go. Fuck only knows how I manage to do that with my hands shaking so much, but I do. Maybe there's someone up there looking out for me. Perhaps it's my mum finally being a mother and protecting me from the afterlife... then again, perhaps not.

By the time Monk and his crew have caught up, I've locked my door and shoved my chair under the handle for good measure. The oxygen that kept me moving, suddenly leaves my lungs and I slump to the floor, angry tears welling in my eyes.

I never fucking run, but this time I did, and I *hate* myself for it.

"Open up, bitch!" Monk roars from the other side of the door, his fists pounding against the wood. It shakes in the frame, but it doesn't open.

"FUCK YOU!" I scream, unable to hold back the rage a second longer. It takes every ounce of willpower not to open the door and launch myself at the bastard. But I have to be smart, and that wouldn't be smart at all.

"I see you've met Monk," a voice says from the doorway of my bathroom.

Stiffening, I swivel my head, not truly believing what I've heard. Hoping and praying that I'm hallucinating.

I'm not.

Leaning against the doorframe, with my sketchbook in hand, is Camden.

18

S crambling to my feet, I lose all self-control. I lose all sense
of *anything*. My anger and fear all funnel towards the boy
standing before me. If my words were daggers, he'd surely be
dead.

"You motherfucking bastard! This was all *you*!" I scream.
I'm vaguely aware that the pounding on my door has stopped,
leaving a gaping silence, as though I imagined it all. I'm
shaking so bad that my teeth are chattering, and my vision is
wobbling with the tears that I know are falling. I swipe at my
face, angry at myself for showing weakness.

I'm so fucking angry.

I never cry and now I am, in front of *him*.

Camden's face is neutral, showing no emotion at my
outburst. He flicks open my sketchpad, holding it gently in his
large hands as he flips through the pages. I know the second
he's found the portrait I sketched earlier today in the library,
because his eyes widen just a fraction before glancing up at me,
a question in his eyes.

"Give that back," I seethe, taking a step towards him.

He closes the sketchbook and throws it on my bed, pulling out my mobile phone from his back pocket. "This is what I came for. Now that I've got it, I'll leave."

"No you fucking won't," I snarl, not caring anymore. He may be big, he may be built, but I'm back in more familiar territory. One-on-one I can do. *This* I can do.

"You'll step aside, Asia. Don't make this harder than it needs to be," he says calmly. So calmly that I want to scratch his eyes out.

"Harder than it needs to be? You set your pack of wolves on me, for *what*? So they can distract me whilst you steal my phone? Whilst you take away the only ability I have to contact my friend!" I bark out a hysterical laugh. "What the fuck are you even doing here anyway? Don't you have a crew to rule, lives to destroy and a town to fucking terrorise?" I'm panting so hard by now that it's difficult to keep myself upright. There isn't nearly enough oxygen in the room for the two of us.

"Number one, that wasn't me. I had nothing to do with that," Camden says, his topaz eyes darkening with... what? Anger? That throws me a little. "Number two, the cops caught Eastern last night, and they have his phone. I'm taking this so you can't get him into any more shit with your messages and texts, and number three, Oceanside is my new home now too, so we'll be seeing a lot of each other..."

"Wait, *what*?" I respond, my anger successfully doused by his response.

"Eastern is in custody," he says more slowly this time. "I can't have you calling him, texting him and getting everyone into deeper shit."

"What, he's been arrested? Tracy never said anything." I know I told him to hand himself in, but now that I know he's

144

been caught I'm afraid for him. So afraid. There are too many people relying on him, Braydon, his mum, my little brothers', *me*. A small sound escapes my throat, and I clamp my lips shut forcing myself not to cry. No more tears. Not in front of this arsehole.

"Tracy doesn't know yet."

"And you do?"

"Yes," Camden says softly, too softly, as though he feels some remorse, some guilt about Eastern's arrest. My eyes snap up, meeting his. For a fleeting moment I see pity, then he shuts it down. His face void of emotion. I see it happen right there in front of me.

"Monk showed me a video of Eastern. It's why I went to meet him. He promised to show me the rest if I went on a *date* with him," I say, spitting the words out in disgust.

"And you believed him? I thought you were smarter than that?"

"Fuck you, Camden. Do you have the video or not? I'm assuming you've got a damn copy. How else would Monk get it?"

Camden sighs. "Yes, I have the video." He reaches into his back pocket pulling out another phone. I watch as he frowns, scrolling through to find what he's looking for. "Here," he says, holding the phone up so I can watch it. He's not fool enough to hand it over, that's for sure.

The video plays again, repeating what I'd seen earlier. Apart from Eastern looking over his shoulder in fear, there's no more footage. It stops just as abruptly.

"Where's the rest?" I snap.

"There is no more. This is all I have."

"You fucking liar!" I shout.

"Believe what you want. This is it."

"But Monk said..." my voice trails off at just how much of a fool I've been. I mentally kick myself. I'm not usually this fucking stupid. "That lying piece of shit."

"Not long after I was sent this, I heard he was caught." Camden shrugs as though it's no big deal. I want to scratch his eyes out.

"You fucking arsehole. You really don't give a shit, do you?"

"He's in custody. Get used to it," he lashes out.

I stumble-walk over to my desk and sit down heavily on the chair. Camden pushes off from the wall and reaches into the pocket of his jacket, pulling out a packet of cigarettes. He grabs one and lights it, drawing in a deep lungful before blowing it out slowly.

"You can't smoke in the rooms," I say, rubbing my hands over my thighs. I don't know why I say that instead of addressing the fact that my friend has been arrested and what that means. I don't actually care that he's smoking, I've lit up often enough, but it's *my* room and he's got no right making himself comfortable. His gaze moves to my bouncing legs. All the adrenaline rushing through me needs a place to go and this is the result. I wish they'd stop moving. To give myself something to do, I open the window behind me then sit back down, forcing myself to keep still. Forcing my breathing to calm down and my thoughts to stop racing.

"It fucking stinks," I say, wafting my hand in front of my face. Not really talking about the cigarette smoke, but about this whole sorry night.

"I don't give a shit," Camden retorts, making himself comfortable on my bed. His gaze lands on the sketchpad. Reaching for it, he flicks it open randomly, showing a drawing of Eastern and Braydon. They're smiling, *happy*. I drew it last Christmas when I joined them for dinner.

It was a good day and my heart squeezes at how shitty everything is now, at how quickly everything can change. You'd think I'd be used to how my life can flip on a coin. I'm not.

"It's a good likeness," Camden remarks, but when I catch his gaze, I don't know whether he's talking about this sketch or the one that made his eyes widen earlier. When I refuse to acknowledge his compliment, a scowl forms on his beautiful, *lethal* face. That's exactly what he is. Sharp, dangerous, deadly, just like the edge of a knife.

I have the sudden urge to snatch up my sketchpad, but I don't. I refuse to do or say anything that would give my feelings away. He's already seen me cry and I won't give him any more of me. He's had enough of a glimpse already. Too much, actually. He's seen more than anyone else has, Eastern included.

Instead, I let the silence fill the space between us. I don't need to have a conversation with him. This is *my* fucking room. If he doesn't like the company, he can get the fuck out. Honestly, I'm in shock that he's actually here right now sitting on my bed without a care in the world. Yet, I've just run for my life from *his* crew only to find out that my best friend is in custody and I can't contact him anymore. Eastern's video message told me not to '*piss him off*' but he wasn't talking about Monk, he was talking about *Camden*. It all makes sense now.

Neither one of us speak. Camden smokes the cigarette right down to the butt, then pinches his fingers over the end putting it out, before chucking it out of my open window. He blows out a plume of smoke then looks at me. His topaz eyes flashing through the haze.

"Eastern was caught delivering speed and amphetamines to a third-party distributor. He fucked up, but he managed to get away. He ran, he hid, and then the police found him and arrested him."

"You say that like it's his fault! You sent him on the job. This is all on *you*!" I shout.

Camden leans forward. "No, this is on *him*. He knew the score and he made his choice. End of story."

"This is bullshit. He has a family to look after, his kid brother is disabled, for fuck sake. His mum doesn't have anyone left. What the hell is she supposed to do now?"

"Not my problem. We all have baggage." There's that coldness again. The I-don't-give-a-flying-fuck-about-anyone-else look. I *hate* it. I *hate* him.

From outside my room I can hear footsteps and talking. There's some laughter too. I'm pretty sure I can hear Sonny cuss out Bram but I'm too angry to try and distinguish what he's saying. My whole body is vibrating with it. "That's it? No apology for fucking up my best friend's life?"

"I don't apologise for something that isn't my fault."

"I *hate* you," I spit.

"Whatever." Camden stands. I get to my feet stepping closer to him.

"And setting your crew on me, I suppose that isn't your fault either?"

"No. Not my style."

"Bullshit," I snap back, not believing him for a second.

"I don't play games, Asia. If I want to take out an enemy, *I* go for the jugular."

"Oh, I get it. I see where we're at. I insulted you in front of your crew, so you set up my best friend. You sent him on a drop that would get him arrested. Is that what you mean by going for the jugular?"

Camden's jaw clenches; I can almost hear the grinding of his teeth. "No. Eastern already made his choice to work for me. To join my crew. I didn't set him up. His mistake has fucked us all over. The final nail in *my* coffin. That's why I'm here, paying for his fucking mistake. He owes me big."

"What do you mean?"

"It doesn't matter. Point is, no one wins. We're all fucking losers."

"Don't try and make out he owes you one. You brought this on yourself. You set my friend up and you sent Monk and his posse after me because I pissed you off. That's the kind of person you are. A fucking tyrant."

He steps closer to me, crossing his muscular arms across his broad chest. "Believe what you want. It's the truth. We might be on opposite sides of the line, Asia, but I respect my enemies. I don't play games. *I* take them out."

"So, we are still enemies then?" I don't know why I ask that, but for some reason I need it clarified. This conversation doesn't feel like the ones I have with Monk, if you can call them conveersations- more like a bully meting out punishment. It's just as well that I refuse to be Monk's victim. I'm his *adversary*, there's a difference. He won't beat me down and neither will this arsehole.

"That was *your* choice, Asia. I offered you a spot in my crew, you didn't take it."

I bark out an almost hysterical laugh. "Thank fuck I didn't if those arseholes are anything to go by."

"I shall say it one more time, I had nothing to do with Monk's games. I had no idea what he was planning."

"I don't give a shit if you did or you didn't. He's part of *your* crew. You're his *leader* and therefore you're responsible for his actions. Now, I want you out of my room. If I find you in here again, I won't be so accommodating."

This time it's Camden's turn to laugh. He laughs so hard that his perfect white teeth flash in the semi-darkness. "I suppose you'll try to hit me again?" he asks, scoffing as he takes another step closer until we are almost toe to toe.

My whole body trembles, but it isn't with fear. Rage, absolutely. Fear, definitely not. I don't know what it is that I feel between us. I'm both livid with anger and consumed with something else... something I do *not* want to try and understand. Jesus, this is *not* how I imagined my evening going. Monk has well and truly fucked with my head and Camden is the cherry on top. I fucking *hate* cherries.

"Yeah, and next time you won't be able to stop me. I'll rule your arse," I say brazenly, way past giving a shit.

Camden shakes his head, grinning like we've just shared a private joke. "There won't *be* a next time, Asia. You don't ever strike the boss unless you intend to win the fight and take the leadership. I don't lose, *ever*." His topaz eyes darken with warning.

"Number one," I say sarcastically, throwing his words back at him, "I'm not in your crew, and number two, you're not *my* boss, so I can do what the fuck I want whenever I want to. If you want a challenge, go fight Ford. I'm sure he'll be more than happy to serve you your arse."

His smile drops instantly. "Ford's here?" he snaps.

"He's here," I confirm, loving the look of shock that's quickly covered by a slow easy smile. "Scared he's going to make a fool of you again?"

"Careful, Asia, you're pushing it."

"I wasn't, but now I am," I snap, surging forward suddenly,

shoving the flat of my hands as hard as I can against his chest. It's like slamming into a brick wall. He grabs my wrists, squeezing tightly. My skin tingles.

"Don't," he bites out, glaring at me.

We look at each other. My breath quickens.

One beat.

Two.

Three.

Four...

I don't move, he doesn't either. Then his head dips down, his beautiful eyes boring into mine. For a fraction of a second I think he's going to kiss me and my stomach clenches with... what? I'm not sure. Hate, *lust*? Jesus.

Then just as quickly, he drops my wrists, nudges me out of the way with his shoulder and reaches for my sketchpad. He flicks through the pages, finds what he's looking for and rips the page out of the book. "I'm taking it," he states, daring me to object.

My mouth pops open, then shuts again. "Have it. It's a shit likeness anyway," I retort.

"See you around," he grinds out.

"Not if I see you first."

Then he strides to my bedroom door, yanks the chair out of the way, unlocks it and flings the door open with a crash. After a beat I rush to the door and watch Camden as he walks away. Monk is waiting for him at the other end of the corridor. He notices me and smirks. I give him the finger.

"Yo, Cam! Good to see you, bro. See you've been catching up with the resident *skank*," Monk says, barking out a laugh. Camden reaches him and, without saying a word, punches him twice in the face in quick succession. I suck in a surprised breath at the sudden unpredictable violence. Monk falls to the floor, knocked out cold.

"Her name's *Asia*, prick," he grinds out, and as if he knew I'd been watching him all along, Camden turns on his feet and looks at me. He nods once, a clipped look in his expression. Then he steps over Monk, unlocks his door and enters his room.

An immediate thought come to mind; I lied when I said the sketch I drew of Camden wasn't a good likeness. I think it captured him perfectly.

19

Sleep evades me. I'm too wired to even contemplate sleeping. Instead, I pull out my tobacco and papers and roll up a cigarette, then sit on my window ledge looking out at the view. Below us, Hastings is lit up with twinkling lights from the houses and hotels peppering the valley below. Nearer the shoreline are the multicoloured lights of the funfair, a permanent fixture along the promenade. A Ferris wheel moves in a slow circle, each seat adorned with different coloured lights whilst a rollercoaster whizzes around and around. I've never been to a funfair; actually, that's a lie. I've been, I've just never had enough money to go on any of the rides. Sighing, I lean my head back against the wall and smoke my cigarette, enjoying the way the smoke fills my lungs and the rush I get from it. I'm addicted to nicotine but at least that's it. I can give or take marijuana. I don't need it like others do. Tonight, however, I wish I had some. It might have helped me to sleep, given it's almost midnight and I'm still wide awake and full of restless energy.

Breathing in the briny smell of the sea, my eyes catch movement below. Sitting forward I squint into the darkness. Someone is jumping off the flat roof of the equipment store at the back of our building. Pooled in darkness it's difficult to see who. So, I watch and wait.

Then a spotlight flicks on from the movement and I see Sonny backing up against the wall, evaporating into the shadows of a doorway. He waits a beat for the light to flick off, then makes a mad dash across the asphalt of the carpark behind our building, before squeezing through a gap in the fence and disappearing into the copse of trees beyond it.

Seconds later, I see more people sneaking out of the back entrance of our residential annex. I'm pretty sure I see Red and Bram and some other members of the No Name Crew. Another couple of minutes pass and more kids appear, this time from the HH crew. My breath catches when I see Camden. He looks up at my window and grins. His teeth bright in the darkness.

What the actual fuck?

Knowing I should ignore the temptation to follow the stream of kids breaking curfew, I throw my cigarette butt out of the window and slam it shut. Whatever they're up to, I don't want to get involved.

Five minutes later after spotting two familiar girls sneaking out the back entrance, I follow suit and head outside myself, curiosity and a sense of adventure getting the better of me.

"Wait!" I whisper, running to catch up with Pink and Kate. Part of me feels a little pissed off that they didn't think to invite me to wherever it is that they're going, but then again I've no real right. I've turned down their offer of companionship numerous times already today.

"FUCK ME!" Pink screeches as I tap her on the shoulder.

"Shhhhh!" Kate hisses. "Do you want us all to get caught?"

"Mother of freaking God, Asia! You scared the shit out of me!" Pink clutches onto Kate, her free hand pressed against her chest as she struggles to catch her breath.

"Fuck, sorry!" I exclaim. It's pitch black in the woods and if it wasn't for the occasional light from a mobile phone (that hasn't been fucking confiscated) I wouldn't have seen them at all. "I was having a smoke and I saw you all heading out this way. Where are you going?"

"The Tower," Kate and Pink respond simultaneously.

"Bobby?" I ask.

"Too fucking wasted on Mary-J. He's passed out cold. The bastard won't be waking up any time soon," Pink explains with a shrug.

"Yeah, I bet," I retort, knowing exactly who provided him with the stash and *why*. Trying not to think about Monk and his pack of wolves, I walk in step beside Kate.

"What about those two security guards?"

"They leave at 9pm each day. Bobby is the only adult in charge." She smothers a laugh at that fact.

"But he's such a dick. I'm surprised Mr Carmichael hasn't sacked him already," I remark. Mr Carmichael doesn't seem like the type of guy to miss a trick. He must know Bobby is up for bribery, surely?

"You'd think so, right?" Kate responds in agreement. "But maybe Mr Carmichael isn't as clued up about shit as he makes out."

"Maybe," I agree. We fall into companionable silence for a while, holding onto each other as we traverse through the woods. Eventually, curiosity gets the better of me and I break the silence.

"So, what exactly *is* the Tower?"

In the gloom I can see Pink look at me with excitement.

"Apparently it's where shit that goes down at Oceanside gets settled…!"

"Yeah, I heard Ford wants to challenge Monk," Kate adds, her eyebrows lifting. She gives me a curious look as if I should know something about it.

"What?" I ask, then swear loudly as I bump into a tree trunk.

"You never did tell us what happened on the field after we left that day," Kate says. I might not be able to see her clearly, but I know what she's thinking, and the giggle from Pink tells me she's thinking the same thing. These girls are nothing but idle gossips, like a pair of curtain twitching nosey parkers. Normally I hate anyone getting all up in my business, but I kinda like that about them. We're just three girls having friendly banter.

"That's because *nothing* happened. We ran around the field, got sweaty, then went inside. That's it," I lie, not willing just yet to give them the details of what actually happened. I'm pretty sure they'd be giving me shit for days if I told them that Ford had tackled me to the ground with a raging hard-on. I'd never live it down. My cheeks flush at the memory; it's just as well it's so damn dark.

"Hmm, whatever you say," Pink giggles.

We fall silent again for the next few minutes as we traverse through the forest. I'm on full alert mode, more than ready to deal with Monk should he decide to pounce. But something tells me that Monk and his cronies expect me to be hiding in my bedroom, so I think I'm safe. For now, at least. That's if he has even come along, given the fact that Camden knocked him out. Perhaps he's laid out in bed, a couple of sad cases from the HH crew looking after him.

Who knows, I really don't give a shit.

Up ahead a group of people are gathering just at the edge of the copse of trees. We head towards them then follow as they start walking across the field that lies beyond the woods. Now that we're out in the open, the full moon and night sky scattered with stars light our way. In the semi-darkness I can see Camden up ahead. He's talking to one of the girls in Monk's crew, I mean *his* crew, I guess. She's laughing at something he's saying and for some reason the attention he's giving her pisses me off. I scowl, simultaneously wanting to attack the girl he's with for no other reason than the fact her laugh is grating on my last nerve, and give her a thumbs up for even attempting to entertain the arsehole.

"Who's that?" Pink asks, pointing to Camden. "He's tall, dark and handsome. If I weren't into girls I'd totally do him."

"*That* is trouble with a capital T. He arrived earlier today. I saw him talking to one of the security guards; they seemed to know each other. Bad aura if you ask me," Kate responds, frowning.

Pink laughs. "This is a reform school for a bunch of fucked up kids, Kate. Who doesn't have a bad aura?"

"You for a start," Kate retorts. She turns to look at me. "And Asia, though I suspect she'd rather we think she did."

"Shut up," I respond, hiding my smile behind a frown. I eye Camden who right at that moment decides to glance over his shoulder. He looks about, then smirks when he sees me. Dick.

"You met him already?" Kate asks, never missing a beat.

"You could say that," I reply, not willing to elaborate.

Pink pulls away from Kate and traverses around us until she falls into step beside me. "You're a dark horse, ain't ya, Asia? You gonna tell us what the deal is with Mr H.O.T, or are we going to have to beg?"

"Mr H.O.T?"

"Yeah, Handful of Trouble."

I can't help but laugh at that. "Later. Let's see if we get through tonight first."

"Why? You think we won't?" Kate pipes up, looking concerned all of a sudden.

Way to go Asia, dousing the fun with your positivity. I internally roll my eyes at myself. Sometimes I need to just stop being such a Negative Nancy. "We'll be fine. Look, just so you know I'm a glass half-empty kind of girl. I prepare for the worst. Every time."

"Nothing wrong with that. Besides, I'm a glass half-full kind of girl, so we balance perfectly," Pink says, a tinkly laugh following her statement.

"I'm neither. So, where does that leave us?" Kate pipes up.

"Pretty evened out, I'd say," I respond.

"Or fucked," she retorts with a wry grin.

"Or fucked," I repeat.

This time we all crack up laughing. After the evening I've had it feels good to laugh.

Less than ten minutes later we find ourselves standing at the top of a hill that leads down to a stretch of beach away from the main promenade in Hastings. In the distance I can hear the commotion of a Saturday night filled with revellers, but right here the pebbled beach meets the sea with a gentle slope and the sound of the waves lapping against the shore.

"It's the sea!" Pink yells, letting go of my arm and running towards the water. Her laughter is warm and genuine. She's like a child at Christmas. I must admit, were I as easygoing as Pink I might've joined in her glee. As it is, I'm still wound up tight from everything that happened earlier. Plus, I'm more intrigued by the stone circular building that Camden and the rest of the students of Oceanside have just disappeared into.

"Hey, Pink, over there," I say, motioning towards the building. She runs up to join us, a stupid grin on her pretty face.

"Anyone would've thought you've never seen the sea before," Kate says with a chuckle.

"I haven't," Pink shrugs, not in the least bit bothered by the fact. "How 'bout you, Asia?"

I stop, breathing in the briny air and stare at the moonlight reflected in the darkness of the sea. "No, only on television," I admit.

"Shit, sorry," Kate says, pulling a face.

"What are you sorry for, girl? Not your fault our parents were obviously total fuck-ups," Pink says, almost cheerily.

Fuck-ups. She got that right.

"If you're coming in, you'd better get over here now. Doors lock in five," a familiar voice says.

"Sonny!" Pink shouts, skipping over to greet him. He's leaning against the stone wall hidden in a little alcove. I'm pretty sure he's been watching us and listening to our conversation this whole time. Great, now he knows that this is the first time I've ever seen the sea and stood on a damn beach. *Perfect.*

"Didn't know you were coming," she says, slapping him on the back.

He grins. "Believe me, when I come, you'll know about it."

Pink laughs, Kate groans, and I roll my eyes.

"Come on. Let's get inside," he says, yanking open the door.

"Oh, my fucking God, do you hear what I hear?" Pink says, as the sound of Grime music filters out of the iron door. "It's a flippin' club! NO WAY!" She squeals, shoving past Sonny, and heads inside. Kate puffs out her cheeks, giving me an 'oh-shit-this-is-going-to-be-a-long-night' look, then follows

159

her inside. I move forward, about to enter, when Sonny grabs me by the arm. "You okay?" he asks, dipping his head so he can look into my eyes. He's doing that concerned thing again, the same as he did on the sports field the other day.

"Why wouldn't I be?" I retort, squirming a little under his scrutiny.

"Monk's in there. So is Camden and Ford."

"You've met him then?"

"I've met him. I make it my business to know who my fellow *students* are," he says with quote fingers.

"Criminals, you can say it you know. It's not a dirty word."

"Criminals then. Just so you know, this night is going to get a little crazy. Ford is gunning for Monk. So am I."

"Why?"

"Because the motherfucker tried to hurt you, Asia. That's why."

"How did you..." I begin, but my words falter as he removes his hand from my arm and cups my cheek. He looks at me intently, heaving out a sigh. Great, not only does he know that I've never seen the damn sea, but now he's heard of my humiliation too. I wonder who told him, Monk? Camden? One of the other pricks who was involved tonight maybe?

"For my part, I'm sorry I wasn't there."

"News sure does travel fast. I bet everyone is having a right laugh at my expense," I say.

"Travel fast? What do you mean?"

It's only then I realise that Sonny's talking about the incident on the sports field, not what went down tonight. Fuck.

"Absolutely nothing. Don't worry about it."

"Asia, if there's something else..." A muscle ticks in his jaw as his eyes search mine.

I shove his hand away. "There's nothing else, okay?!"

Sonny nods tightly, but I can tell he doesn't believe me. "You shouldn't have had to deal with that prick alone," he says after a beat.

"Don't sweat it. You don't owe me shit, and that's the way I like."

Sonny frowns, shifting back. "Sure," he mutters.

In this light, his eyes are less of a baby-blue and more of a midnight sapphire, as dark and as deep as the ocean behind us, and full of hidden depths. Now look at me, fucking waxing lyrical over some boy and his baby-blues. Jesus, someone get me a drink.

"Are we going in then or what?" I snap.

"After you," Sonny says opening the door, but he doesn't stop looking at me like he knows I have something to hide.

"Very gentlemanly," I offer, as we step into a wall of heat and noise.

20

Inside the Tower there's a makeshift DJ booth set up in one corner, the equipment powered by a generator. Strings of fairy lights are hanging from several beams that criss-cross above our heads, as well as some random flashing neon lights giving off a cool club vibe. I'm actually mildly impressed.

To the left of me and built into the wall is a wooden staircase that curves upwards towards the roof. If I look up I can see all the way up, any other floors this building might've had are long gone. On one side of the circular room is a portion of flooring that has fallen away with another couple of beams of wood crossing it that looks like a makeshift bridge of sorts. Below there's a ten-foot drop. Not high enough to kill, but high enough to injure should someone happen to fall into it awkwardly. Fortunately, that part of the building has been sectioned off with an iron railing, preventing drunk teenagers from tumbling into the hole and doing severe damage to themselves. I make a mental note not to get too close to that particular area, especially since Monk is here.

Speaking of which… I search the crowd. It doesn't take me long to spot him. He's in the corner of the room, sporting a dark purple bruise on his face. I can't help but smile. Good. I hope it fucking hurts.

"You want me to get you a drink?" Sonny shouts over the music, successfully drawing my attention away from Monk and the six guys he's surrounded by, the same guys who hounded me earlier. *Fucktards.*

"They actually have alcohol here? How?" I shout back.

Sonny takes my elbow and manoeuvres me through the crowd. I spot Pink and Kate dancing and wave. They wave back, both of them have a bottle of beer in hand. Even Kate's grinning. Well, at least they're enjoying themselves.

"This place was originally set up by previous students of Oceanside a few years back when the academy first opened. It's become the place to be with the local kids in these parts. Not everyone here is from the Academy," Sonny explains.

"And you know this how?" I'm always so amazed at his knowledge. He's only been here a couple of days more than me, so how the hell does he know all this stuff?

"I keep my ear to the ground. I ask questions. It's just the way I am."

"A nosy bastard, you mean?"

Sonny barks out a laugh. "Pretty much," he agrees with a shrug.

We head over to a shady looking teenager who's standing next to a metal tub, not unlike one of those old tin baths people used to wash in years ago. In it are bottles and cans of beer. The cheap stuff granted, but alcohol, nonetheless. He hands over two cans to us without preamble. Sonny snaps back the tab and takes a deep glug. I do the same, trying not to wince at the taste. Disgusting.

"This stuff is like drinking lighter fluid," he says, reading my mind.

"You can say that again," I agree, but take another mouthful anyway.

"Want to dance?" he asks me after a beat.

Do I? Do I want to dance with Sonny? I scan the crowd. In one corner I can see Camden still chatting to that girl he was walking with earlier. I think her name is Diamond, but I can't be certain. She's in the HH crew and no doubt one of his *girls*. She looks pretty happy with all the attention, and is pressed flush against him, trailing her fingers down his arm. Any closer to him and she'll be riding his cock for everyone to see. He's giving her an encouraging smile. Then, as though he knows he's being watched, he flicks his gaze to me, grins salaciously before drawing the girl towards him and kissing her roughly. My face heats with... *annoyance.* Yes that. *Definitely* that.

It reminds me of the time I first met him when he had his finger buried inside Jade and was practically fucking her in front of everyone at Sasha's party. I'm beginning to think this guy's an exhibitionist. He gets off on it, I swear. *Urgh.*

"Well," Sonny prompts.

Dragging my gaze away from Camden and back to Sonny, I shrug noncommittally.

Sonny cocks his head to the side, frowning. "Is that a yes or a no, Asia?"

"It's a fine, I'll dance," I retort, my gaze flicking back to Camden who's now shoved the girl up against the wall and is crowding her with his body. Seems like that's his signature move.

"Come on then," Sonny says, placing his palm on my lower back, and pushing me gently into the growing crowd of kids. I snatch my gaze away from Camden and look about me. Sonny was right, there are faces here that I don't recognise at all and most of them are paired up dancing in couples, grinding against one another in time to the music.

Sonny steers me to a spot a little distance away from Kate and Pink, then starts moving to the music. He doesn't instantly grab me and use this as an opportunity to get into my pants, and honestly, I'm surprised to see that he can actually dance. He kind of loses himself to the beat of the music, closing his eyes, bending his knees and swishing his hips in a seductive way that has me alternating between chewing on my lip ring and swigging back more mouthfuls of the foul tasting beer so that I have a distraction. There's no way that I want him to have any idea that I think he looks hot right now. No fucking way. His head will expand to gigantic proportions and he'll never let me forget it.

We dance for a long time, and as the minutes pass the tenseness I've been holding evaporates. I let the music and the shitty booze relax me. I'm still furious over what Monk and his cronies tried to do, but I'm not fearful anymore. Nope, my head begins to fill with thoughts of revenge.

Monk has it coming. That much I do know.

"You sure can move, Asia," Sonny murmurs into my ear as he steps up behind me seamlessly. I can feel the heat of his body warming my already hot back. A bead of sweat rolls down between my shoulder blades as he makes his move. I have a second to decide whether I want to put some distance between us or let him get close. For whatever reason, I choose the latter. *Fuck it.* When Sonny rests his hands on my hips, I don't step away. When his palm slides across my waist, I let him inch his fingers beneath my t-shirt. They feel warm and strong and despite my feelings towards him, towards anyone who tries to get close to me, I let him do just that.

"Well, you know what they say about being able to dance well..." I retort with a smirk. Flirting isn't usually my thing and flirting with Sonny really shouldn't be something I'm entertaining. But I do it anyway. I let my inhibitions go and lean back into Sonny, allowing him to hold me tightly against his body. It's not the worst thing I've ever done. In fact, it feels kind of... nice.

I swig back the last mouthful of beer before Sonny grabs the can and chucks it towards the pit. It disappears over the side, hurtling into the darkness just as the beat picks up speed into something more primal. I feel the change in Sonny, the spark of something coming alight between us. For the longest time we just dance, my back to his front. It's slow, sensual, bordering on illegal. He's hard, I'm hot and achy. I've no clear idea what's going on. Perhaps this is my way of dealing with the ordeal earlier. Like some weird kind of fight or flight response. I survived. I need to feel that I survived, so I'm getting horny with a guy I promised myself I wouldn't even give the light of day, let alone close access like this.

"Fuck, Asia," he whispers.

In response to his almost guttural reaction to me, I arch my lower back pressing my arse into his groin. "If you can't take the heat, Sonny, I suggest you step away from the fire," I smirk, loving that he seems to be losing his mind a little.

"Oh, baby, I can take all the heat you're able to give," he responds, his fingertips feathering beneath the waistband of my jeans, "And turn it into an inferno."

I'm pretty sure I should be moving away, but I don't do that. I let him hold me, enjoying the feeling of his body pressed so firmly against mine. When his lips brush along the curve of my neck, I don't stop him. In fact, I let out a low moan of my own, my lips parting on a breath as his teeth scrape across the sensitive skin.

"Looks like we've got an audience," Sonny whispers into my ear, as his arm slides around me tighter. Across the room Ford is watching us, fire blazing in his eyes. He looks royally pissed off. In fact, he looks as though he's about to commit murder.

What's that all about? Then I remember his comment to Monk about me being *his girl* and for reasons unknown to me, I want to test that sense of property. Looking at him dead in the eye, I smile suggestively then turn in Sonny's arms so that I'm facing him, before resting my head against his chest, hip to hip. He smells even more of the ocean now in such close proximity. I breathe him in, feeling a little drunk on the shitty alcohol, on *him*. If I'm perfectly honest with myself, it turns me on that he's turned on, and it makes me feel good knowing that Ford is watching. Maybe Camden is too? Fuck, where did that thought come from?

"Why are you doing this, Asia?" Sonny asks half a minute later. His hand slides down my back and rests on the top of my arse.

"This is what you want, isn't it?" I respond, swirling my hips against his. Fuck knows what's got into me. Really, this isn't my style and for a brief moment I wonder if the beer was spiked. Given I've still got great control of my body, even if my mind has decided to do a one-hundred-and-eight-degree turn, I know it wasn't.

Fuck it. I think for the gazillionth time since I set foot inside the Tower.

I'm always worrying about everyone else. Tonight, after all the shit that's gone down, I'm going to just go with it. Aside from Ford, everyone else is oblivious to what's happening between us. Actually, that probably isn't true given both Pink and Kate are staring at me open mouthed now. They're going to give me the third degree later. Oh, well.

"Don't get me wrong, I like the attention, but I'm a little surprised by it," Sonny admits, frowning. "Up until half an hour ago, these dimples of mine and my charm wasn't having much effect. I thought I was losing my touch."

"The dimples are nice," I say, reassuring him, because honestly they are, "But the charm could do with a lot of work. I don't like arrogance. Confidence, however, is a whole other ball game."

He grins, showing me those very attractive dimples to full effect. "Dimples are a go, arrogance is a turn-off, but confidence is not. Have I got that right?"

"I like your eyes too," I suggest with a little smirk.

His grin widens... and then, just as quickly it falls. "What do *you* want?" he says to someone behind me.

"Looks like our resident skank is up for a bit of something-something tonight."

Monk. I should've known the bastard wouldn't leave me alone for five fucking minutes.

Sonny shifts me in his hold so that I'm shoved behind him.

"Up for a gang-bang?" he questions lasciviously.

Without a moment's hesitation, Sonny grabs Monk by the throat and squeezes. "Back the fuck off, Monk," he seethes. Monk doesn't back off. Instead he raises his fist and slams it into the side of Sonny's head.

A fraction of a second later, all hell breaks loose.

I'm thrown to one side, stumbling into the crowd of people that have gathered around us. Pink and Kate reach for me, shock and a little bit of glee lighting their faces.

"Fuck, Asia, look what you've started," Pink says, grinning.

"You've got Sonny defending your honour. The guy has got it bad."

"I don't need defending," I retort, moving towards the two of them who are now laying into each other. The sound of bone meeting flesh and muscle, and the jeers and excitement from the crowd drowns out the music. "This is my fight, not his!" I shout to anyone who'll listen. Only one person is.

A hand grabs my arm, pulling me back.

"This is *Sonny's* fight, not yours," another familiar voice counters.

I look up to see Ford standing next to me. He doesn't even acknowledge me, instead he has his gaze trained on the fight even though he's firmly gripping my arm. The crowd steps back, forming a jostling circle around Sonny and Monk. Everyone wants to watch the fight.

"Fucking do him in!" one of the HH crew members cries out, fist pumping in the air.

"Make him bleed!" another shouts.

"Hit him, Sonny," Pink screams, letting him know he has people on his side.

The two are similar in width, but Sonny is a few inches taller than Monk and it gives him a slight edge. Pretty soon the crowd is working itself up into a frenzy, the atmosphere changing from the fun of a few minutes ago to downright feral. It's like something out of Mad Max, that film Tracy liked to watch on repeat mainly because she fancies Mel Gibson so much.

"This *is my* fight," I repeat.

"Sonny laid hands on Monk first and now he has to end it. Those are the rules."

"Rules?"

"Of the Tower," Ford explains.

"Pink said this place was used to settle scores."

"That's right. He insulted you and Sonny decided to defend you. So, let him. It's about time someone taught that prick a lesson given his own leader won't," Ford growls, seeking out Camden, his eyes narrowing when they find him.

"You don't understand. Monk set upon *me* earlier tonight. This really *is* my fight and I want my fucking revenge," I bite out.

"What the fuck, Asia?" Ford snaps, his gaze focusing back on me. He yanks me around to face him, drawing a snarl from my lips.

"What is with you and manhandling me?" I grind out, glaring at him even though inside I'm on fire.

"Don't avoid my question. What are you talking about, Asia?" he asks, dropping his hand, but not apologising for grabbing me.

"Monk and six of his gang tried to jump me earlier this evening. Monk set me up, telling me to meet him on the third floor of the annex."

"Why the fuck would you do that?" Ford snaps, anger darkening his grey-green eyes. "That was *stupid*."

"He had a message from my friend, Eastern. I agreed to meet with him so I could see it. I should've known fucking better. So, yeah, fucking stupid. It won't be happening again. I've learnt my lesson."

A muscle jumps in Ford's jaw. "So, that's where he went. I should've known. I thought he was with Camden, seeing as he arrived tonight."

"No, he was *trying* to terrorize me."

"And did he?" Ford asks, searching my face.

"No," I half lie. He did fucking scare me though, even if it was for just a bit, but I'm not about to reveal that and neither am I going to tell Ford that Camden witnessed me crying about it either.

"Good. Never let them know they've affected you."

Turning away from me, Ford continues to watch the fight. He holds his whole body stiff but makes no move to step in and break up the fight. I'd love to know what he's thinking, perhaps our sessions with Mr Burnside will eventually open him up enough for me to see beyond his toughened exterior.

Before us, fists fly, knees jab, feet kick. It's a dirty fight and with no referee to cut in, both sides are injured. Blood seeps from a cut in Sonny's eyebrow and Monk's lip is split. When Monk hits Sonny with such force that he stumbles backwards slightly I move forward instinctively.

"They're going to kill each other," I grind out. I really don't want Sonny to get hurt on my account. Ford reaches out once more, but this time instead of grabbing me, he slides his arm around my back and draws me into his side. I'm acutely aware of his thumb hooking under the waistband of my jeans and the gentle, almost cajoling stroke of his fingers against my hip. He doesn't say a word but despite everything that's happening, it's a distraction. Heat swirls outwards from my stomach and settles between my legs. What the fuck is up with me tonight? I'm like a dog in heat.

Monk punches Sonny in the back not far from his left kidney, and the power behind the punch forces Sonny to his knees. For a second Monk just prowls around Sonny spitting blood and spittle on the floor whilst the crowd goes nuts. Everyone bar me, Kate, Pink, Ford and, weirdly, Camden remain closed-mouthed. Monk even has the audacity to look over at me and point.

"You're next," he says smiling, his teeth coated in blood.

A rumbling growl releases from Ford at the same time that Sonny pushes to his feet. He's a little wobbly, but he stands.

"I need to help him," I protest, trying to step out of Ford's hold. He tightens his arm around me, refusing to let me go.

"Sonny's got this. Monk is strong, yes, but he has no stamina or common sense. Wait," he urges, and for some reason I do. Though it hurts me to see Sonny take the punches. The realisation that I don't like seeing him hurt is a bit of a shocker, given before tonight I hadn't even considered Sonny more than an irritating gnat, least of all a friend. Sometime during this evening, that changed.

Across the other side of the room, I can see Camden watching the fight play out and I wonder what he really thinks about this whole display. Earlier today he defended me against Monk, at least I think that's what he did. But perhaps he was just him reaffirming his power as leader. Yeah, that's more likely. Now his gaze slips from the violent brawl and lands on us both, specifically me and Ford's arm wrapped around my back. His attention makes my skin ice over then heat up all in one fell swoop.

"When this is over, Camden and I are going to need to have a little chat," Ford states. "I'm not down with this bullshit Monk's playing. One-on-one in a fair fight is one thing, fucking seven on one. No way. No fucking way."

My response stills on my tongue as Sonny hits Monk square on the nose, blood spraying from his face at the impact. I'm pretty sure it's broken. Monk falls to his knees ending the fight just like that. It's been bloody and vicious. Sonny hasn't come out of it unscathed, but he has won, and that's all that matters right now. Some of the HH crew crowd around Monk, helping him to his feet and dragging him over to the far side of the space. It doesn't go unnoticed that Camden doesn't move towards him, and neither do a vast portion of the HH crew. The division is obvious. A couple of minutes later, the music gets turned up once more, and the crowd fills the floor and begins to dancing as if nothing happened.

"Jesus, that was intense," Pink says, breathing out slowly as though she were holding her breath the whole time.

"I'm gonna have that chat now," Ford says, squeezing my hip once before letting me go. He walks past Sonny, gripping him briefly on the shoulder before disappearing into the crowd.

"Uh-oh, here comes Mr H.O.T number two," Pink says, nudging me in the side.

Sonny approaches us with a split eyebrow and a nasty bruise forming on his cheek. He's holding onto his side as well. He's pretty fucked up.

"Pink was right, he sure has got it bad," Kate mutters before Pink pulls her away, leaving the two of us alone once more.

"You didn't have to do that," I state. It comes out sounding ungrateful, I don't mean it to. I'm just not used to people coming to my rescue. This is the second time he's stuck up for me now and I don't like it. He has no business taking on my shit like that.

"He's a prick. He deserved it. Besides, I couldn't let him speak to you like that. It isn't right."

"Is there a toilet here? You need to clean that," I say, pointing to the cut on his brow and the blood dribbling from the wound, trying my utmost to ignore the intense look he's giving me.

"No toilets, but there's a whole ocean outside."

"Come on then," I say, taking his hand in mine and pulling him through the crowd. "Let me clean you up."

21

Sonny and I head down to the shoreline. Outside the air is cool, crisp, but given it's so hot inside the Tower, I welcome the sea breeze and the sharp sting of the salt spray. The water's a little choppier now, reflecting the turmoil I feel.

"Sit down," I urge Sonny, who's looking at me with a guarded expression now. He's normally so expressive. Actually, he's normally full of innuendo and bravado, but it seems right now that part of him is remaining tight-lipped. Maybe he took note of what I said earlier or maybe the punches to his head have had more of an impact than either of us realise.

"Shit, I've got nothing to clean you up with," I say. It's not as if I'm carrying a bloody first-aid kit with me. I'm betting the Tower doesn't have anything useful either.

Sonny strips off his t-shirt, handing it to me. "Use this," he says, a tiny sparkle lighting his eyes as my gaze roves over the firm muscles of his chest and arms. He's got a tattoo, a rather large one actually, of an eagle spread out over his chest. The intricate wings are tattooed into his pecs whilst the body and head of the bird are centred between them.

"Nice tattoo," I say, trying not to trip over my words, or drool as I walk the few steps to the water. That wouldn't be cool.

"Thanks," he mutters, a tiny little smirk twitching his lips when I look back up at him. Perhaps the arrogance hasn't quite been knocked out of him yet. Bunching up his shirt, I dip it into the water making sure it's nice and soaked before ringing it out a little. Then I return, kneeling between Sonny's parted legs and lift it to his face. He winces the second it touches his skin.

"Fuck." He jerks a little, but I cup the back of his head with my free hand, keeping his head still.

"It's pretty deep. You might need a couple stitches."

"Fuck that. I'll stick a plaster on it when I get back."

"Sonny…"

"If Mr Carmichael finds out I've been brawling then I'm out."

"Monk fucking tried to hit me and ended up punching Pink, *he's* not out," I say, pressing a little firmer against the cut. Sonny sucks in a sharp breath but this time he doesn't pull away.

"It's part of my deal, Asia. I can't brawl, ever. If they get wind of what happened then not only am I putting the Tower in jeopardy, I'm also on a one-way ticket out of here and into some secure unit for kids with *anger* issues." He smarts at that, rolling his eyes. "Not to mention Bryce will fucking kill me."

"What do you mean, part of your shit?"

"I'm not just here because I have light fingers and love the rush of stealing. I'm also here because I get into fights, Asia. A lot of fights. Let's just say Monk isn't the first person I've fucked up because the rage takes over. And by fuck up, I mean put into hospital."

"Shit," I say, not having any other words.

"You're surprised by that?" He looks at me behind guarded features and I'm pretty sure no one else is aware that's why he's here at Oceanside.

"Actually, no. I get it now. It makes perfect sense." I pull back my hand, turn the t-shirt to a cleaner spot then wipe at the blood caking his face. "There, that's as good as I can get it," I say, lowering my hand and dropping the t-shirt onto the pebbles. Sonny stares at me for a bit, then lifts his hand to swipe a stray hair behind my ear. His warm fingers burn a trail across my cool cheek.

"What makes perfect sense?" he asks, tipping his head to the side. He reaches around his back and rubs at his side. I worry a little that Monk has done damage to his kidney.

"Is that hurting?" I ask, frowning. "Let me see."

Leaning forward, Sonny lets me inspect his side. I run my fingers over the spot he was just touching and gently press against the area. "That hurt?"

"Not now it doesn't," he murmurs, catching my fingers in his. "Seriously. It's fine. I've taken knocks like that before, I'll survive."

"Okay." Sitting back on my haunches I draw my lip ring into my mouth. He watches me carefully.

"You didn't answer my question. Tell me what you meant about it making perfect sense."

"The humour, the charm, the jokes and the dirty talk. I figured you were hiding something underneath all of that," I reply with a shrug.

"You did?" he asks, a little surprised given the look on his face.

"I did," I retort, not elaborating further. Not explaining how he's been infiltrating my thoughts these past few days or that I've sensed that anger rumbling beneath his skin. "How are you going to explain this away?" I ask, pointing to his cut and the bruise blooming on his cheek.

He shrugs. "I'll say I had an accident in the gym. Ford will back me up."

"And they'll believe you given Monk's face is black and blue?"

"Probably not, but they've no proof and Monk won't blab. He's a dickhead but he isn't a snitch. Camden won't allow it. What happens in the Tower, stays in the Tower."

"Is that so?"

"That's so."

I shift on my haunches a little, not sure what to do next. I've cooled down sufficiently that I now feel a little chill. Goosebumps rise across my arms and I rub my hand against my skin in an attempt to warm me up.

"You cold?" Sonny asks me.

"I should be asking you that since you're practically naked."

Sonny grins. "Don't forget I'm full of fire, enough to start an inferno," he says, those dimples back.

"Ha bloody ha," I retort moving to stand, only Sonny rests his hands on my shoulders pushing me gently back down.

"Don't go, stay here for a bit," he says. The flash of vulnerability he shows has me ignoring common sense. I stay.

"Thank you for this," he says, pointing to his cut that's still bleeding a little.

"Sure, it's the least I can do given that should've been me fighting Monk and not you."

"You're kidding, right? The guy fights dirty, there's no way I'd let you brawl with him."

"Just as well that you have no say in the matter. I *can* fight, Sonny. I'm not your average girl ready to hide behind her man."

"Her man?" he repeats with another grin.

"You know what I mean… *some* man."

"There's more to fighting than rage, Asia. You've got to be smart," he says, tapping his temple.

"Have you been talking to Ford because he used the exact same line as you?"

Sonny laughs. "Yeah, I've been talking to Ford."

"How do you know each other?" I ask, shifting myself so that I'm sitting on my arse, rather than the backs of my legs. I'm still cold so I kind of wrap my arms around myself and draw my knees up a little. It doesn't really help, but I can deal.

"He's my second cousin twice removed or something," Sonny says, lifting a brow at the look of shock on my face.

"You're *related*?" I kind of saw a resemblance, but given they've hardly been friends I thought I was wrong.

"Yep, 'fraid so. We both have shitty parents in the family. Though until I arrived here, I hadn't seen him since we were kids."

"Fuck, that's awkward."

"It was a bit at first, but now we're cool. Except maybe…"

"Except maybe what?"

"Except we might not be cool over you."

"What?"

Sonny frowns, and if I didn't know any better I could've sworn his cheeks are turning a little pink, but perhaps that really is the cold. "What?" I repeat, kind of wanting to know what he's thinking and not wanting to know. Okay, that's bullshit. I want to know.

"You might be an issue for us. He likes you, Asia. *I* like you."

"Like me, like me?" I ask, chewing on my lip. I know what he means, I just can't quite believe it. I mean, I can believe that he wants to get it on with me, but liking me, that's something different.

"Yeah, as in I really give a shit about what happens to you kind of liking…"

"In a protective friend kind of way?"

"Yes and no. Yes, as in I want us to be friends, and no, as in I want more than just friendship. This is the kind of liking that makes me really, *really* want to kiss you right now."

"You want to kiss everyone," I say with a soft laugh.

"But I don't care about everyone," he responds just as softly. "And I'm pretty sure Ford's been wanting to do the same thing since he pinned you beneath him on the field that day," Sonny adds with a wry grin.

"He told you about that?"

"Fuck no, the guy's a closed book! I saw it happen. Once I dropped off Pink and Kate at the medical room, I went back outside to look for you and to make sure the HH crew wasn't giving you shit. I saw what went down."

"He was trying to prove a point, that's all."

"Yeah, and the rest. He got you beneath him and he kept you there." A dark shadow crosses Sonny's face and it unsettles me a bit.

"It didn't mean anything," I say, not really understanding why I'm trying to reassure him or why I'm lying. It meant something.

"Either way, he has the hots for you. Just like me."

"Sonny, you've taken a few whacks to the head. I'm not sure you know what you're saying." I laugh to cover up the strange feeling in my chest.

"I know exactly what I'm saying," he retorts firmly.

"You're just desperate. I mean, it's not as though there's much choice and I'm pretty sure you've worked your way around most of the girls already in such a short amount of time. I'm the last one available, right?"

"Wrong. I *like* you. I don't really know why given you've pretty much blasted me, but I do."

My teeth begin to chatter, but I can't respond because he's suddenly reached over and pulled me into his lap. "Sonny!" I exclaim, a small smile pulling up my lips.

"I'm freezing and so are you. Let's warm each other up," he says, wrapping his arms around me as he shifts me into a more comfortable position across his lap. My arse slides between his parted legs and my hips can definitely feel how much he likes me. Jesus. I flush warm, suddenly not feeling the cold anymore.

"You're freezing," I exclaim, leaning back slightly so I can look at his face. My hand finds itself on his chest just over the eagle's head and his thumping heart.

"So are you. Makes this a good idea, right?" he questions tentatively, his eyes darkening with lust even though his voice remains neutral and not at all jokey.

"I'm not so sure about that..." I start to say, but when he slowly leans in to kiss me, I don't push him away or tell him to stop. I let him.

His lips are slightly warmer than his skin, but pretty soon both are heating up as our kiss deepens. He doesn't try to do anything other than explore my mouth with his. It's a tentative kiss at first. A kiss that's more of a flicker than a flame. It's searching, gentle, and entirely surprising. That gentleness is a shock. I'm used to being kissed quickly as though it's just a formality to get out of the way before everything else. Not Sonny. I can tell by the way he explores my mouth that he likes to kiss. That it may even be his most favourite pastime. I can deal with this. I can deal with a kiss. Relaxing into his hold I allow myself to enjoy the moment. After a while, as his lips slide over mine and his tongue strokes against my own, I find that I have to press my thighs together to ease the throb between them. And even though I know how it sounds, I wish he'd move his hands away from my arm and my thigh to other places that ache for his touch. But he doesn't do anything more than bite gently at my lower lip before soothing it with his tongue. Fuck. A little groan escapes me and I'm pretty sure he's smiling, but I don't want to pull away to check. I'm enjoying this way too much. If I'm honest, I would never have put him down as a gentleman, but then again, he's already shown me there's more to him than what he presents to the world. I like that.

Without removing my lips from his, I angle my body so that more of me is I'm facing him, then reach up and wind my fingers in his hair, cupping his head. I'm more than aware that my tits are now pressing into the firm planes of his chest and that my nipples are hard as marbles, partly due to the cold, but mostly because I'm turned on. This time it's his turn to groan.

With a last slow sweep of his tongue, Sonny pulls away, flashing me that dimpled grin. "If I'd known how fucking epic a kisser you were, I would've laid it on a lot thicker and a lot sooner, Asia."

"Shut up, you idiot," I respond, slapping him lightly on the arm before jumping up and helping him to his feet. Knowing that if I don't move now, this kiss may lead to way more and

I'm not in the habit of shagging someone after only knowing them a week. That also might be a lie. I've fallen into bed with guys before after only a few hours in their company. I don't want to do that with Sonny.

He gets up, wincing from the pain but still he smiles, a flop of dark blonde hair falling into his eyes.

"Does this make you mine now?" he asks, the cockiness back. My mouth opens to speak but my response is interrupted by a certain someone who sounds far from happy.

"No, it fucking doesn't," a voice behind us says. It's Ford.

We both turn around, looking back up towards the Tower. Standing watching us both is Ford and beside him, Camden. One looks thunderous, the other entirely amused, except that amusement is a thinly veiled disguise of his true feelings. At least that's how it seems to me. I'm not sure who's reaction annoys me the most. The out and out anger at me kissing someone of my own choosing, or hiding that anger behind laughter and cheapening this moment with Sonny.

Screw them.

Actually, perhaps I *should* screw Sonny, that would really get their goat.

22

The following Thursday afternoon, Sonny and I are sitting in an English lesson with Mr Collins, a middle-aged, grey-haired man with a dyed black beard. He's trying way too hard to look distinguished, but instead looks like a Lego character with a stuck-on beard. I'm not sure I understand why he's let his hair go grey but has kept his beard dyed, but Sonny says it's probably something to do with the fact his beard is slightly ginger, and no one wants a ginger beard.

"That makes no sense whatsoever," I whisper behind my copy of Oliver Twist. We're supposed to be discussing the social injustice committed to orphans during the Victorian period, but instead we're discussing ginger beards.

Sonny grins at me, his baby-blues twinkling with mirth. "Most men get a bit of ginger in their beard no matter their hair colour. You should see Bryce. He's got black hair and still has a bit of ginger going on. It's weird as fuck."

"Bryce, as in your guardian? That fit guy who was at the court with you?"

"The one and only."

"He seemed alright, even if he's got a ginger beard."

"Maybe, but he's not my dad," Sonny shrugs.

"What happened to him?" I blurt out.

"He died."

"How?" I murmur. It's unfair of me to ask him such a personal question knowing I would never reciprocate, but I ask it anyway.

"Wrong place, wrong time. He tried to break up a brawl in a bar, he got stabbed in the heart instead of the man the arsehole was aiming for. My dad, always the fucking hero."

"I'm sorry."

"Me fucking too, Asia. Me too."

For the rest of the lesson we listen to Mr Collins drone on about how circumstances forced Oliver into a life of crime, but that his strength of character helped him to make the right choices. It's obvious what he's trying to do. The thing is we're not characters in a damn novel. Oliver got his happy ending. He escaped a life of crime. Not one of us can say the same.

Except maybe Sonny. Those guys he lives with seem alright and they're rich, after all. When all is said and done, he'll leave here and go live in some mansion and the rest of us will return to our council flats if we're lucky. He'll forget about us, about *me*. One kiss isn't going to change that. People have a habit of leaving me, so this time I make a decision to be the one to leave. It's better that way.

When Mr Collins informs us the class is over, I stuff my books into my bag and rush out of the room ignoring Sonny's shouts for me to wait up. I rush down the hallway, past the rec room and into the girls' toilets. Thankfully it's empty and I step into one of the cubicles, locking the door behind me.

"Asia, what the fuck?" I hear Sonny say as he walks into the room a few seconds later. "You ran off. What's up? You got the shits or something? I've been feeling a bit gassy myself since lunch."

"Oh my god, *gross*!" I yell at him.

"Too much information?" he asks, chuckling.

"Yes, *way* too much information. Let's keep a bit of mystery please."

Beneath the door I can see his feet, one crossing over the other as he leans against the door, making himself comfortable. "Did you know the average person passes about half a litre of farts a day?"

I can't help but laugh. "You're really are full of useless information, do you know that?"

"Yep, so I've been told..." He pauses, then coughs. "Seriously though, Asia. You sure you're alright?"

Nope. No, I'm not. Eastern's in custody. I miss my little brothers. Tracy is freaking out and my mum's fucking dead. I don't have some rich guardian and a safe future just like Oliver fucking Twist. Monk is gunning for me and I'm sitting in a toilet like some little twat because I don't want to share any of this, with anyone.

"I just need to pee."

"If this is about the kiss..." His voice trails off, uncertain how to proceed given I've gone deadly quiet. I want to tell him the kiss was nice. That it was fucking great actually. But I'm not one for expressing how I feel, obviously, given I'm hiding in a goddamn toilet.

"I want you to know that I'm not the lothario you think I

am. I mean I like women, a lot, but I also like you, so... I meant what I said on the beach that night."

"Jesus, Sonny. Will you just sod off, please? I'm about to piss myself, pretty sure you won't want to kiss me then."

He barks out a laugh, pushing off from the door, it shakes a little as he moves. "Okay, okay, I can take a hint. Maybe we can pick this conversation up another time. For now, I'm going to head to the canteen. Want me to save you a spot?"

"Sure," I mutter. He waits a beat, then realising I'm not about to say any more, leaves.

I hear the door slam shut and breathe out a sigh of relief, then decide that I do actually need to pee and do exactly that. Just as I'm pulling up my jeans and flushing the toilet, I hear the door open once again. Rolling my eyes, I unlock the cubicle and yank the door open. "Fuck sake, Sonny, can't a girl pee in peace?"

Except it isn't Sonny, it's two of the girls from the HH crew and they're out for blood. Mine, specifically.

"She's here," one of them says, pulling the door open slightly. Beyond I catch a glimpse of the girl who had smirked when I cussed out Monk on the field. She gives me a pitying look just before the door closes and I can't help but wonder what kind of circumstance led her to the HH crew.

"Get the fuck out of my way, Little and Large," I sneer, making sure to give both my most cutting glare. They really are little and large, like total opposites of one another. One's tall, almost Amazonian and attractive in a fierce don't fuck with me way. The other is petite, slightly curvy, pretty, but with a dark look that tells me she'd rather cut her own mum than be disloyal to her crew.

"Nah, don't think that's gonna happen," the tall girl says. I'm pretty sure her name's Diamond. It suits her. Beautiful, sharp, perfectly flawed. She was the girl eating Camden's face the other night. I dislike her even more now.

I roll my eyes, leaning against the sink and feigning boredom. "I'm kinda tired of the same old shit. Would've thought that between you two there'd be some originality to the cuntish behaviour. Jumping me in the toilet? You do realise sticking someone's head down the loo is so 1980's, don't you?"

"You sarcastic little…"

"Bitch?" I finish for her. "Yep, like I said. Un-fucking-original. Anything else you'd like to add before we get down to it?"

Emerald, the shorter of the two, smiles slowly as Diamond boxes me in. "Yeah, which toilet?"

"Oh, you really don't know who you're fucking with, do you?"

Ten minutes later I walk into the canteen not a hair out of place. The same, of course, can't be said for Emerald and Diamond. Pretty sure they've swallowed enough toilet water to keep them in bed for days. Did they honestly think they'd could jump me and get away with it? I'm sick of people thinking I'm a pushover. Sonny stepping in and fighting Monk has done me no favours. It made me look weak. Let's see if my rep changes around here now.

"What are you smirking at?" Sonny asks just as Ruby, the girl who was on lookout, comes rushing into the dining room. She heads straight for Monk, who's sporting two black eyes and tape across his nose, and whispers in his ear.

"Let's just say after you left the toilet, things got super interesting with a couple of the HH girls," I respond, sitting down and swiping a donut from Sonny's tray.

"They jumped you?" he snaps, pushing back his seat.

"Hey, don't sweat it. I'm not. They got what they deserved."

A sudden loud crash sounds as Monk swipes his tray off the table in his rage. He points at me before raising his finger to his neck then sliding it across his throat.

"Fuck, dramatic much," I state, not in the least bit worried about his threats. I probably should be, he seems like the type to follow through, but I'm not. Now who's being cocky?

"Motherfucker," Sonny snarls, moving to stand, but I clock the canteen staff watching him and grip his arm.

"Don't, we're being watched. Not to mention, you got me into this shit in the first place by jumping to my rescue with Monk."

"He insulted you. I dealt with it," Sonny responds, watching Monk as he storms from the canteen.

"Yes, *you* dealt with it, not me. It was my fight, Sonny."

"Well, sorry if I didn't want to see you hurt," he snaps.

"It isn't about me getting hurt or not. This is about me showing them all I'm not a fucking pushover, or weak. I understand the rules of the street, Sonny. I've had to live by them regardless. Those pricks will keep gunning for me if I don't fight back."

"I get it, Asia. But I can't stand by and see them go for you. I *won't* do that." He lays his hand over mine, squeezing gently. "Some people are worth fighting for. *You're* worth fighting for."

My skin prickles under his touch, but I'm prevented from responding as Pink and Kate slide into the seats next to us. Pink looks like she's about to self-combust with excitement.

"Tell me you shoved their heads down the toilets like everyone's saying," Pink says with glee.

"Is that what you did?" Sonny's mouth drops open, then he leans back in his chair and laughs, his whole body shaking with mirth.

"That's what they had planned for me, I just happened to get to it first." I shrug, drawing a low whistle from Kate.

"You sure know how to fuck with them," Kate says, looking at me in awe.

"What, you never got into a fight?" I ask her, genuinely wanting to know. She's alluded to issues at her previous school but has never gone into detail. I've respected her wishes and never dug for more information, until now.

"Not one I've ever won," she responds, her cheeks flushing.

"Then you're friends with the right people. I'm totally down for assisting you in that department."

"Thanks. I'll think about it."

"Uh-oh, here comes trouble," Pink mutters, looking over my shoulder. Sonny's eyes narrow and he tenses. I twist in my seat. Camden is striding straight towards me.

"A word. Now!" he demands, flashing a dangerous look at Sonny.

"Don't come in here ordering-" Sonny starts, but I cut him off.

"We're being watched, remember," I remind Sonny, nodding towards the canteen staff who are looking more and more concerned by the minute. I bet they've seen all sorts of shit go down in here over the years. Any minute now they'll be calling security and we don't need those arseholes descending on us.

"What is it, Camden?" I smile sweetly. His gaze darkens.

"You fucked with my girls. You do realise what you've started?"

I bark out an incredulous laugh. "What *I've* started? Are you actually mentally impaired?" I hiss under my breath. If we hadn't got the whole of the dining hall's attention before, we have now given Camden has grasped my arm and Sonny is on his feet and by my side in less than a second.

"Your *girls* tried to jump Asia in the toilets," Kate says perfectly calmly from her spot at the table. I see a thread of fear in her eyes, and I hate that. She shouldn't feel afraid.

"What the fuck are you talking about?" He narrows his eyes at her and out of the corner of my eye I see her kind of fold into herself. Jesus, whoever fucked with her at her previous school managed to do a right number on her. I make a mental note to speak with her about it someday soon.

"Why would she lie?" Pink adds.

"Is this true?" he asks me.

Sonny scoffs. "You're either a great liar, Camden, or fucking clueless. Do you have *any* control over your crew at all?"

"Is. This. True?" he bites out, completely ignoring Sonny and stepping far closer to me than is necessary. I stand my ground, not allowing his sheer size and presence to scare me.

"If I said it was, would you even believe me?"

He looks at me for far longer than is comfortable, as though trying to see the truth inside of me, then steps back and drops my arm.

"I'll deal with this," he says, before striding off.

And something about the conviction in his voice leads me to believe that he will, but why is a total mystery. We're enemies, *aren't we?*

23

For the next few weeks, Camden is true to his word and I'm left alone. I'm not sure what he's said or done but there have been no further attempts to jump me.

Don't get me wrong, Monk still gives me evil looks every chance he gets, and the name calling hasn't let up but everything else has stopped. At least for now. Monk is still part of the HH crew, that hasn't changed, but there's been a very significant shift in the group dynamics. Not that I care, gang politics aren't exactly on my list of things I give a shit about.

Instead I use my time to get into a rhythm of sorts. Every day I spend breakfast, lunch and dinner with Kate and Pink and now we've established an easy-going friendship. Sometimes Sonny will eat with us, sometimes he won't. I've avoided spending time alone with him, not certain what to do about the kiss we shared and this growing intensity between us. He's a distraction and I really, *really* need to keep focused. If I concentrate on keeping my head down and doing my work, then maybe I'll be getting a day out of this place. *Soon.*

Avoidance is my only strategy right now when it comes to Sonny and his fucking dimples, and I don't even want to think about Ford or Camden. Trouble is, all three violate my thoughts all the damn time. I'm sick of thinking about them. Sonny reminds me a little of Eastern, they both have a wicked sense of humour and a streak of protectiveness that could get them into trouble. Camden and Ford too are alike in so many ways, guarded, mysterious, dangerous... They keep their true selves tightly under wraps, so tightly that I wonder if they even know who they really are beneath it all.

But I don't care about them... *I don't*. Eastern, yes. The others, no.

That's what I tell myself over and over whilst I sit and wait for Mr Burnside to enter the therapy room with his usual cup of bitter smelling coffee, leather notebook and pen.

"Sorry I'm late, Asia. Got caught up on an important phone call. Won't happen again," he adds, sitting in the leather armchair opposite me. Between us is a low coffee table covered with art gear which I'm assuming is for me. There are some beautiful acrylic pens that I'd love to get my hands on. Even the sketchpad is one of those expensive ones with thick paper, and as far as you can get from the cheap stuff I usually buy from the pound store. There are even some really expensive pencils. This stuff is the real deal and something I could only dream of buying for myself.

"No skin off my nose," I retort, tapping my finger impatiently on the armrest and pretending not to be impressed by the expensive art gear laid out before me.

"You want to tell me how your day has been or anything about your stay so far at Oceanside?"

"Nope." I hate these therapy sessions. I don't like talking about my shit. I don't like talking about anything to do with my past, present or fucking future. It really is a waste of time. His and mine.

"These sessions are for your benefit, Asia. Nothing goes beyond these walls. I'm legally bound to keep anything you tell me between us. You *can* trust me."

"I don't trust anyone."

"No one at all?"

"I trust Eastern..." I blurt out after a second.

"And he is?" Mr Burnside asks.

"My best friend. But that's all you need to know."

Mr Burnside nods. "Thank you for sharing."

I scowl, pissed off that I did share but he isn't put off by rudeness or my reluctance.

"So Eastern is your best friend. How about you tell me a happy memory of him." He looks at me with a neutral expression and waits.

"No."

"It can be anything you choose. It doesn't even have to be about Eastern. Perhaps something small. So, for me, one of my happy memories is of getting a whippy ice cream every Sunday afternoon during the summer. It was my Sunday treat. I'd always get chocolate sprinkles and sauce. It became a tradition."

"Well, lucky for you. I didn't eat much ice cream growing up."

"No?"

"No, ice cream was a luxury we couldn't afford."

Mr Burnside nods, scribbling something down in his notepad.

"Okay, so no ice cream. How about something you did with your mum that made you happy."

"There wasn't anything..." I shrug, feigning boredom when

really I feel sick inside. I have a handful of happy memories of my mum, one of which sits within my cheap sketchpad. But I don't want to share them, they're too precious. *Too painful.*

"Just a small thing, *anything*…?" Mr Burnside asks gently.

I make the fatal mistake of looking at him, unnerved by the sympathy in his voice. When I see the pity in his eyes, something inside reacts to it. I hate pity. He studies my face and waits.

"Where I come from, most kids like me don't have happy memories," I snap, annoyed by the pity in his eyes. "We aren't all spoilt little brats who get what they want when they want it…" I leave that hanging between us.

"That's quite a statement to make, Asia. You grew up on a council estate in Hackney, yes? Are you saying all the kids on your estate had family difficulties, had no happiness whatsoever?"

"Yes, I grew up on a council estate, but you know that already. Don't pretend you haven't seen my file and read all about my dirty, fucked up past. And, no, not all the kids I grew up with have shitty lives like mine. But a lot do. *A lot.*" *Too fucking many*, I think.

"Care to elaborate?" he persists.

"No, I don't." I snatch my gaze away, looking at the table with the beautiful new sketchpad and acrylic pens. "I don't want to talk about my past or my memories. Happy or fucking otherwise. *I don't want to.*"

"Then don't. Draw them." Mr Burnside says, pointing to the art equipment on the table. He leans forward, picks up one of the acrylic pens and holds it out towards me. When I don't take it, he places it back on the table.

"Look, I'm not an idiot. You're not as fucking sneaky as

you think. Why would I give you what you want?" I ask, folding my arms across my chest, glaring at him.

"Because I can help you, Asia."

"These memories I have. My past pain and happiness are *mine*. Not yours, not Mr Carmichael's, my social worker's, the judge who stuck me here or the kids at this fucking school. They're *mine* and who I choose to share them with is up to me. I will not be bribed into telling you anything so that you can tick some fucking box and tuck my shit away in another file."

"So, you *do* have some happy memories then?" he asks, ignoring my tirade. "Do those happy memories include your younger brothers?"

That fucking pisses me off. He has no right to bring up Sebastian and George. I clamp my mouth shut and draw my feet up onto my chair, folding my arms around them. Effectively shutting down.

Mr Burnside looks at me for a moment before placing his pad and pencil onto the table between us. He takes a sip of his coffee then lets out a long sigh. "They're okay you know…"

My head snaps up as I narrow my eyes at him. It's been weeks since I've talked to my brothers or heard how they're doing. I've felt a constant pain in my chest at not knowing how they are. I bet they've changed so much already.

"They still think I'm at some boarding school for the magically gifted?" I ask, despite myself.

Mr Burnside smiles. "They're happy. They're *okay*," he insists. "If you want, I'll call their foster mother regularly. Give you updates. Would that help?"

I nod, gratefully. "Yes, it would help," I murmur.

That doesn't make my heart ache any less though. I miss them. I miss them so damn much. Pressing my forehead against my knees, I will the tears away. I won't break. Not here. After a long silence, Mr Burnside speaks.

"Nothing good ever comes from holding pain inside, Asia. I can help you if you let me. But I see that your trust is something I must earn before you're willing to share. So, here's the thing, I'm going to tell you something that only Mr Carmichael knows about. I might be making a huge mistake, in which case I shall deal with the consequences, but I'm going to share this with you anyway."

"And I suppose after you're going to want me to tell you something? Is that it?" I retort, hugging myself harder and wishing he'd just shut the hell up.

"No. After I finish, you're going to take that sketchpad and those pens and you're going to leave my office. Because once I tell you this, I'm going to need time to myself."

I don't say anything, so Mr Burnside does. He breathes in deeply before letting out a long, steady breath. I notice that his hands are shaking, and he clasps them together in his lap.

"When I was ten years old I was molested by my father's best friend. He was looking after me for the weekend whilst my parents celebrated their twelve-year anniversary. I didn't tell my parents. I didn't tell them because they loved this man as much as they loved me. When they returned and asked me how I'd been, he'd looked at me and said: *just perfect*. I was *just perfect* dozens of more times like that over the years. He abused me from the age of ten until I was fourteen. During that time, I fell in love with him. He was a monster, a paedophile, and someone who I never should've loved. But he was, by my parents and, eventually, by me. It was twisted and messy and nothing I'd ever wish on another human being. He stopped the abuse when I showed signs of becoming a man. I mourned for his attention as though I would the end of any relationship. It took years of therapy, of love, *real love* to understand I had been a victim of abuse. Without that therapy, without allowing myself to be loved in the right way, I would never have survived my past. That is why I became a therapist, to help others. I *want* to help you for no other reason than because I understand what it's like to be betrayed by the people we love. I understand, Asia."

The pain in Mr Burnside's eyes is so unbearable, so real that I can only stare in the face of it with complete and utter horror. He doesn't say any more to me, he just raises a shaking hand and pushes it through his hair.

"I'm sorry he hurt you…" I mumble, placing my feet on the floor. He nods tightly whilst I look between him and the items on the coffee table. "I won't share it with anyone else because it's not my secret to tell."

"I appreciate that," he says eventually.

Minutes tick by as we regard each other, until eventually I break the growing silence.

"You were right when you said you needed to earn my trust, but that's something very rarely given by me," I say, standing. I look at the items on the table with longing, but my pride refuses to let me take them. "Too many adults have let me down. One story, however sad, isn't going to change the fact that you could let me down too. How can you guarantee that you'll be any different? That you won't let me down like everyone else has?"

Mr Burnside chuckles sadly. "I can give you my word, but I understand for you that isn't enough."

"No, it isn't," I agree.

"Then somehow, I have to prove it to you that I care. I will earn your trust."

"Don't say something you can't possibly live up to."

"I won't let you down, Asia. *I promise*. Please, take those," he says, pointing to the items on his desk.

I shake my head. "Gifts are superficial. Promises are breakable. Anyone can say they care. Many people have 'cared' for me over the years and all of them bar a couple have hurt me."

"Then what can I do?"

I think of my mother's actions, how she chose heroin over me. I learnt from a young age that her love for heroin was more than her love for me. She couldn't fight her addiction because I wasn't enough to fight for. I think of Eastern and his actions, how he chose to run drugs for his mum and Braydon because he loved them enough to ruin his own life to support them. I think of Sonny and Ford and how both stood up to Monk for my honour; Ford on the sports field and Sonny in the Tower. Words might be beautiful. They might bring life to a story or a poem, creating something magical, powerful, unforgettable, but they only reveal the truth of someone's *mind*. Actions have the power to show the truth of someone's heart and that, that is what *I* trust.

"Actions speak louder than words, Mr Burnside. On the street every action has a reaction, a consequence for kids like us. Rightly or wrongly, we live and we die by the choices we make, and the actions we take. Can you say the same?"

Mr Burnside is silent for a long time, then he stands too. There's a determined look on his face, one that I appreciate. This man is not a quitter. He won't give up. I like that. Both he and his partner, Mr Carmichael, seem like good men. Then again, I've met lots of people who pretended to be good and weren't. See, *actions*.

"You're right, Asia. Actions do speak louder than words. So, here's my first action; I will stop deducting credits for those who refuse to share their stories in the joint therapy sessions I take. I will let everyone sit in silence if that's what they choose. I will *only* insist on attendance, even if no one participates. I will also give back the deducted credits. How does that sound?"

"It's a start..."

He nods. "Good. I can build on that. Same time next week?"

"Same time next week," I respond, heading towards the door.

"Oh, and Asia..."

"Yes?" I look over my shoulder at him.

"I disagree with one thing," he says.

"And what's that?"

"Words do have meaning when they're spoken from the heart. Don't discount them completely."

"I'll think about it," I concede, pulling open the door and shutting it behind me. But he's wrong. Words are just that, words. They mean nothing unless they're backed up with action.

24

I don't go back to my room like I was planning to do. Instead, I hook a left and take a walk past the classrooms on the same floor as Mr Burnside's office. This is my free period and as far as I'm aware, everyone else is in lessons except a few kids who I'm not particularly worried about.

When I pass the open door of Ms Markin's Maths class, I'm accosted with my usual greeting around here.

"Skank!" Monk calls, whilst the rest of his wolves' howl. Everyone except Camden, who's just staring at me, makes some kind of comment as I walk by.

"Fifty credits deducted for the whole class and you, Monk, can accompany me to Mr Carmichael's office after the lesson," Ms Markin says, giving me an apologetic smile as she shuts the classroom door. I catch a glimpse of Camden who's leaning over and talking to Monk just before the door shuts. Neither look particularly happy.

When I get to the end of the corridor, I can either head towards the gym and swimming pool or outside to the back of the building and the formal gardens beyond. Whilst I've looked at the gardens plenty of times from Pink's room, which is on the opposite side of the annex to me, I haven't ever bothered checking them out. I'm a city kid at heart. Give me concrete and skyscrapers any day of the week. Today, however, after my session with Mr Burnside, I feel the need for air, space. The fact of the matter is, I'm itching for my cans. To spray paint something, *anything*. I need to switch off, I need to get rid of this constant unsettled feeling inside from being here, for all the weeks of shit I've had to endure. I miss home... I miss my little brothers, Eastern, Tracy and Braydon. I wish I didn't feel anything, but I do.

Pushing those thoughts aside, I head outside hoping that this time the fresh air will blow away the cobwebs like Libby, my foster carer, would often say. God, if she knew I was taking a walk in the park (because, let's face it, these gardens are practically a fucking park) she'd have a fit. She was always trying to get me to go out for fresh air with her. Now look at me.

After a couple of minutes, I find myself at the entrance to the maze. I've seen it countless times from Pink's bedroom window that overlooks the gardens and not the car park like mine. Each time I've looked out of her window I've never seen anyone enter.

Peering into the entrance, at the high hedgerows and pathway that seems to end in another wall of green hedge, I chew on my lip. My gut, which is generally always right, is telling me to back off, but my sense of adventure and that familiar adrenaline rush that I usually only get when graffitiing is telling me to go for it.

I go for it.

For the next half an hour I lose myself in the maze, and I

like it. My head is so preoccupied with finding the centre that I don't think about anything apart from that. After taking several wrong turns and having to retrace my steps on a number of occasions, I finally find the heart of the maze. Except when I get there, I'm not alone.

"What are you doing here?" I stammer, completely thrown by the fact that Camden is sitting on a bench in the middle of the maze as though he's been there the whole time.

"Skipping class," he shrugs.

"I can see that. But how the fuck did you get to the middle so fast?" And more importantly, why is he here? Did he follow me or something?

He gives me a meaningful look. "There are two entrances, two paths to follow to get to the middle. I took one, whilst you took the other. We've still ended up in the same place."

"Is that supposed to be significant or something? It's a fucking maze, Camden. That's all." I turn around and stride towards the gap I entered by. There's no way I'm staying whilst he's here. Especially not since we're on our own together, and I have no fucking clue what his agenda is.

"Where do you think you're going?" he asks, and even though I quicken my pace he's in front of me in seconds. I raise my gaze to meet his and to avoid the sharpness of his nipples beneath his thin grey t-shirt. It's cold out, evidently.

Thing is I'm not cold… I'm the complete opposite of cold. I feel warm, *alive* and I'm not sure I like it. Actually, what I should be saying is that I'm positive I hate it. though, truthfully, I'm somewhere in the middle.

"You're running again… Isn't that what you did at Sasha's party that night?"

"Have you got some weird case of amnesia or something? I *stayed*, remember. Pretty sure I called you out too."

He laughs, showing that pretty gold molar. "Only after I challenged you. Do you always follow people's orders or just mine?"

"Don't flatter yourself. I'm going to my room. So, if you wouldn't mind," I snap, trying to step around him. He simply mirrors me, and I'm faced with a wall of muscle and a determined look. "Get out of the way," I insist.

"Not happening," he whispers as his topaz eyes glower with a mixture of challenge and… lust. There it is again. What the fuck? Inside, that flame ignites.

Spinning on my heel, I run to the other gap in the hedgerow on the other side of the central square. This time Camden isn't fast enough to stop me and I hook a left sprinting as fast as I can, acting on instinct. I can hear his heavy footsteps right behind me and feel his heavy breaths as though he's mere inches from me instead of metres. Following my gut, I race through the maze. I've no idea where I'm going just like I've no idea why I'm so intent on running from Camden. Is it because of the way he looked at me? Is it because I'm genuinely afraid of him? Or is it because of the way my heart pounds not in fear, but in excitement? This is a dangerous game I'm playing.

I might lie to others, but lying to myself? I've never done that until now.

When I turn the next corner, I'm faced with a dead end. Camden is on me in a matter of seconds. Like me, like most kids who live their lives on the street, he's not even broken a sweat. Being a criminal keeps you fit. We might generally stay and fight for our honour and reputation, but we run to save our arses from the law. Except, I'm not running from the law. I'm running from Camden when I should've stayed to fight. In all honesty, I'm pretty sure I liked the chase.

"You're quick, but I'm an expert at hunting, Asia." He steps closer, crowding me. My back hits the sharpness of the hedge, little branches dig into my back scratching at my skin.

"Back off, Camden," I whisper.

"Why?"

"Because I hate you. Because you're an arsehole, ruling over a bunch of arseholes. Because you destroyed my friend's life. Because we're enemies. Because you hate me. Because you confuse me..." I admit.

"How so?" he asks, the tenor of his voice lowering. He's so close I can smell him and the deep musk of his cologne. It's expensive and smacks of riches stolen not earned. Fakery. I wonder what his real smell is like beneath the heady aftershave he's wearing. "Why do I confuse you, Asia?" he persists, crowding me more. Spikes of fear and... excitement run amok inside my chest. *Fuck sake.*

"Every time Monk hurts me or tries to, you've stepped in... Why?" I grit my teeth and force myself to look into his eyes. My throat constricts as he stares down at me.

"Asia..." he whispers, bowing his head so that it's only inches from mine

"Yet you let him try and hurt me time and again. I don't understand. Be my enemy or be my friend, you can't be both. You can't straddle the line, one which *you* drew in the sand, not me," I remind him.

"I think you'll find that was you forcing my hand."

He leans forward suddenly, invading my space further. His chest heaves, but not from the running. There's emotion in his eyes, so much emotion; anger, fear, lust. All of it swirling, I'm not sure what I'm going to be left with. I wait. It's like watching the reels on a fruit machine turn, waiting for three of the same to hit the fucking jackpot.

Eventually he blinks, and just like that all the emotion is gone, replaced instead with that look I've become accustomed to. Blank, uninterested. He steps back, but I won't let him get away with this bullshit. Not today. Today, I'm done. Mr Burnside tried to pry me open with his gifts and promises and words. I need *action*. Camden is a man of action, even if it's the kind I have to defend myself from. At least I know where I stand with that. I don't know where I stand when he looks at me the way he just did.

"What do you fucking *want*, Camden? You hate me, then protect me. You turn a blind eye when your crew disrespect me, but study me when you think I don't notice. You chase me, but don't hurt me. WHAT THE FUCK DO YOU WANT FROM ME?"

Something seems to snap inside him. I see it behind his eyes, I can almost hear it crack.

"Fuck!" Camden growls, grabbing my arm with lightning fast speed then yanking me against his chest. With the other hand he grasps the back of my head, cupping it roughly. One word slips from his lips before his mouth crashes against mine: "*This.*"

The kiss is rough, quick, overpowering, *devastating* and over before it's really begun. Camden steps back, the muscles in his arms taught, the sinews jutting out against his dark skin.

"You bastard," I spit. "How fucking *dare* you!" I'm so angry. I hold onto that, because if I don't I might just step back into his arms and kiss him back and that I won't do. *Can't.*

"Just claiming what's mine."

"I'm not yours, Camden. I turned you down, remember?"

"Yes, you are," he insists, anger blazing in his eyes now.

"I don't belong to anyone, just like you don't belong to anyone either," I remind him.

"Belonging to someone and being *owned* are two very different things," he responds quietly, and for a moment I'm pretty sure he isn't talking about me, but about himself.

We stare at each other, neither of us willing to step away, caught somehow in this dangerous attraction.

"Back the fuck off, Camden."

Camden twists on his feet at the same time I step out from behind him. Ford is staring at us both like he's about to commit murder. Had he seen us kiss? Correction, had he seen Camden kiss me? I most definitely did *not* kiss him back.

"Or what?" Camden taunts.

"You know exactly what I'm capable of. Do you want a repeat of what happened that night in Grim?" Ford steps forward, his fists clenched. Camden does too.

Oh, fuck. Here we go. They can't fight here, not on school grounds. Not like this.

"Stop it. Stop! Not here." I shout, getting in between them.

I'm tired of this shit. My head is all over the fucking place. This day has gone from bad to fucking worse. I press the flat of my hands against both of their chests. Beneath my palms their hearts battle for my attention with the thudding and the pounding. Anger oozes from them both and perhaps something more, ownership, jealousy? Maybe both?

"Why? Let's deal with this once and for all. Right here, right now," Ford snaps. I see the violence in him then. I feel it in the tremor of his body beneath my hand. It's a thousand times more powerful than Camden's. That surprises me.

"No. I'm done today. No more." I grit my teeth, trying not to let my emotions get the better of me. Mr Burnside successfully dragged out unwanted emotions and memories, and now Camden has had the audacity to kiss me, leaving me reeling. The violence pouring off Ford is too much. I don't need to bear witness to this fight. I don't.

"I'm *done* today," I repeat.

"Who are you protecting right now, him or me?" Camden asks, glaring at me.

"Neither," I snap, refusing to be drawn into the argument. *Both*, I think. But why? I should let Ford kick the shit out of Camden. I should, and yet I don't want to.

Ford's nostrils flare but he steps back, heeding my request, surprising me. He schools his emotions, keeping the rage under wraps. I watch as he shuts it down. And Camden? He leans into my hand, baring his teeth at Ford. "Stay the fuck out of my business," he snaps.

"I won't do that, not when it comes to Asia," Ford retorts, glancing at me.

"Then things will only get worse around here."

"Bring it on, Camden. I'm not scared of you or your pack of wolves."

"Just go," I snap, glaring at Camden.

"Me?" he says, pointing to his chest. "You want *me* to fucking go?"

I scoff, an hysterical laugh pushing free from my lips. "Are you fucking kidding me?"

"What makes Ford the better option?" he asks.

"*He* doesn't want to hurt me..." I respond instantly. I might be wrong. I might be very, very wrong but I'm going with my instincts here. Besides, Camden is still my enemy, after all. One rage-filled kiss doesn't change that fact.

He glares at us both. Then shoves past Ford, pushing against his shoulder. "This isn't fucking over, not by a long shot," he snaps and I'm not sure whether he's talking to Ford or to me now. He rests his gaze on me, and I wince at the beauty of his topaz eyes and the bruising memory of his kiss. "Don't think for one second that Ford won't hurt you. He's capable of inflicting more pain than you could ever imagine."

With that last parting shot Camden stalks off, disappearing into the maze and leaving me with Ford and making me question whether my instincts were right after all.

25

A s the weeks crawl by and the weather turns cooler, fights continue to break out around the school between the opposing gang members. Over the last day or so there's been whispered talk about an organised brawl at the Tower between Ford and Camden to settle the score once and for all. The dislike between them is thick and toxic, causing the atmosphere around the place to worsen a thousand-fold.

Just this morning at breakfast, Mr Carmichael went apoplectic after finding out that two kids had to be sent to the hospital last night to fix broken bones. He pushed for someone to come forward. No one admitted to anything. No one said anything. Even though the crews are enemies, the rule on the street remains the same in this setting just as it ever did back home: no one rags, ever.

Believe me, it's a stupid fucking rule. Aside from that one time on the field when Monk hit Pink, I didn't tell any of the staff about what happened later that week with the stunt Monk pulled. I won't either. I want revenge on *my* terms.

By the end of his rant, and ten minutes of waiting for someone to step forward, Mr Carmichael realised that he was dealing with a bunch of kids whose skewed sense of loyalty remained fierce. You can take the kid out of the street, but you can't take the street out of the kid. Of all people, he should know that. But it would seem he's forgotten his roots no matter how much he tries to convince us all otherwise.

Every single one of us had fifty credits deducted.

Fifty bloody credits.

Now my overall score is back down to one hundred and ninety. I'll need to earn back the fifty credits I lost and gain an extra ten more to get my day trip out of this place. I'm desperate for a whole eight hours where I can do whatever the fuck I want. Granted, I've escaped Oceanside to visit the Tower, but that's not the point. It's a risk every time I do that and whilst the thrill of getting caught is part of the fun, I do actually want to spend time outside of Oceanside without having to keep looking over my shoulder.

Honestly, I need to *breathe*.

It's begun to get a little stifling in here.

"Penny for your thoughts?" Sonny asks, plonking himself next to me in the art studio where I'm sitting now.

"You'd have to pay a lot more than a penny," I retort.

If only he knew. The truth is all four of them consume my thoughts and it's driving me fucking mad. Camden has barely acknowledged me since the afternoon in the maze. But I know he's got his eye on me. I feel it every time I walk into a room. That hasn't changed.

Danger is creeping up on me, I feel it like a nightmare that I can't prevent, but this time I won't leave myself vulnerable again. Camden appears to be losing his hold on Monk and his wolves and I've no doubt Monk is going to go after me soon.

When he does, I'll be ready. I have a plan and I'll have Ford to thank for that. Well, I hope so anyway.

After lunch, I've arranged to meet Ford in the outhouse that borders the edge of the sports field. The space is used to store the sports equipment, but a portion is empty and that's where we've agreed to meet so he can teach me how to hone my fighting skills. I've not told anyone about our arrangement, least of all Sonny. A nervous kind of energy runs through me at the thought.

"Asia, shit. If I knew kissing you would make you clam up like this around me, I might've thought twice about it."

"I'm not clamming up. I just have stuff on my mind, that's all."

"Is this who you have on your mind" he asks, tapping his finger on the portrait of Eastern I'm sketching.

"Yeah," I admit. *That and three others, including you.* Though I don't say that thought out loud.

"Who is it?"

"My best friend, Eastern," I explain. The tight expression on his face relaxes.

"Ah, phew. There's me thinking I had more competition." He grins, then his face falls when my grimace gives my feelings away. "More than friends then?" he asks, trying to be all cool and relaxed but failing miserably.

"It's complicated. Let's leave it at that."

Sonny taps his fingers against the table, then puffs out his cheeks. "I know I should respect your wishes and all, but I kind of want to know who I'm up against. Don't tell me a guy as pretty as that is built like a brick shit house," he responds, playfully. Though it isn't really playful, not when he's looking at me so intensely. "The list is getting longer and longer. I need to up my game."

"What are you talking about?"

"There's me, your best mate Eastern, and *Ford*," he adds with a little growling noise.

"Ford isn't interested in me like that..." I insist, ignoring the flutter in my chest. Although, the way he'd looked at me that night he and Camden caught us kissing told another story.

"I told you before, Ford likes you. The guy might be a closed book, but I'm not an idiot. Neither is Camden. He sees it too."

"How so? And more to the point, how do you know what Camden does or doesn't see?"

"There's something about you, Asia. Don't you notice how they both watch you?"

"No. No, I don't," I lie. *Yes, yes I do*, and it feels weird. Good weird in the case of Ford, and strange, I've-no-idea-what-to-make-of-it-because-I-hate-Camden-I-really-fucking-do, in the case of the notorious HH gang leader.

"See? Competition," he insists.

"Look, we're not together, you and me. We shared a kiss ages ago, that's it." I wince at how harsh that sounds.

He nods tightly and stares at me as though he wants to counter that statement with something more serious, instead he grins. "It was a fucking great kiss though. Want to share another?"

"Do you ever let up?" I ask, a whole lot frustrated and a little flattered. Plus, I kind of *would* like to share another kiss too, but he really doesn't need to know that.

"When it comes to you, Asia, never."

With that, he returns to his own sketch and remains quiet for the rest of the lesson.

A<small>FTER LUNCH</small> I head out to the sports field and the outhouse beyond. When I arrive, Ford is already working out. He's skipping, wearing nothing but a pair of shorts and trainers. I slip inside the room quietly and stare at him, enjoying the view of the tight muscles across his back and arms as he moves. He's light on his feet and fast, the rope whizzing beneath his feet and over his head quicker than I can see. I'm pretty sure he knows I'm here, but he doesn't stop what he's doing.

Is he putting on a show for me right now? Was Sonny correct about Ford's interest in me or are we both getting all the wrong signals? Ford doesn't give much away, and he's still refused to open up in Mr Burnside's group therapy sessions when the rest of us have conceded and shared a little. I doubt Ford will ever get enough credits to escape Oceanside. He barely even tries. I'm not sure he really gives a damn about that though. Something tells me that this place is just a stop gap within a life he won't give up. Being here is meant to change us. Mr Carmichael's vision is to get us all to see the error of our ways and be a useful part of society. Which is already kind of insulting, I *am* useful.

Ford is just doing his time. Playing the game to a certain extent by following the rules he wants to follow, but ultimately I get the distinct impression none of this really matters. I would, however, like to know what does. He's the perfect definition of a dark horse; mysterious, aloof, intriguing, wild, but completely untouchable.

Eventually, after another five minutes of perving, I cough. "Hey," I say, not quite able to get out much more than this feeble greeting.

After another minute, he drops the rope and turns to face me. Sweat slides down his face and falls from his chin. For some reason I expected him to be covered in tattoos, but apart from a small one on his right collarbone that says *'Bad Boy'* there aren't any. Unless of course you count the countless white scars scattered across his chest. They're round, some of them are puckered, some smooth, all of them suspicious. I hold my breath.

He drops his gaze from me to his chest, his finger tracing across one of the nastier looking scars just beneath his rib cage. "Cigarette burns courtesy of my parents," he says, without a trace of emotion in his eyes.

Fuck.

"I'm sorry," I mutter, not sure what else to say but suddenly feeling the urge to pull him into my arms.

"What for? You didn't do it," he counters, picking up a hand towel hanging from a hook on the wall. He wipes his face, then hangs it back up.

"I'm sorry anyway," I whisper. He catches my gaze, his face impassive. His grey-green eyes void of emotion. He seems to make a decision though and swipes a hand through his sweaty hair before laying himself bare.

"My mum was abusive, my father too, though to a lesser degree. I've lived in care since I was ten. Ten years too late, if you ask me. I don't fit in anywhere. I'm distant, abrasive, cold. I don't like to talk about my past. I don't like to talk about my feelings. Instead, I train, and I fight. I'm here because I like to fight too much, not because I get taken over by the rage like Sonny and lose my mind, but because fighting *focuses* it. My crime…? I'm an illegal ring fighter. I'm notorious in the underground fight clubs in London. *Grim* Fight Club is my home away from home. I fought Camden there once before and won. That's why he dislikes me so much. That's why our crews are at war now because he knows I'm a threat. That's about it," he reels off leaving me gasping.

"Damn," I say. Talk about information overload. I mean, he's just revealed a shitload about himself and he's not even blinked. There's no emotion. None. The guy's a machine. Plus, what the fuck is Grim fight club? My gaze flickers to the 'Bad Boy' tattoo. It's not particularly professional looking, just two words etched into his skin. "Is that what you are?" I ask, motioning towards it.

"That's what I'm told. That's what my parents called me every damn day for ten years. It's a reminder they sought fit to scar me with." He shrugs. No emotion. Nothing.

Fuuuckkk. "I'm…"

"Don't. No pity."

"Okay, no pity." God only knows I understand his need for that even when I can't understand the lack of emotion.

"Now you," he states, pointing a finger in my direction.

"What?"

"You know what. I can't help you be a better fighter if you don't lay it on the line for me. That *is* why you're here, right? I need to know where the rage comes from so I can help you to hone it into a useful weapon. Talk."

"You're kidding me, right? You're not Mr Burnside and this ain't no therapy session."

"Not kidding, not in the slightest. Talk, Asia."

"I can't," I say, shaking my head and backing up against the door. I reach for the handle, my gut twisting with anxiety. I can't switch off the emotion like he can. I can't reel off my past hurt as easily and emotionless as he just did. There are some things I'm just not willing to share, and despite the little snippets about my life that I've given up in Mr Burnside's therapy sessions, they're nothing compared to what I've kept hidden. *Nothing.*

"Then I can't help you," he says flatly.

"Can't or won't?"

"Won't help you," he rephrases.

"Then I'm out," I say, turning my back on him and reaching for the door. I'm running. Again. What the fuck is it with this place? I don't run ever, and yet I find myself doing it once more.

26

"Wait," he snaps, drawing me back around to face him again.

"Why? You said you won't help me unless I spill. I can't. So, we're done."

He sighs, his fists curling at his sides. I notice them, he notices me noticing them, and he releases his fingers. I watch as he wiggles them, losing some of the tension that his body still holds.

"You might not have realised it, but that was hard for me. I've told you more about my shit than I've told anyone. Like I said, I don't share. I just did. You owe me."

"I don't owe you anything. That was your decision, I didn't ask you to tell me shit. I came here to *train*. I didn't agree to sharing." I turn my back on him once more and pull the door open. He's on me in seconds. I'm yanked back against his chest, the door slammed and locked before I can do a thing about it.

"Ford!" I shout, but his name is snatched from my lips as

he twists me around to face him, forcing me backwards. I'm trapped between the wall and his body. His firm, sweaty body. He smells like a man. I'm not sure how else to put it. He may only be my age, but Ford is *not* a kid. Not in any sense of the word. "What the fuck do you think you're doing?" I grind out trying to shove him off me. He's too strong. Wily fucker.

"Lesson number one. When I ask you to do something, you do it or face the consequences."

"What consequences?"

For a split second he seems to consider something. Then he shows me.

Fisting my hair in his hand, he yanks my head to the side, then runs his tongue up the length of my neck before biting my earlobe. "Every time you disobey me, I'll deny you what you want the most," he whispers, grinding his hips against my own. Hitting the spot that's been tingling from the moment I stepped into this room, even though I'm only just realising that now. It's like my brain has finally caught up with my body. "But if you do as I say, do as I ask, then I'll make you see stars."

Motherfucker.

"Get off me," I demand, but neither he nor I believe that's what I really want.

"You're good at lying to yourself, aren't you, Asia?"

"Fuck you."

"Is that an invitation?" He stares at me intently, the heat between us growing. He loosens his hold.

"Get off me," I repeat, but when I don't take the opportunity to escape, his nostrils flare at the silent approval. How have I ended up here again? Camden in the maze now Ford in the outhouse. The only person who didn't steal a kiss from me was Sonny, and I've been avoiding him for days now.

"Make me," he growls, crowding me again. My hips jerk as

he reaches between us and grasps my heated crotch over my leggings. I'm embarrassingly wet.

"Get your fucking hands off me," I shout, but I don't move. I don't and I have no idea why.

"Make me, Asia," he repeats, running his mouth against my jawline. He pulls back, his lips hovering over mine as he captures my gaze with the heat of his. Between us his hand is gently moving against my mound. I'm about half a second away from jumping his bones, but something in me knows that's exactly what he wants. He wants me to lose my inhibitions.

"I'm touching you like this and you're letting me?" he kind of states, almost surprised by the fact. The thing is. I don't really want him to let go. I *want* him to touch me. I've been wanting it ever since he pinned me beneath him on the field the first week I arrived here, and all those times since when he's stood up for me. Except, of course, that truth is harder to share.

"Enough," I push his hand away roughly, giving him a shove. But it's half-hearted and he knows it. He cocks his head, looking at me with fascination then steps back into my space and cups my mound once more.

"*Tell me* something, Asia," he repeats, his circling finger making me go mindless. If this is how he can make me feel with his hand over my clothes, I can only imagine what it'd be like when he gets beneath them. Damn, I'm in trouble.

"I'm not telling you shit," I grind out, goading him. Let's see how far he's willing to go.

"I was hoping you'd say that."

The heel of his palm presses firmer against my crotch, right on the spot that makes me squirm. A moan escapes my lips, colouring my cheeks, and I do what he knew I would. I lose my inhibitions. He pulls back slightly, watching me as I grind helplessly against him. Sensation swells outwards from that tiny nub between my legs, scattering up my spine and prickling my scalp. My mouth pops open, another moan escaping as he increases the pressure. What the fuck is happening here? Okay, stupid question... But, really, what the fuck is going on?

His breathing quickens with mine, as though I'm touching him in the same way he's touching me. Except my hands are pressed against the wall behind me, my nails digging into the stone as I hang on for dear life.

"Do you always wear your emotions on your sleeve, Asia? Or are those ones just for show? Do you have hidden depths just waiting to be discovered?"

I can't answer him. All I can think about, all I can *feel* is the swell of an orgasm teetering around the edges of my consciousness. It builds deep within me, curling outwards, upwards. I push back against Ford's hand, wanting to chase the pleasure. Needing it like I've never needed anything. Just as it's about to expand and shatter, Ford pulls his hand away and my eyes snap open. His pupils are dark, and just for a second it's as though I can see right into his soul. There's a glimmer of something there, something worth knowing.

"Ford...?" I manage to pant, my pulse racing. He closes his eyes briefly and when he opens them again the hollowness is back.

"Don't bother looking, Asia, there's nothing to see," he says, placing his hand back between my legs and cupping me once more. I move against his hold, out of my mind with need. He allows me a few moments of blissful torment before grasping my hips with his free hand and forcing me to still.

"The decision as to whether I let you come is down to you. Give me something to work with and I'll give you what you've been dreaming of ever since our tussle on the field. Then and only then will I teach you how to fight."

"I know how to fight. I have no idea why I even came here today," I bite out, trying not to launch myself at him and kiss him until his mouth is bruised.

"You're a scrapper, Asia. You're not a fighter. There's a difference. Besides, we both know why you came here today, and it has less to do with learning how to fuck up Monk once and for all and more to do with the heat between your legs. So, are you going to share now so I can make you come?"

"No," I respond reflexively, the word releasing from my lips before I can even think about his offer. It's a knee-jerk reaction and one I instantly regret.

He lets me go, backing up. "Get out."

"Wait, what?" I kind of stumble forward, my head all twisted up, my fucking body on fire and my clit throbbing for release. Every single part of me *burns*. I've never, *ever* felt like this before. Who is this guy?

"You heard me. GET OUT!" he shouts, startling me.

But I don't move. I can't.

"Do you have a problem with simple instructions, Asia? I said get the fuck out." He's mad. So damn mad, and I have absolutely no idea why. I mean, I do, I *guess*. But this seems like so much more than me not willing to tell him a little bit about my past. I don't understand.

"I don't understand," I repeat out loud this time. Shaking my head, I force away these sudden feelings of disappointment and confusion that stirs within me.

I want to come.

I don't want to leave.

I want him to teach me to fight.

I don't want to share my past.

I *need* revenge.

I'm so fucking confused.

"You're not making any sense." I take a step towards him. "Finish what you started, Ford."

Now it's his turn to deny me. "No," he bites out, turning his back to me. "You're not worth the trouble."

The rage descends.

I don't know why it happens so suddenly or with such force, but it does. It grips hold of me and forces my feet towards him. Within two strides I'm grabbing his arm and yanking him around to face me. Without a second's hesitation, I raise my hand and slap him across the cheek as hard as I can. The sound of my palm hitting his skin is deafening, but nowhere near as deafening as the silence that follows. I'm breathing heavily, my body shaking with denied pleasure and pent up emotion. There's a sudden chill and a darkness in his eyes that makes me regret my actions immediately.

For the first time in a long time, I cower.

"There she is," he bites out, stalking me.

I back away not understanding what's happening between us. He's just flipped on a dime and I have no idea how to handle him.

"That rage you just felt, that *emotion*, it makes you weak, Asia. Vulnerable. It will get you killed. You cannot rely on any kind of emotion to win a fight. Do you understand?"

"I'm *not* vulnerable. I'm *not* weak," I insist, even though that's exactly how I feel right now.

"No?" he questions, pressing me back up against the wall, aligning his body perfectly against mine, his hands pinning my arms to my sides. Somehow he's right. The sudden rage is gone as quickly as it appeared, and I'm left empty, wanting, cut open, raw, helpless.

Bereft somehow. All of that.

"Tell me one thing, *something*," he says, his gaze softening. Not enough to let me really see him, but enough to let me know he isn't a monster.

"My mother was a heroin addict. When I was born, I was too..." I whisper the words, releasing them before I'd even made a conscious decision to do so.

Ford nods once, then presses his forehead against mine and reaches between my legs once more. He doesn't try to kiss me even though I really, really want him too. Instead, he slides his hand beneath the waistband of my leggings and knickers. His fingers find my slick heat and my eyes flutter shut at the sensation of his skin against mine.

"Look at me, Asia. Don't take your eyes off me," he demands. His voice is thick with feeling. With *lust*. It breaks me that little bit more and as much as I want to keep my eyes shut, I can't deny him this. Right at this moment, I'm not sure I'll be able to deny him anything.

My eyes snap open as he pulls back slightly, watching me react to the way he's touching me. His finger finds my clit, circling gently. I moan, and he bites down on his lip in response, his chest heaving. I wonder why he's holding back, why he doesn't try to kiss me. I want to ask, but the feeling he's stoking within me won't let me concentrate on anything but how fucking good I feel. I'm so damn wet. So hot for him. He's dangerous for my heart, this one. I understand that simple truth in the moment, but I don't care.

When his fingers circle my entrance, I whimper at his gentleness, at the way he's coaxing me, drawing my orgasm out. I've never experienced anything like this before.

My lips part as he sinks his finger inside me right up to the knuckle, the pad of his thumb pressing on my clit gently as he does so.

I let out a low, steady moan.

He leans in closer, flicking his gaze between my eyes and lips. I want him to kiss me so badly, *so fucking badly*. But I'm so caught up in his gaze and the sensations as he moves his finger in and out of me in a gentle rhythm that I can't move.

"That's it, Asia. Come for me," he mutters.

As his lips hover over my own, his soft breaths fluttering across my skin, I do exactly what he asks and see stars.

AN HOUR later I'm a sweaty mess. My muscles are roaring with pain at the strenuous exercises Ford has made me do and I'm barely standing on wobbly legs. Whilst he too is sweaty and panting, he's nowhere near as physically affected as I am. We've sparred. He's taught me how to punch with conviction and where. I've learnt a lot.

Ford hands me a bottle of water. I take it from him, open it up and drink the whole lot in one go.

"You did good today," he says. It's a throwaway compliment, but I take it.

"Thanks."

I'm completely drenched in sweat and know that I must look like a complete mess. My t-shirt is completely stuck to my chest and I feel disgusting. Stupidly, I hadn't thought to bring a change of clothing. Looking like this is bound to raise questions especially since I'm nowhere near the gym. I guess I could say that I've been running around the field. Then again, for the last hour there's been a P.E. lesson going on outside, one that's not on my timetable for this double period.

"Next time bring a change of clothes," Ford states, grabbing his t-shirt from the back of a chair in the corner of the room. He chucks it at me. "You can wear this."

Grabbing it, I pull a face.

"It's clean. If that's what you're thinking."

Actually that isn't what I was thinking. I was thinking that I'm not sure how I'm going to be able to school my feelings when I slip his top over my head. Even now, holding it against my chest I can smell him on it.

"What about you?" I ask, gesturing to his bare chest.

"I've got a sweater," he walks over to the duffle bag perched on the seat and pulls out a black sweater. He yanks it over his head, his hair falling into his eyes, then waits.

"Your turn," he murmurs, his chin jutting out a little towards the t-shirt I'm holding.

My cheeks heat at the implication. I mean, I'm wearing a bra and all, but still…

"Shy?"

He had his hand down my pants not more than an hour ago, I shouldn't be. Yet, I am.

"No," I lie, clutching his t-shirt between my thighs and pulling off my top. I'm wearing a simple t-shirt bra, black with no lace. It's probably about as sexy as a pair of granny knickers, but then again what does it matter.

"You've got tattoos," Ford remarks. It's a statement really, not a question. He has a habit of doing that.

"Yes. I have three. One on my thigh, one on my back and the one you see here," I say, pointing to the bleeding heart with a dagger stabbed through the centre of it. It sits right in the middle of my chest between my breasts.

"What's that mean?" he asks, pointing to the heart and dagger tattoo. He steps closer, to get a better look I assume.

"If I don't answer, are you going to do what you did before?" I ask tentatively.

"What, deny you an orgasm?" he asks, not in the least bit disturbed by how that sounds or the easy way he refers to that intense moment between us earlier.

"Well, yes…"

"Do you *want* it to be like before? I can make this question that kind of question if you'd like?" His eyes darken as he lifts his hand to his face. For a second he breathes in, then drops his hand, a tiny smirk playing about his lips. Does his hand still smell… was he just smelling…? Oh, my days, he was.

Holy Mother of God, this guy. I don't know whether to be embarrassed or turned on. I think I'm both.

"So, *do* you?" he repeats, stepping closer, that intensity back again.

"Do I what?"

"Do you want me to make this question like the one before and if you answer me truthfully, I make you see stars. I make you *come*, Asia." He spells it out for me. There's no beating around the bush with Ford. I like that about him. I know where I stand. But then he follows it up with a cocky smirk. The evil, rotten, bastard.

"No." *Yes*, I think. "No, definitely not."

I turn my back to him, pulling his t-shirt over my head and trying not to breathe in too deeply. It smells of him, of sweat and man and musk and… *power*. It's intoxicating, just like him.

He barks out a laugh. It's a funny sound that is even stranger coming from him. I'm getting the impression he doesn't laugh all that often. Smiling is even rarer.

"Fair enough. Do you want to tell me what it means, no strings attached? That one on your back is of a dove, you willing to share the meaning behind that one too?"

"Not today. I think I've shared quite enough for one day," I say, grabbing my dirty top and heading out the door.

"Same time next week, Asia?" he asks me.

"Sure."

"And Asia..." he says, the tone of his voice making my steps falter.

"Yes?" I twist on my feet to face him.

"You're beautiful when you come."

27

"Congratulations, Asia, you've enough credits for a day trip out of Oceanside," Pink says, imitating Miss Moore, my art teacher, as we rifle through her clothes a week later. Today, after almost two and a half months confined to the grounds of Oceanside I get to leave for the day without looking over my shoulder and worrying if I'm going to get caught out. It's a crisp Saturday morning, but it isn't raining and whilst cold, it's still quite a nice day for an outing.

"Look at you, delinquent turned swot. Mr Carmichael must be creaming his pants over you," she adds with a wink.

"He's gay," I remark, rolling my eyes.

"Yeah, duh! I meant you're his perfect pupil." She grins, wiggling her eyebrows which she's somehow managed to die light blue just like the new streak in her hair.

"I'm not so sure about that. I haven't spoken to the guy since my first day here. He's elusive as fuck."

"Do you want to speak with him or something?" Pink asks, shaking her head in disbelief.

"No, not particularly."

"Good, I really was worried you'd turned into a swot for a minute there." Pink picks up one of the items of clothing strewn across her bed. "So, what's it going to be? Off the shoulder green top paired with this denim mini-skirt and your DM's, or how about this cut-out pink tee with my orange leggings? You'd look hot in both."

I give her a look. I appreciate colour, I do, but I'm not an out and out colour freak like Pink. She's off the charts with her mix 'n' match attitude when it comes to clothing. "It's nearing the end of October, Pink. I'm not wearing a bloody mini-skirt and risk the chance of my clit falling off from the cold. I happen to quite like that little piece of flesh."

Pink bursts out laughing, falling backwards onto her bed and clutching her stomach. "You're a gas, do you know that? There's me thinking you're one step up from being a nun, and all along you been plucking that clit of yours like it's a violin getting tuned."

"Hey, who said anything about *me* plucking it?" That shuts her up.

She sits upright, grabbing my arm. "Please tell me the rumours are true."

"What rumours?"

"You're kidding, right? *Everyone* is talking about you. You've got the whole damn academy up in arms. For someone with as much street smarts as you, you're frigging oblivious, Asia."

"I'm going to wear my black jeans and that green top if that's okay?" I say, trying to steer the conversation in a different direction.

She waves me off. "Of course, it's okay. What's mine is yours, we're friends remember... but back to the topic at hand. Don't you *want* to know what they're all talking about?"

Do I want to know? Not really. Gossip doesn't tend to be positive, especially when it comes to me. I shrug and Pink takes that as a cue to let me in on the gossip. *Great.*

"So, rumour has it you've joined No Name crew and that you've been shacking up with Ford *and* keeping Sonny as your bit on the side..." she pauses, studying my reaction. When I keep a straight face, she presses on. "A certain someone ain't too happy about it."

"Let me guess, Monk?"

"Monk? No. I mean yes, he certainly ain't happy about anything you do, but it's not him."

I shake my head in confusion. "Look, let's get shit straight. I've not joined Ford's crew."

"You haven't?"

"No, I haven't. I meant what I said before, I don't do crews."

"Well, tell that to Camden, 'cause I heard he's pissed as fuck."

"Why?"

"Haven't got the faintest idea. Only, all these fights breaking out between the two sides..."

"Yeah?" I prompt, frowning.

"All because of you, Asia."

"Oh, for fuck sake," I respond sitting heavily on her bed. I don't want anything to do with this shit. I just want to do my time and fucking leave. That's it.

"But..." Pink sing-songs, looking at me as a smile nudges her lips. "You *have* been mucking about with those two hotties, haven't you? What did you think would happen when you kiss

Sonny and meet with Ford for a *one-on-one* session?" She wiggles her eyebrows again, then bursts out laughing.

"You know about that?"

"About the kiss at the Tower or the one-one-one session?"

"Both."

Pink smiles. "Pretty obvious to me that you'd end up snogging Sonny after that hot-as-fuck dancing you two were doing. The Ford thing… I wasn't sure, until now."

"Oh, shit…"

"I'd say your secret's safe with me, but given the whole school knows about it, it's kind of a moot point."

I swear multiple times under my breath which only makes Pink laugh more. Then her expression turns serious. "Never seen Sonny's pride hurt so much though. The guy's a fool over you, Asia. It's eating him up that you went to Ford for help."

Oh boy. I'm not sure how to address that, so I don't. Instead I ask the only question I want answering right now. "What exactly are people saying?"

I sincerely hope that it's the training he's given me that has got people talking and not the orgasms. Or should I say *orgasm*. He hasn't attempted to touch me like that since the first time. In fact, Sonny has backed off too, and even though I'd wanted him to in the beginning, I'm kind of missing his persistence. Now, I understand why he has. He thinks Ford and I are an item.

"He's been teaching you to fight… right?" Pink narrows her eyes at me. "*Right?*"

"Yep, exactly that."

"You sneaky bitch," Pink teases, her mouth dropping open. "You *have* hooked up with him, haven't you?"

Standing, I snatch up the green top willing my body not to

give me away. "Thanks for this," I mutter, before striding from the room, her laughter following me out.

▟▙▟▙▟▙▟

"ROOM FOR A COUPLE MORE?" Sonny asks, climbing into the cab and sitting opposite me. Behind him Ford and Kate follow. She gives me a sheepish grin.

"Surprise," she says, waving her hands about.

Ford scowls. Sonny grins. I groan. It's not that I don't want Kate here, actually it's pretty fucking great she is. But Ford and Sonny? After my conversation with Pink, I'm not sure how to act around them both knowing what I do now. I'm not dating Ford, and I miss Sonny's tenacity.

"I didn't know you'd earned enough credits," I say, as she settles in the seat next to me. Ford folds down the other seat in front of us both and proceeds to roll down the electric window, not bothering to meet my gaze. He looks epically pissed off.

"I didn't, neither did Ford here but he asked me a favour and I obliged. It's good for my hacking skills." Kate whispers so the cab driver can't hear.

"You didn't? Fuck, Kate, if they find out…"

"They won't. I'm that good."

"Yeah, *thanks* Kate," Sonny mutters, sarcastically. Ford continues to play with the electric window ignoring us all. "I didn't realise there were black taxis in Hastings, they're normally a London only form of transport," Sonny continues as the driver pulls off, oblivious to the tension building in the cab. Then he catches my gaze and I realise not only is he aware of it, he's trying to diffuse it.

"Retired down here, son. Couldn't give up my cab. Besides, I got to earn my pocket money, right? Ain't no way the missus is going to fund my Friday night drinks." the driver says, his London accent familiar and warm. It makes me a little homesick.

"I don't blame you, mate. It's roomy," Sonny remarks, winking at me.

"So, where to?" the cabbie, asks.

"Hastings beach front," I respond before anyone else can.

"The beachfront it is."

We arrive at our destination twenty minutes later after Paul, the cabbie, finds the best shortcuts to avoid all the traffic. He rolls down the window when we climb out of the cab. "I'll pick you up right here at 9pm, don't be late or it's my arse on the line and I really, really, need that pocket money. Know what I mean?"

We all laugh, except Ford. Ford just scowls.

"So what do you want to do?" Kate asks, looking like a fish out of water. She is staring at all the people milling around. Even though it's freezing and the sea is grey and squally, the seafront is still busy. At least it isn't raining.

"I'm going to go over there," I say, pointing to the pebbled beach.

"You're going to sit on the beach? Are you mad? It's so cold," she responds, wrinkling her nose.

"Yeah, I am," I shrug.

"Well, sounds like… *fun*?" Sonny says, grinning. He winks at me and I just know he's thinking about the last time we sat on the beach together. And even though we've been to the Tower on several times since I kissed him, we've not done it again. I flick my gaze to Ford, who's staring intently at me.

"I like the sea too," he says, still scowling, but doesn't elaborate more than that. The guy's a mystery, just like the bloody sea he appears to like so much.

Kate pulls a what-the-fuck-you-guys-are-nuts face at me. "Fine, we'll sit on the beach. I'll grab some hot drinks. Who wants a cup of tea?"

"Me, please," I say, digging in my pocket for some coins.

Kate holds her hands up. "Hey, I can shout us all a cuppa. Sonny? Ford? Want one?"

"Sure," Sonny responds. Ford just grunts, drawing a laugh from Kate.

"I'll meet you over there somewhere," she states, waving her hand in the general direction of the beach just by the basketball courts on the promenade.

So that's where we head to.

Sonny plonks himself down just behind the basketball courts, his back leaning against the concrete foundations. The beach slopes downwards here, so the spot is sheltered by the wind. I sit next to him, not too close, but close enough to feel a little awkward. Ford drops down on the other side of me. Shifting closer when he notices Sonny do the same, until I'm sandwiched between them both. The warmth of their arms making me feel slightly brain numb.

"Well, this is cosy," I mutter. Awkward much? On one side is the guy I kissed, and on the other the guy who had his hands down my knickers. My skin prickles at the thought of them doing the same, right now... *together*. Oh, shit. I'm in deep trouble. I really should friendzone them, but my heart won't let me. Actually, make that my clit... my clit won't let me and right now with all the throbbing she's doing I'm powerless to argue.

"Do you think Atlantis exists? I mean, imagine a whole city under the sea. I bet the mermaids are fucking hot. Also, how do they... you know, *fuck*?" Sonny asks suddenly, successfully distracting me from my clit.

"Does your brain *always* go straight to sex?" I respond, rolling my eyes but grinning nonetheless.

"Not *always*... sometimes it's preoccupied with other things. Actually, of late, one thing in particular." He looks at me and there's no joke to follow up the statement this time. My thighs press together in response and I swallow hard. Goddamn it.

Deciding my only option right now is to break up the tension with something jokey because, you know... *tense*. I make a statement of my own.

"I heard that if you strip completely naked, stand waist deep in the sea, and blow through a conch shell you could get lucky and attract a mermaid..."

"Oh yeah?" Sonny smirks.

"Yeah, then she'll grab your cock and depending on how big it is, will decide whether you're worth dragging back to Atlantis for hot underwater sex or drowning because it's such a disappointment."

"Reckon I need to find me a conch shell then, because my cock is *mammoth*." Sonny grins, holding his hands up so that they're at least a metre apart.

Ford barks out a laugh. It kind of bursts out of him and sounds more like he's choking than actually laughing. Sonny and I are both so surprised by it that for second we don't react. Then I let out a snort of laughter followed by a belly laugh and Sonny joins in. By the time Kate arrives with the tea, we're all laughing hysterically. Even Ford. It feels good, great actually. But, of course, it was never going to last.

28

B y the time we arrive back at Oceanside we're all quiet, reflective. It's been a good day. We mucked about on the beach for a while, spent some time in the kid's playground being… well, kids. Then Kate and I had dragged Sonny and Ford around all the little boutique shops. I even managed to pick up some spray cans from a hardware store in town, and once the sky had darkened and most people had gone home, left a little piece of me on one of the more rundown beach huts. I wasn't stupid enough to tag my graffiti art given my circumstances and all, but it felt good to just step back and look at something once so dull and lifeless transformed into a work of art. Whoever owns the beach hut, I hope they appreciate it.

"Well, I'm beat. I'm going to head back to my room. You coming, Asia?" Kate asks me.

We're all standing in front of the residential annex, the lights of the cab pulling away, leaving us in semi-darkness.

"I'm going to grab something to eat from the rec room first.

See you at breakfast?" I respond. I'm actually not that hungry, but I suddenly want a minute alone with Sonny and Ford. Stupid idea really, and I'm not really sure what I'm playing at, though I go with it anyway.

"Okay. Thanks for today," she says almost shyly, squeezing my arm before nodding to Sonny and Ford and heading inside.

For a beat we stand awkwardly, the three of us, until I break the sudden silence. "Right then, I'm going to get that snack." I say, hesitating, feeling a bit of an idiot standing here waiting to see if they'll take a hint. I'm not going to ask them to come along, but I do want them to.

"I don't think you should go there alone," Ford states as I start to walk away. I'm not sure if he's offering to come with me or not, but when he jogs to catch up with me, I figure that means he is.

"Good point. I could do with something to eat too," Sonny agrees, resting his hand lightly on my back when he reaches me. My skin immediately heats under his touch and my body temperature rises even more when Ford scowls at Sonny and says, "We agreed no making a move on Asia today..."

"That's right we did, but our agreement was whilst out on the day trip. Just as well it's over then, isn't it?" Sonny laughs and keeps his hand where it is, giving Ford a challenging look. What the actual fuck?

"Wait, *what*?" I blurt out, looking between them both.

"We'll explain inside," Ford snaps, anger blazing in his eyes. For someone who's so adamant that rage should be kept in-check, he's really not that good at it himself.

"He's just pissed that he's off his game," Sonny whispers in my ear, successfully sending a shiver down my spine. We've been flirting all day, bantering back and forth. I feel at ease with him, more so than with Ford, and when he's not talking about women all the time, he's actually pretty intelligent. Apart from his question about Atlantis and merwomen earlier he hasn't once talked about the opposite sex. It's been refreshing. I like this Sonny. And Ford? He's been way more open today. Joining in on conversations, having an opinion on stuff. He even laughed more than once, but despite that slight lowering of his walls, he was still intense, on guard for the most part. Spending time with him today has just intrigued me more. A couple of times I caught him staring at me when he thought I hadn't noticed. It made my skin heat up from the inside out each time. When he looks at me now, like he wants to devour me, it does the same thing. I'm beginning to understand that today had been some kind of challenge of who can get the girl. Thing is, I'm not a prize to be won. I deserve to be a willing participant. Yes, I might be attracted to them both, but that doesn't mean to say I lose my right to be a master of my own life.

We head towards the rec room. The lights are out, and the room is thrown into darkness. In fact, it's suspiciously quiet given it's still an hour until curfew.

"Where is everyone?" I whisper. I'm not sure why I keep my voice low. Instinct maybe? I feel like we're about to get jumped or something.

"No idea," Sonny responds, stepping closer to me.

Ford's shoulders are tense underneath his hoody. "I don't like it," he mutters, glancing at me and giving Sonny a look. He steps closer too.

"Do you want to tell me what's going on?" I say.

"I'm not sure yet. Just stay behind me," Ford responds, pushing open the door to the rec room. He flicks on the light switch and I walk straight into his back.

"Fuck!" he swears.

"Shit, sorry..." I begin, then my mouth drops open before my skin goes ice-cold as all the blood drains from my body.

"Jesus fucking Christ," Sonny says, reaching for me. I shake off his arm reflexively.

"Don't!" I snap.

The rec room is filled with drawings from *my* sketchbook. Except they're all copies, enlarged and doctored, turned *ugly*. My sketch of Braydon, smiling in his wheelchair, has been drawn all over with black marker pen and pinned to the noticeboard. Someone's written '*spaz*' right across his beautiful face. I stumble towards it, my heart tearing open. I rip it from the wall, staring at it dumbfounded.

"No," I whisper.

Twisting on my feet, I grab the next doctored sketch. This one of my little brothers holding hands and grinning. I sketched it one afternoon from a photograph I was given by their foster mum. I remember feeling gutted that I hadn't been there to witness such love between them. Now, that love has been twisted and ridiculed with the words '*gay boys*' scrawled across it. I choke back a sob.

"Asia, let me help you clean this up," Sonny offers, his voice quiet, careful. He knows I'm on the verge of tears. I blink them back, refusing to let them win.

Breathe, Asia. Just breathe.

On the coffee table is another blown-up copy of the sketch I drew of my mother. The only sketch I've ever done of her. This one was from a memory, one of the only happy memories I have of her. She's sitting on a chair next to her bedroom window smoking a cigarette. Even now, I remember how the morning light filtered through the glass surrounding her in a kind of ethereal glow. She'd been sober for three months at that point. It was the best three months of my life. Now some arsehole has drawn a cock in front of her face and written *'Hackney's Whore'* in capital letters beneath it. I gather that one too, gripping hold of it tightly as I scan the room.

Stuck to the fridge with masking tape is my sketch of Eastern. It's one of my favourite drawings of him. I remember the moment well. It'd been a boring Sunday afternoon and I'd been doodling in my sketchpad when he'd offered to pose for me. I remember showing it to him once I'd finished and my cheeks matching the redness of his own. That day my feelings for Eastern had changed from just friends to something more. Now, his eyes have been blacked out and a gun drawn against his temple. The words *'dead meat'* stamped across his face.

This can only be the work of one person... *Monk.*

"That motherfucker!" I scream, storming around the room and ripping off the remaining pictures with unbridled fury. "I'm going to kill the bastard!"

Blown up images of Ford, Sonny, Pink and Kate are also strewn about the room, all of them doctored, all of them having a nasty slight or comment inked across them. The humiliation is just too fucking much. Not only has that bastard done this, but he's got my sketchpad. He's got my damn sketchpad. That pulls me up sharp. *No, no, no, no, no.*

Twisting on my heel I storm out of the room, Ford and Sonny calling after me. I've never felt such rage. How dare he? How fucking dare he? I can take the jibes, the food missiles, the fucking threats even. But this? This goes beyond that.

This fucking hurts...

Those pictures are like a personal diary to me. They're my fucking soul spilled out onto a page for everyone to see. That fucking bastard Monk.

Then I remember that he's no longer the leader of the HH crew, Camden is, and though this stinks of Monk going rogue, ultimately Camden is responsible. Hasn't he done enough fucking damage?

"Asia, wait!" Ford shouts, running after me as I leg it back to the annex. He catches up to me just as I get to the lobby of the main building. Standing there waiting is Monk and the same six guys who jumped me that first week I arrived. Pink and Kate run into the lobby behind them. Pink is teary-eyed, her mascara black ribbons down her face. Kate looks pale. Haunted.

"I see you found our new gallery. What, don't like the artwork?" Monk sneers. His pack of wolves burst out laughing behind him.

"You, *motherfucker*, are dead!" I seethe, my fingers curled around the paper in my hand.

"Is that a promise?" he asks, leering at me.

"Prick, you'd better start running because I'm more than happy to finish what I started," Sonny bites out, stepping up beside me.

"No! Not this time," I snap, "This is my fight, Sonny. *Mine!*"

Pink is sobbing now, and I wonder why she's so distressed. Then I look at what she's holding... My sketchbook. "I'm sorry, Asia." She holds it up, all the pages have been ripped from the binding, it's empty. "I thought you'd got back early because your bedroom door was open. It's a mess, there's *shit* everywhere. Kate found me trying to clean it up. I didn't know. I would've tried to stop them..." she rambles.

Shit? As in my stuff thrown about or real, *actual* shit? I'm not sure I want to know. All I want are my drawings. "Where are they, arsehole?" I bite out, rounding on Monk. I take several steps forward, but Ford's hand clasps around my arm holding me back.

"Not here, Asia. Not now," he warns me.

"Get off me, Ford!" I shout turning on him.

"Oh look, trouble in paradise," Monk says, drawing more laughter from his gang.

"Fuck you, prick! This isn't over," Sonny snaps, his whole body is vibrating with anger. Just like mine is. Just like Ford's is too.

More people arrive, the lobby filling with students. Amongst them are Bram and Red looking far too delighted by what's going on. A look is exchanged between Bram and Monk. It doesn't go unnoticed. Ford's grip tightens on my arm and I hear him swear under his breath. Is this a joint endeavour? It wouldn't fucking surprise me. I yank my arm out of Ford's hold, turning on him.

"Is that why you came today, pretending to be my friend when in reality your bastard crew helped Monk set this up?"

Ford looks shocked. "No! Fuck, Asia, no!"

He seems sincere, but I don't know what to believe. Bram and Red exchange glances, then start to back up into the crowd. It's too late though, Ford is already on them both. He grabs Bram by the collar yanking him out into the open space.

"Stay the fuck there!" he orders Red, who stills, her eyes wide with fear. Kate and Pink step in behind her, preventing her from leaving.

"What the fuck did you do?" Ford is eerily calm. His voice low, threatening.

"Only what that bitch deserved. Wasn't like you were going to do it... too busy thinking more about your cock than the rest of us," Bram blurts out, hate seeping from every pore. He looks at me then. "Fucking whore!" he spits.

Ford lifts his arm, pulls his fist back and punches Bram on his cheek, sending him sprawling. Red screams, pushing past the bystanders. She drops to her knees beside her boyfriend who is currently groaning and clutching at his face.

"You're out," Ford snaps, those two words gutting Red and Bram like a knife would a fish.

"Ford," Red begs, her eyes wide, lips trembling.

"You knew about this?" he questions.

She winces. "She's a bitch," is all she can say.

"Then you're both done."

"We've been friends since we were kids and you'd drop us, for *her*?" she spits, her trembling lips and moist eyes replaced with daggers and gritty determination. She isn't done, not by a long shot. This will only fuel their hate more.

"Well, well, well, if there isn't dissention in the ranks. Looks like you're losing your grip, Ford," Monk sneers. His laughter cutting through the air.

"Fuck you, Monk," Ford snaps. The pain of losing two of his friends flashing in his eyes. I see him shut it down quickly, shut all his emotions down. I know what he's doing, he's preparing himself mentally to fight.

"This is my fight, Ford," I warn him, just the same as I did Sonny.

Behind us a door slams open, echoing through the lobby. The crowd parts and Camden strides in.

"What the fuck is happening here?" he asks, addressing Monk directly. His gaze flicks between us all, apparently assessing what's going on. *As if he doesn't know.*

"This is what's happening," I shout, chucking the pieces of paper on the floor. They scatter like petals. My soul ripped out and ruined for all to see. Camden's eyes darken as his focus lands on the sketch I drew of my brothers and the words 'gay boys' scrawled across their innocent faces.

He looks at Monk with narrowed eyes, then at Bram and Red before finally resting his gaze on me. For a long time, he just looks at me. Then his gaze flicks to Sonny and Ford who are standing on either side of me. He seems to make up his mind about something.

"You went against my explicit orders?" Camden says to Monk. Like Ford, he remains calm, holding his temper, but I see the anger bubbling just beneath the surface.

Monk sneers at him but doesn't respond. So, Camden turns to me instead. "Monk has wronged you, so I'm going to give you *one* chance and one chance only at retribution. None of my crew will intervene. *None!*" Camden snaps when some of the HH crew mumble their distaste. He turns to face them. "If any of you motherfuckers have an issue with that, I suggest you speak up now and face the consequences. I'm done being lenient."

Not one person does, except Monk.

"What the fuck are you doing, Camden?" Monk asks, looking somewhere between shocked and downright livid. "This ain't going to go down well with the..."

"Shut the fuck up, Monk!!" Camden roars.

Monk flinches, his hate focusing on Camden now who is oblivious as he regards me.

"You can choose your punishment, Asia, and I will guarantee no interference from me or any of my crew, but I have one rule and one request."

"And what are they?" I snap.

"You cannot ask that I cut Monk from the HH crew and you spend the rest of the evening with me."

"Over my fucking dead body," Sonny snaps, stepping forward. I grab him by the arm, squeezing hard.

I daren't look at Ford because I know that if I do he'll lose the very precarious hold he has on his rage.

"And if I refuse?"

"Then all bets are off, everyone chooses a damn side and we settle this right here, right now."

Pink and Kate gasp, their shock palpable. I can't do that to them. *I won't.*

"Don't do it, Asia," Ford finally says, breaking his silence. "Don't play into his hands."

But what choice do I have? I don't want my friends dragged into this mess.

"I accept your terms," I respond.

"So, how do you want to play this?" he asks, drawing a surprised gasp from Monk and the rest of his crew, not to mention the half dozen kids from the No Name crew who are watching the whole sorry exchange.

"The Tower. Me against Monk. A week today. If I win, Monk leaves me and my friends the fuck alone."

"And if you lose?" Monk smirks, puffing out his chest.

"I *won't* lose."

Monk laughs, his wolves laugh with him. Camden fucking glowers.

"If you lose, *when* you lose," Monk corrects himself with a smirk, "you get to be *mine.*"

"The fuck I do!" I shout. This is not what I'd intended.

"Done," Camden states. He glances at me with an emotion I can't read.

"Fuck this," Ford shouts, moving forward.

"No, Ford! It's done. I *will* win. I'll never be his."

Ford shakes his head. Sonny grits his teeth. *"I'll win,"* I repeat.

Monk laughs like a man who's already won the fight. Well, screw him. He has no fucking idea what I'm capable of. None. With that, I storm out of the building leaving them all gaping behind me.

29

Pink was correct my room *is* full of shit, fortunately not the human or animal kind, just the trash kind. It's as though they've upended a whole dustcart worth of trash in my room. There are empty food packets, half eaten mouldy food, cigarette butts, used tissues, and *condoms*. Fucking *used* condoms. I try not to gag as I kick aside the rubbish then curse like a fishwife as I tread on a rotten piece of meat, maggots wiggling in the mouldy flesh. It fucking stinks. In the corner of the room I notice a black bag, already half filled up with rubbish.

"Don't go any further, Asia. Let us clear this up," Pink says, as she follows me into the room, Kate, Sonny and Ford all behind her.

"I'll do it," I bite out angrily. It's not her fault, but I'm so full of hate and rage that I can't be anything other than short with her. "Is the bathroom just as bad?"

"It's worse. Don't go in there, please," she begs.

Of course, I ignore her, knowing I should heed her warning

but unable to help myself. I want to know what they did in there too.

I need to see.

It's like a sick sense of fascination, you know, just like staring at an accident on the motorway. You know you shouldn't look, that it's better if you don't, yet you can't seem to stop yourself. When I push open the bathroom door, I nearly pass out at the smell coming from the confined space. It seems to be coming from the toilet, so I do something stupid, I lift the lid. Puke immediately fills my mouth. The toilet is filled with used tampons and sanitary towels. It's fucking disgusting.

"Bunch of bastard cunts," I swear, rushing from the bathroom and slamming the door shut.

"I'm so sorry, Asia," Pink whispers.

"Not more than Monk will be when I finish with him," I retort.

"They even cut up your clothes," Kate murmurs, her hands sifting through the torn material on my bed. Literally all I have left to wear are the clothes on my back. It's not as if I had much to begin with. Now I have even less. Everything else has been cut up and dumped on my bed alongside slithers of paper…

My drawings. My drawings are in tatters, but my heart is not. I harden it, refusing to let them break me.

I refuse.

Monk will rue the day he decided to fuck with me. They all will. Every single one who's wronged me will pay.

Tonight, that starts with Camden.

Speaking of which… leaning against my doorframe with a blank expression on his face is Camden. Anger bubbles up my chest, but I push it away, smothering it. Can't say the same for Sonny though.

"You fucking nasty piece of shit," Sonny snaps, rounding

on his feet and striding towards Camden. Once again, I find myself stepping in to prevent a fight.

"Wasn't me," he bites out.

"Nothing's ever you, *is it?*" Sonny snaps back. "Fucking own your shit, you coward!"

"Asia, I'm waiting," Camden says turning to face me and completely ignoring Sonny and the evil glares from everyone else in the room. Out of the corner of my eye I can see Ford staring at me, trying to figure out his next move no doubt.

"We have to do this now?" I ask, still shaking, still enraged.

"Yes, right now."

"Fine," I snap.

"No!" Ford shouts, narrowing his eyes at Camden. He wants to kill him. Well, now that makes three of us.

I look at him, shaking my head. "I made an agreement, Ford. I'm doing this."

We look at each other, both of us knowing I can't back out, understanding the rules of the street. I made an agreement and I must follow it through. Ford grits his jaw, nodding his head. "You hurt Asia, you're *dead,*" he spits. Camden nods in understanding.

"I won't."

Ford snarls at Camden's response. He doesn't believe him any more than I do. "Be careful," he says to me. Sonny swears under his breath whilst Pink and Kate gape at me. They can't believe I'm going through with it but if I don't, they're still at risk. All three of them. Camden will make them choose and I can't, *won't* do that to them.

"*Be careful,*" Ford insists.

I don't respond, we both know that whilst I can promise him I'll be careful, I sure as fuck can't promise him I'll be safe. Not with Camden. Especially not with him.

"WHY ARE we going to the Tower now?" I ask Camden for the third time as we traverse through the woods beyond the carpark behind the annex building. Like both times before he ignores me. When we get to the edge of the woods and I start trudging across the field in the direction of the Tower, Camden grabs my wrist.

"Not there," he snaps, tugging me along behind him. When I fall into step beside him, he loosens his hold but doesn't let go. My skin burns under his touch.

"Won't Bobby send out a search party for us or something? We left before curfew. You want to get us expelled? Is that the big plan?"

"Bobby won't be doing jack shit apart from cleaning up your room."

"Why would he do that?"

"Because I fucking told him to."

"He's firmly in your pocket then?" I ask, wondering what Camden has over him, wondering why he'd even bother to make the fat bastard do anything for me.

"Not mine, no…"

"Then whose?"

"Stop asking questions, Asia, and keep up."

After that, Camden refuses to answer anything else I throw at him, practically ignoring my existence. If he weren't holding onto my wrist so tightly I would've thought him oblivious to my presence.

After another thirty minutes we end up walking down a steep path onto a section of beach that is little more than a cove with sheer rock surrounding us. The tide is out, and the water dark, highlighted only by the smattering of stars peeking out from the gaps between thick clouds.

"Why are we here?" I ask as we step onto the pebbled beach. The smell of the briny sea air is stronger here, reminding us both that we are so very far from home. Camden's nostrils flare as he draws in the smell, as though it's clearing the fogginess from his mind. I know that since living here I feel physically better in my body, and more importantly my lungs, enjoying the fresh air and lack of smog.

Camden shrugs off his backpack, his expression hidden by the absence of light and the shadows of his hoody pulled up over his head. "Sit down," he orders, pointing to a rug that he's just pulled out of the bag and laid down on the stones.

"Why?" I question, not liking the fact he's ordering me around. Not to mention, I've no idea what the fuck he's up to. He better not think this is some romantic date under the moonlight.

"Just do as you're told for once!" he snaps, whipping around to face me. The wind has picked up, causing my hair to flutter around my face as I glare at him. The strands are like tiny little whips that slash across the delicate skin of my cheeks, then soften to a tickle as the wind dies down momentarily. That's what I feel when I'm around him, like I'm being whipped then caressed. It's fucked up. One minute I'm left reeling, the next drawn in.

"Fuck off, Camden," I retort, fed up with this constant confusion.

He sighs, yanking his hood off his head. "*Please*, Asia. Just sit down."

"Fine." This time it's my turn to sigh, not liking the way my stomach flips at the intense look he gives me and the gentle tone of his voice. See? Whiplash.

"Thank you," he murmurs, the deep cadence of his voice rumbling in his chest, or maybe that's mine? Either way, he turns his back to me and bends down, rifling through his bag.

From my spot on the blanket I watch him as he sorts through his bag with his back to me. He seems to be lining some items up on the pebbles in front of him. Then he reaches in his bag and puts something over his face. It's too dark for me to see what, but when he turns around, I gape. He's wearing a white nose and mouth mask, the kind I use when I'm about to do some graffiti art.

"Why are you wearing that?" I ask, my gaze following his as he nods to the items on the floor. An assortment of spray cans are lined up. I frown, confused.

"You're not the only one who's a graf writer, Asia."

My mouth drops open.

He laughs. It's a bitter, painful laugh. "Ever heard of *Bling*?"

Is he fucking kidding me? Of course I've heard of Bling. He's notorious in the graf world. His identity is as secret as Banksy's. If you look at the most dangerous spots in the whole of London you'll find his tag, his artwork. On the side of bridges, train cars, high up on buildings. The guy's a legend. But more than that, he's talented, like seriously talented. I've coveted his work for the past two years ever since I started graf writing seriously. Then six months ago, he stopped putting up new pieces of work. Rumour had it he was arrested and sent to prison, but no one knew because no one knows who he is...

I narrow my eyes at Camden, not believing what he's insinuating. He *can't* be Bling.

Camden bends down and picks up a can. He holds it comfortably in his hand, giving it a quick shake before pressing sharply on the cap. A spray of paint erupts from the nozzle.

"You aren't telling me that you're…"

"*Bling*? Yes, Asia, that's exactly what I'm telling you."

"No way. There's no fucking way…" I mutter, shaking my head. He can't be the artist I've admired from afar all this time. He just can't be.

"My girls… all precious stones, all nicknames. Ever wondered why?"

"*Bling*… a slang word for flashy jewellery…"

"That's right, Asia, my girls are now the bling that adorn me like the beautiful jewels they are. Or, at least that's what I'd thought. Some of them are no more than poor imitations." He gives me a look and I can't help but think of Diamond and Emerald, the two bitches who tried to shove my head down the toilet. Actually, what am I thinking? I can't even believe I'm entertaining this.

"I don't believe you're Bling. No fucking way," I say, folding my arms across my chest.

"That's what I'd thought you say," he responds with a smirk.

He picks up two cans, tucking them inside the pockets of his zipped-up hoody then trudges across the pebbles. Once he reaches the stone wall of the cliff face, he reaches up and grabs hold of a jutting piece of stone and pulls himself upwards, finding a spot to grip with his foot. I watch in shock as he scales the rock face with his bare hands until he finds a slim ledge about twenty feet up. He settles himself precariously against the stone, feet turned outwards as he pulls out a can and begins to paint. Is he like Spiderman in disguise? This is nuts.

"Camden, are you insane?" I shout, getting to my feet.

"Nah, I'm *Bling*," he shouts back, humour in his voice. It's light and carefree and doesn't sound like the person I've come to know in the slightest.

Fuck sake, he *can't* be.

Over the next hour he shows me that he is. There's no denying it.

Camden *is* Bling. Someone I've admired from afar for the last two years. Someone who produces extraordinary graffiti art.

Someone who's my enemy, my nemesis, my fucking *idol*.

By the time he's finished, his tag brightens the black rock with six foot white and blue lettering, diamonds and gems falling over the piece like raindrops falling from the sky expertly spray painted across the uneven surface. I can only sit and stare.

He's *Bling. Holy shit.*

I watch as he climbs back down the wall as easily as he walks towards me. He chucks the now empty cans on the pebbles and sits down lighting up a pre-rolled joint that he pulls from his pocket. After he takes a deep toke and blows out the blue-grey smoke, he regards me. "I've seen your work around Hackney. I've admired it for a long, long time, Asia. That was the reason I didn't allow my crew to rip you to shreds the night of the party. I knew who you were, even if you had no idea who I was. Out of respect for your talent, for you as an artist, I protected you despite how that made me look."

"And now, do you protect me for the same reason?" I ask, swallowing heavily.

"Partly…"

"And the other part?"

Camden, or should I say Bling, looks out to sea drawing on his spliff once again. "Because I owe you for Eastern…"

When he offers me the joint I take it, needing the

combination of nicotine and marijuana to edge out the mixed-up feelings in my gut. I draw on it heavily, loving the almost immediate feeling of relaxation that filters into my bloodstream. I shuffle on my arse, turning to look out to sea mesmerised by the gentle caress of the waves against the shore. Camden shifts beside me, reaching over as I pass him back the joint.

"This changes nothing you know. I still hate you," I mutter, hugging my knees to my chest. There's no conviction behind my statement even though Camden believes there is.

"I thought you might."

"So why bring me here? Why bother?"

"Because I needed you to know that I'm not just the arsehole who rules Hackney's Hackers. I'm not just the guy who can't cut out the cancer in my crew."

"Can't?"

"Yes, *can't...*" He sighs again, and I want to ask him why but instead he continues.

"I *am* Bling. I'm the guy who scales impossible walls to share his art for every kid who ever dreamed of something more. I'm the guy who once believed that there was more to the world than just the postcode I rule over now..."

"Once the guy?" I say, scuffing some pebbles with my toe.

"Yeah, once the guy. I can't be Bling anymore. I can only be Camden: leader of the Hackney's Hackers, the most feared gang in London. That's who I am now. That's who I have to be to survive... There is no other way."

I nod, understanding that he's bound by the rules of the street just as much as I am, but knowing there's something far more significant in what he isn't telling me, perhaps can't tell me. "That's why you turn a blind eye to what Monk has done because you have to be this person everyone expects?"

Camden draws on the joint once more, inhaling deeply then

holding his breath. When he blows out his whole body seems to relax, the drug spreading out into the extremities of his limbs, making him languid. He lies back, looking up at the sky.

"The first time when he jumped you, I honestly had no idea. The second time when he stole your sketchpad, when he ransacked your room, I found out too late. He's made me look a fool, Asia, and I have to rectify that. When you get to my position you cannot be viewed as weak. Monk is making a mockery of me. *You* are making a mockery of me whether you intend to or not. It's gotta stop."

"I have no control over Monk. I'm only reacting to him."

"I know that." He scrapes a hand over his face, rubbing at the stubble on his chin.

"So what do I do? I'm in an impossible position."

"You beat Monk. You join my crew. Then and only then will it be over…"

He rests his hand on the blanket mere inches from mine but doesn't try to inch closer or kiss me like he had before. Instead, he studies the water just the same as I do, trying to make sense of the world we live in and the rules we must follow to survive.

Getting to my feet, I look at his tag high on the cliff face then back to Camden. "I'll beat Monk. I'll prove that I'm not a victim or a pushover once and for all…"

"But…"

"But, I will never join your crew," I say quietly.

"I know that too." He nods his head once then turns his face away looking back out to sea. I walk away from him, from the artist I admired once and the guy on the other side of the line wishing, not for the first time, that life wasn't so fucking difficult.

30

I t's first thing in the morning on Friday and just like every
day this week, I'm training with Ford and Sonny in the
outhouse just beyond the sports field. It's cold out, frost has
begun to settle on the grass and shrubbery making everything
crunch underfoot. Before long it's going to be Christmas break
and I'll be able to see my baby brothers for the first time in
ages. That thought should be on the forefront of my mind.
Instead, I can't help but think about this fight with Monk and
Camden's revelation.

"Asia, arms up, don't lose concentration," Ford snaps,
lightly jabbing me on my chin. It doesn't hurt. It's a mere
whisper of a touch but it brings me back to focus.

"Fuck!" I exclaim, dropping my arms and turning my back
on him. A bead of sweat dribbles down my spine, pooling at the
top of my leggings and the growing patch of sweat there. It
might be freezing cold outside, but I'm burning up inside and
not just because Ford and Sonny have put me through my
paces.

"You need to focus," Ford adds, stating the obvious.

"I know that," I snap. It's not his fault.

"Ford, give her a sec, okay? We've been pushing Asia hard all this week. She can sit this out for a bit, yeah?" Sonny says, trying his best to calm the situation.

"Fine. If you want to take a break for a while then watch instead. Sonny, get over here and let's spar. Asia needs to see it from this point of view anyway. It helps to visualise the fight."

I sit down on the chair in the corner of the room and pull my knees up, perching my feet on the edge of the seat. Resting my chin on my knees, I watch Sonny and Ford bounce up and down on their toes.

"You want to remain light on your feet," Ford begins, eyeing me thoughtfully. "Monk might be strong, and he can throw a meaty punch, but he's like a fucking elephant. You, Asia, need to be a gazelle."

"A gazelle is the bloody prey, Ford," Sonny remarks, rolling his eyes. He looks at me with his baby-blues, his dimples deep in his cheeks as he smiles. "Be a fucking lion, Asia. A *lion*," he reinforces with a light laugh.

"You know what I mean." Ford retorts, punching Sonny on his shoulder.

"Fuck, dickwad, ease up will you?" Sonny rubs his arm, grimacing.

"Nope. Deal with it."

For the next twenty minutes I watch Ford and Sonny spar, and whilst Sonny is good there's no doubting who's the better fighter. If Sonny's a lion, then Ford's a goddamn mythical creature. He moves with intelligence, power and an almost magical grace. He really is very impressive and a complete turn on.

Pretty soon my worries over the fight tomorrow night are

replaced with awe for the two men before me, and they really are men, not boys. They might only be my age, but everything about them screams manliness. The two might be similar in looks but when it comes to fighting, they approach it completely differently. There's an edge to Sonny that comes to life when he fights, a hardness that is in complete contrast to his usual easygoing nature. He's untamed for the most part, reacting on instinct. I suspect he could be as good as Ford if only he'd learn to control the wildness within. Ford, on the other hand, is calculated, clever and entirely controlled in every move he makes. That, and the fact he is insanely talented, gives him the edge. I find myself wondering what would happen if he were to let go, really let go. I'm guessing he would be far more dangerous than any of us suspect.

By the time they finish sparring, both are dripping with sweat and pumped up with a restless kind of energy. I feel it wash over me when they both, almost simultaneously, turn their attention to me. Sonny grabs a towel and wipes his face, then rips off his shirt showing me his glorious eagle tattoo. Ford cracks his knuckles, then rolls his head on his shoulders. I get the distinct impression he could go all night.

My cheeks heat up at where that thought takes my imagination.

"You ready to go again?" he asks me, a question in his eyes.

Blowing out a long breath, I nod. Though what I'm ready for isn't sparring... The testosterone in the room is high, causing my hormones to go crazy right about now.

"Come here then," he utters, and I suddenly feel as though his gentle request is more of a command. A command that I can't say no to, and just like that, the atmosphere changes from friendly to downright sinful.

Pulling up my metaphorical big girl's pants, I walk towards them both readying myself for more sparring.

"You have to clear your head of all your emotion, Asia. As you've been able to see for yourself, Sonny's a good fighter. One of the best, actually. But he is ruled by emotion and instinct. Like I said before, that will only get you so far in a fight. You must funnel any emotion you feel, hone it into a deadly weapon and above all else, use your head," Ford says, tapping his temple with each word. "If you do that, you *will* win."

"Sonny, hold her," Ford says, suddenly.

Before I even have time to figure out what the hell is happening, Sonny has his arms wrapped around me from behind. I can feel his damp skin against my back, causing heat to surge upwards from my core.

"What are you doing?" I ask.

"What I've wanted to do for some time..." Ford's voice trails off as he steps closer, so close that I'm sandwiched between them both. Sonny's hot breath flows over the skin of my neck, and when his lips press gently behind my ear it's all I can do to stop the moan erupting from my lips.

"And what's that?" I manage to utter, my lust-filled voice betraying me.

"Sonny tasted you. Now, it's my turn," he responds, cupping my face in his hands and pressing his mouth against mine. The second his tongue seeks out mine, I know I'm lost as red-hot heat rips up and outwards from my core, scorching every single part of me. I'm acutely aware of Ford's hands finding my hips as the tip of Sonny's tongue trails against my neck and up to my earlobe which he bites at the same time Ford bites my bottom lip, sucking it into his mouth.

Between them, I'm a ball of feeling, emotion, but most of all

I'm lustful and horny. So horny that I reach for Ford's arse and
yank him closer. Sonny growls, biting on the delicate skin of
my neck in mock jealousy. I'm pretty sure he's enjoying this
moment as much as I am if the thick ridge of his cock digging
into my lower back is anything to go by.

I'm not religious, but after this encounter I'm going to need
to go to confession.

Just when I'm getting to the point of no return, they both
step back, entirely synchronised, leaving me breathless,
confused and wanting.

"What are you…?" I begin.

"Now fight," Ford says, raising his fists.

"Wh-what?" I manage to mumble.

"No emotion. Switch it off. Do it now," Ford insists.
"Funnel what you feel, use it. Fight me, Asia."

The thing is I don't want to fight him. I don't want to fight
Sonny. I want their lips and their hands on me once more. But
I guess that's the point. Ford knows me better than I know
myself. Emotion does rule me, and if I want to survive, I
mustn't let it.

31

Saturday night rolls around quickly and there's a restless kind of energy that distracts every pupil at Oceanside. We're all on edge, me more so than anyone. Yesterday, Ford showed me how emotion can be a distraction, and whilst Sonny has trained alongside us both, he still tries to persuade me to back out. Even now, as we approach the Tower he's doing the same. If I could be a lover, not a fighter, I would. But I can't.

"Monk's a fucking beast, Asia. He nearly took me out…"

"Are you saying just because I'm a girl that I'm not a good fighter?" I retort, whilst Ford stays silent.

"No, that isn't what I'm saying. We both know you can fight, Asia. I also know that Monk has a mean fucking punch. If he hits you right, you're out cold."

"I know that…"

Sonny stops, pulling up sharp. "Look, I give a shit about you, Asia. Goddamn it. Let me or Ford stand in for you," he begs.

"No fucking way. I back out now, I'm done."

"Ford, you need to tell her to stop. This isn't a game."

Ford looks between us, the moonlight casting a shadow across his face. "Asia is right. She can't back down. She must fight and she *will* beat him." His features are tight, determined.

"Asia..." Sonny starts, exasperated.

"No. I've made my decision, Sonny. This fight is happening whether you like it or not. Nothing you can say will change my mind."

Pink and Kate give me worried glances, but they don't try to persuade me to change my mind. They know me better than that. For the rest of the walk we all remain quiet with our thoughts.

The Tower is jammed full by the time we arrive at midnight. There are people spilling out of the open metal door and more on the beach surrounding the building. I stop to stare at the horde of kids who've all come to watch this fight. Every student from Oceanside is here, alongside the same amount of local kids. News sure travels fast around here.

"Are you *sure* about this?" Pink asks, gnawing on her bottom lip with her teeth. "Monk's gunning for your blood, Asia. The guy's unhinged."

She's right, of course. This may be the single most stupid thing I've ever done. I might've had fights with boys before, but they never really lasted that long. Someone would always come and break it up; an adult, the police, other kids. Here in the Tower the rules are simple. Fight until someone can't stand up again.

That's it.

I need to make these lessons with Ford count because no one is going to step in to stop it.

"Asia, you can back out. No one would think any worse of

you," Kate says, even though she doesn't believe that one little bit.

"You know that isn't true. I *need* to do this. I need to show them all I'm not weak. Monk went too far last week, and I'm done with it. So, no Kate. I *will not* back down."

She nods tightly, glancing at Pink worriedly. Silence descends as we enter the Tower. The crowd parts, forming a ring around us and now Monk, as he strolls into the open space with a glint of unbridled joy on his face. The guy already thinks he's won.

"Skank," he says in greeting.

"Prick," I retort, not to be outdone.

The majority of the crowd hisses and boos, their hate directed at me.

"Enough!" Camden shouts, and they all fall silent as he jumps down from his raised seat overlooking the room and heads into the space alongside me and Monk. Pink and Kate filter into the surrounding crowd, whilst Sonny and Ford remain by my side. Camden eyes the three of us with distaste. Bling is not here; he's hidden behind the face of the notorious gang leader. Tonight, his expression is dark, bitter and filled with violence of its own.

He's wearing nothing but a pair of low-slung joggers and the latest huarache trainers. I notice that his chest is covered in a sheen of light sweat as though he's just arrived from a workout. Low on his stomach is a tattoo of a lion, its mouth open in a roar. My eyes rove over the intricate tattoo that slides beneath the band of his joggers. I wonder how far down it reaches.

"Listen up," he commands, "A score will be settled tonight. Monk from the Hackney's Hackers crew versus Asia." The crowd erupts into excited jeers and catcalls once more. The majority seems to be on Monk's side, and I can't help but notice Emerald and Diamond as they glare at me with obvious hate. Camden lets the noise continue for a short while before he places his fingers in his mouth and whistles. The room falls into silence once more.

"Like all fights at the Tower, there are rules." He holds up his fist, lifting up a finger one by one as he reels them off. "If anyone intervenes, the fight is void. If any weapons are used, the fight is void. This is fist-on-fist only. *Got it?*" he looks at Monk, who growls but removes the knuckle dusters from his hand. The dirty, rotten, bastard.

"The fight will end when one side submits or is knocked out. Each side will give their terms and once the fight is over and the winner revealed, the terms will be obeyed. These are the rules of The Tower. These are the rules we live by. No exceptions, not even for you, Asia." Camden adds. I guess his respect for me as a graffiti artist has finally had its day. He looks between Monk and me. There's no emotion. None. It's scary, honestly.

"Do you both understand?"

"I understand perfectly," Monk sneers, delight lighting his eyes. He thinks he's going to win. The motherfucker is deluded.

Or, perhaps that's me?

"Asia?" Camden turns to face me, his face blank, unreadable.

"Got it," I retort, straightening my shoulders and nodding tightly.

Camden raises his arms out to the side, indicating for the crown to give us room. They move back so that just Monk and I remain in the centre of the circle.

"Give them space to fight. Those who fail to listen, who try and intervene, will be chucked out of the Tower," Camden shouts over the growing chatter, though his gaze lands firmly on Ford and Sonny standing just behind me now. "If there are any last-minute conversations to be had, I suggest you have them now."

Low bass music begins to play in the background, fuelling the already tense air as Monk and I glare at each other. One of his cronies steps in to whisper something in his ear, and he grins slowly. His resulting laughter grating on my last nerve.

Ford appears in front of me, blocking my view. Sonny beside him. Both look at me grimly.

"Monk is strong, Asia. He has a powerful punch, but he's slow, heavy on his feet. You have the advantage of speed and stamina. Tire him out as much as possible," Ford says, resting his hand on my shoulder, squeezing gently. "When he's run out of steam, aim for his weak spots. His face, kidneys, groin. Don't waste your time on his torso. If you can take out his legs, get him on the ground then hit him until you can't anymore." Ford grabs something from his back pocket. It's a roll of masking tape. "This will keep your fingers from breaking," he explains, wrapping it around both my knuckles. It's tight but it gives me some form of comfort. It's naïve to think it won't really hurt hitting Monk, but at least this will help to lessen the damage.

"I know you want to do this, Asia. I get it. But you can walk away. We'll protect you from him. I promise," Sonny adds vehemently. He grabs my hand willing me to listen to him. I shake my head, pulling it free from his grasp.

"You can't. You know that, right? It will never end if I don't stand up to him. It doesn't matter what you promise. He will keep coming for me."

"Fuck!" Sonny swears before bending down and kissing me

roughly. It's a quick kiss; bruising, brutal, and the complete opposite to how he kissed me before. When he pulls back, Ford is staring at us both, fire blazing in his eyes.

"Take your lip and nose ring out. Do it quickly," Ford says, holding his hand out. I do as he asks, dropping them into his palm. He pockets them. "Don't lose focus. You've *got* this."

I nod tightly. *I've got this.*

"Enough!" Camden snaps. When I look over at him, that same fire burns brightly in his gaze. I wonder if he can see it in me too. For a moment I see something flicker within the fire. Respect, definitely. Regret, perhaps that too. It doesn't matter now anyway, this is happening.

"Begin," he adds abruptly. Then I lose sight of him in the crowd.

A hush descends. The tension rises alongside the heat rolling off the onlookers. As I step forward, my body hums with repressed rage. It's welcoming, an old friend. Something I've come to rely on over the years, but rather than letting it take me over like I usually do, I force the storm within me to coil tight. I funnel it into something useful, something deadly, just like Ford has taught me.

Monk is the first to make his move, rushing forward and throwing a punch that I avoid with ease. He sprawls into a few of the onlookers behind me, knocking them over with the force. Twisting to face him, I bounce lightly on my feet.

"Slippery bitch!" he snarls, his face red with anger as he runs at me again. I dodge him.

He spins on his feet, charging at me like a bull would a red rag. I dodge him once more, barking out a laugh as he tumbles into the crowd showing himself up.

"You gonna fight, bitch, or are we just playing here?" He

BEA PAIGE

scrambles to his feet, pushed forward by a few of the onlookers behind him.

"That's what I thought we were doing, only you keep ending up on your arse," I retort, beginning to enjoy myself. I *can* do this.

Monk lets out a roar and this time when he goes for me, he doesn't miss. I manage to get out of his way just enough to feel his fist meet my shoulder and not my face. But *damn* does it hurt. I stumble back a little, but right myself quickly enough. Out of the corner of my eye I see Pink draw in a breath and Sonny start to step forward. Ford grabs him back, shaking his head. One thought flies through my head right at that moment. If Monk does manage to punch me in the face, I'm gonna be out. Game over. The force behind his punch will win.

Shaking out the pain, I duck his next punch and then throw two of my own. My uppercut manages to find his jaw whilst I twist beneath him and punch him in the kidneys as hard as I can. That makes him grunt with pain, but it isn't enough to end him. The guy's a beast.

The crowd fucking roars.

The next five minutes is a blur of me trying to avoid Monk's punches and attempting to gain the upper hand. I manage to get a few more punches in, and some kicks too, but more often than not I'm the one avoiding his attempts at knocking me out. He responds with a few hard punches as well, and a couple of times I'm left reeling as his fist meets my chest and my chin, even my fucking tit. But somehow, I manage to avoid the worst of it, and am able to keep him on his toes without being nearly as exhausted as he is. Ten minutes into our fight and Monk is already on the verge of buckling. I can see that in the heaviness of his steps and the shortness of his breath. He runs hot and fast, no doubt winning fights with brute strength and one punch knockouts, whereas I'm more of a slow burn building to an inferno thanks to Ford and all his training.

"Bitch, I'm done playing. This is over," Monk shouts after stumbling into the crowd *again*. The guy fights without a lick of sense. A worthy opponent would have figured out my tactics by now and used them to their advantage. Not Monk; he's thick as shit, thank fuck.

Taking one last charge at me, I see my opportunity and take it. This time when I dodge him, I swing down low and sweep my leg out, taking his out from beneath him. He goes down with a crash and the whole room erupts.

The crowd lets out a frenzied roar.

Some of them are baying for my blood, whilst others are finally backing me. Either way, I take Ford's advice and leap on top of him, raining blows on his face with all the strength I can muster. My clenched fists land punches to his cheeks, his chin, his nose, his temple, his forehead. I hit hard and fast knowing this is my only opportunity to have a chance at winning.

I don't let up.

I don't stop.

All the rage I've been holding back pours from inside me and like a storm that cannot be contained, I wreak havoc. He attempts to throw me off him at one point, but I clench a hold of his torso and arms between my thighs, refusing to let go, knowing that if he were to flip me on my back like Ford had on the field that day all those weeks ago, he'd win. If I'm honest, I'm not entirely sure where my strength comes from. Looking at us both, the winner should be obvious. He's three times the width of me. He's strong, built, muscular. Yet, here I am beating him. Like David and Goliath.

"FUCK HIM UP!" someone screams, the crowd now

roaring with frenetic energy fuelling the bloodlust in me. It takes me over until I become someone I don't recognise. Someone who could kill given half the chance. By the time I'm finished, Monk's face is a bloody mess and I can no longer feel my hands. When I know he's finally beat, I stand up on wobbly legs, glaring at the crowd. They're going wild. My chest heaves as I look around the room as my body begins to shake uncontrollably. Pain starts to register beneath the adrenaline. Before me, faces mingle with one another. I pant, my focus blurring.

"Monk tried to fuck with me." I yell, pointing to his prone body on the floor. "Let this be a warning to you all, this is what happens when you do!" I make sure to look specifically at Camden then. He doesn't look away, accepting the gauntlet I've just laid down.

Kate and Pink step forward, and I stumble towards them, my body giving way. But it isn't either of them that catches me when I fall, but Ford. I'm vaguely aware of him lifting me up and striding out of the Tower. Once the cool air hits me, I finally lose consciousness.

32

"Asia, can you hear me?"

I'm vaguely aware of a familiar voice talking to me through a thick haze of pain.

Everything hurts.

Every-fucking-where. Why do I hurt so bad…?

Then I remember the fight.

I remember Monk and the screaming arseholes surrounding us all baying for blood, *my* blood in particular. But most of all I remember the feeling of relief when it was all over.

I beat him.

I stood my ground and showed everyone what I'm made off. Fuck him, fuck all the bastards who've tried to make my life a misery.

"Asia, here, have some water."

I groan, my eyes flicking open. But I'm not in the Tower, and I'm not on the beach… I'm pretty sure I'm lying on a bed.

"Where am I?" My voice sounds weak, soft.

"My room," Ford responds gently. He leans over and cups

the back of my head with his hand then rests the water bottle against my bottom lip before I can ask how the hell I got here. Pushing the bottle away, I sit up. My head spins a little at the sudden movement.

"What happened?"

"You passed out. I carried you back here." He shrugs, like that isn't a big deal.

"Are you like Superman or something? You carried me all the way back here, on your *own*?"

"Yeah. My cape's in the wardrobe, want me to put it on?" There's a glimmer of amusement in his eyes and a tentative smile drawing up his lips. The fact that he's trying to crack a joke at all is kind of endearing. He's always so bloody serious. Now he seems almost at ease in his loose tracksuit bottoms and vest top that shows off strong arms and shoulders.

"Didn't you know Clark's my middle name?"

"Hey, don't listen to that arsehole. I helped carry you," Sonny says, stepping out of the bathroom.

"You're full of shit," I say to Ford, smiling, then wince when my jaw hurts. I lift my hand to my face, gingerly pushing against the sore spot. "Motherfucker, that hurts."

"It's gonna bruise. Pink said she'll help cover it up, so you don't get questioned by Mr Carmichael," Sonny explains, pulling up a chair next to me. He looks at me with concern, worry creasing his eyes.

"Is Monk...?" I ask, looking between them both.

"Completely fucked. The guy's never going to mess with you again, Asia. You were amazing tonight." Ford's grey-green eyes blaze with pride, but honestly, I don't know how to react now the storm has passed and the anger is gone.

"I don't feel amazing," I say heavily.

"It'll feel better in a few days," Ford says, looking at his watch that is flashing 3.17am. I've been out for a few hours at least.

"You'll need to rest and stay in bed," Sonny continues. "Think of me and Ford as your personal butlers. We'll get you anything you want, so long as you rest, starting right now."

"What, like Butlers in the Buff?" I deadpan.

"Whatever tickles your fancy," Sonny responds, in a faux posh voice. He winks, I smile, and Ford rolls his eyes.

"Seriously guys, I appreciate your concern, but I'll get over the pain. It's just…"

"Just what?" Ford asks, frowning.

"Fuck, I *know* Monk's an arsehole and I *know* he deserved everything he got but I don't like the fact I had to beat him to a pulp in order to survive here. That fucking sucks. I'm always fighting. When will it stop?"

Ford looks at me with a serious expression on his face. "Listen, Asia. He had it coming. You did what you had to do."

"I know that. I'd do it again… I just wish I didn't *have* to."

"We all wish that, but this is the life we live. If we don't fight we die, either literally or on the inside… I don't plan on doing either, even though I've been close to doing both," Ford murmurs. It's quite a revelation. One that sits heavy between us all. Fight or flight, live or die. Beat or be beaten. Run and hide, or stay and fight. This is how it is for us. This is how we live our lives. The delinquents. The rejects. The misfits.

"How bad is Monk?" I sigh, knowing Ford's right.

"Hospital bad," Sonny explains.

"Then I'm fucked. My time here is done. There's no way Mr Carmichael is going to let this slide. Too much shit is going on around here. He'll know I was involved… look at me."

I stare at my hands, at Monk's blood caked across my

knuckles. I still have the masking tape wrapped around them. I want it off. Now. Tugging at the tape, I wince at the pain I feel.

"Let me do that," Ford says, taking my hands and holding them for a moment. I try to pull them from his grasp, but he refuses to let me go. "It's okay, Asia. You've done the hard part. Let us help you with this."

But he's wrong. The hard part will be surviving what I've done. It always is. Nodding once, I force back the sudden emotion I feel. I can't let it out, not here. Not in front of Ford and Sonny. Shutting down my emotions I watch Ford as he slowly peels off the masking tape from around my knuckles.

"No one's going to talk. There's a code of silence we all live by, you know that."

"But how will Monk's injuries be explained away? Mr Carmichael isn't an idiot."

Ford flashes me the tiniest of smiles; it's like glimpsing the sun behind stormy clouds and I suddenly yearn to see its full beauty.

"Camden had a little bet of his own, apparently. If Monk lost he would have to confess to escaping from Oceanside and getting mugged."

"Really? Why would Camden do that?" I can't help but be suspicious of his motives.

"Monk disobeyed him. This is his punishment."

"But he refuses to get rid of Monk from his crew. Why?"

"That I don't know. If he were in my crew, the prick would've been gone the second I found out what he did to you."

"Ouch." I wince a little as the tape pulls at a split in my skin, a rivulet of blood runs down my finger. Ford grabs the hem of his t-shirt and presses it against the wound. The blood seeps into the white material, marking it.

"I'm sorry about Bram and Red. They're your friends... even if they're arseholes. You didn't have to do that for me," I suddenly blurt out.

"Correction, Asia. They *were* my friends. They also know the rules No Name crew abides by and they broke them out of pettiness and jealousy despite being my oldest friends. *Loyalty* means everything to me. *Everything.* When I give my all to someone, I expect the same in return. No fucking questions. No fucking excuses."

"I'm still sorry. I seem to fuck everything up."

"No!" he snaps. "No. This isn't on you, Asia. This is on *them*. You're just trying to survive. I understand that... I *get* it. Fuck knows I do," he insists. And he does understand. I see it in the emotion that he tries to hide. It's fleeting, but it's there. His past has scarred him. Just like mine has.

When the last piece of tape has been removed Ford holds my hands in his. "How does this feel?" he asks, pressing gently against each knuckle with the pad of his thumb.

"Sore, but not agony," I respond, staring at him whilst he inspects my hands. His dark blonde hair falls forward, covering his eyes and brushing against his straight nose. It doesn't look like it's ever been broken. I wonder how that's possible given his history.

"I don't think they're broken. That's good." He looks up, catching me staring and sees me blush.

"Asia?" He cocks his head, a question in his eyes.

"I should get back to my room..." I pull my hands from his and stand suddenly, regretting it instantly as pain blossoms in my chin and my shoulder where Monk hit me. "I really want a shower and a change of clothes. Is Pink back?" I blurt out. She's been lending me her clothes, seeing as I no longer have any of my own thanks to Monk.

"Yeah, she left me her key so you could stay in her room. She's bunking up with Kate tonight. The girls are a little freaked out by all this shit. I said I would knock for them once you came around. But it's way past three in the morning now. They're probably asleep," Sonny explains.

"I guess I should go to Pink's room then?" I don't know why I phrase that as a question rather than a statement, but that's the way it comes out.

Ford swipes a hand through his hair, glancing at Sonny. "We'd prefer it if you stayed here. Besides," he says, turning his back to me and walking to his wardrobe where he grabs a pair of clean black jogging pants and a grey t-shirt. "I've got clothes you can borrow for tonight, and we'd only come stay with you in Pink's room, so you don't have to leave…"

He lets that hang in the air as he passes me his clothes. "Feel free to use my shower. We'll wait out here."

"You sure?"

"Yeah. I wouldn't say it if I wasn't."

"Thank you, *both*. For everything," I whisper, then hold the clothes against my chest and head into the bathroom.

Twenty minutes later, clean and dressed in Ford's clothes, I step into the bedroom. Ford is lying on his bed, his arms pulled up behind his head. His muscles bunched are up, the sinews in his forearm defined. My gaze follows the curve of his arm to the dark blonde of his underarm hair. He looks incredibly sexy lying there like that. Sonny has brought a duvet and pillows and is lying on the floor.

"That doesn't look very comfortable," I say.

"I nicked Pink's duvet as well as my own. I'm good," he grins.

"She'll murder you for taking her duvet and covering it

with your smell," I smile, imagining Pink's reaction in the morning.

"She'll get over it."

"Feeling better?" Ford mutters, watching our exchange carefully.

"I'm cleaner, though I don't really feel better. Everything's stiffening up already." I stand awkwardly at the foot of the bed, trying to work out where I'm going to sleep.

"You can lie down on the bed, Asia," Ford says, watching me carefully. Sonny makes a kind of weird rumbling noise and when I look at him, he's scowling.

"Where will you sleep?"

"I'll take the floor with Sonny." He shrugs.

"Errr, no..." Sonny grinds out.

"That doesn't seem very fair... I'll just go to Pink's room. It'll be fine." I frown, shifting uncomfortably on my feet.

Ford chews on his lip then looks at Sonny. He slides his legs off the bed, pulling the duvet and pillows with him. "Get up a sec," he says to Sonny.

I watch as he adds that duvet to the others then arranges the pillows so that there are three in a row. *Three in a row...* Then proceeds to settle himself on the right, whilst Sonny takes the left, leaving the middle just for me apparently.

"Lie down, Asia. We won't touch you, promise." Ford twists on his side, making room for me. Feeling a kind of nervous fluttering in my chest, I lie down between them looking at the ceiling. After a beat, Ford begins to talk.

"I want to apologise for something..." his voice trails off and I feel him shift closer to me. Sonny seems to do the same.

Oh, my fuck.

Even though neither are touching me, I can feel the heat of

their bodies along the length of mine. "Apologise for what?" I whisper.

"Touching you the way I did."

"You did what?" Sonny snaps. I daren't look at him. I daren't look at either of them. Nope, I'm keeping my gaze fixed firmly on the ceiling and the little piece of paint peeling next to the light fixture. Ford heaves out a sigh as I stiffen with tenseness, not because I'm afraid that he'll do the same thing again like he did back in the outhouse, but because I want him to.

"I liked the way you touched me." The words are out before I can stop them.

Sonny sits up. "Shit, I'm gonna leave you both to it," he says, hurt evident in his voice.

"No. Wait!" I say, grabbing his arm.

"I liked the way you kissed me too and I don't know what to do about it. I don't know what that means…" It's barely a whisper, and I can't look at him, but I know he's heard because he lies back down, facing me this time. What am I supposed to do about these feelings I have for the both of them? Does it make me the skank Monk tells me I am because I like them both, want them both? *Jesus.*

Ford shifts beside me, propping his head on his arm so he can see me better. Out of the corner of my eye I can see him glance at Sonny.

"I'm not proud of myself, Asia. I manipulated you to get what I wanted, and I promised myself I would never do that to someone I like."

"Fuck, man," Sonny grinds out, tension oozing from him.

My own heart thuds like the bass drum of the Grime music I love so much. "Why do it then?" I ask quietly.

"I needed to know something about you, something from

your past. Not just because it would help me to teach you to fight, but because I collect people's memories so my own don't seem so bad. Sick, right?"

"Ford, you prick," Sonny says on a heavy sigh.

I turn to face Ford, my heart now in my throat as I look at him and see the first true sign of vulnerability since we met. This time he allows me to see it, just for a bit. Reaching up I cup his face before I can even think about what I'm doing. It's instinctual.

"If you wanted to know something about me you should've just asked."

"I did, you refused," he smiles then, and just like the sun it blinds me. Jesus, his smile... warm, genuine, fucking life bringing. Oh, I'm so screwed. My heart pounds loudly as the storm I carry within me always turns into a cloud of butterflies.

"That's true." I laugh lightly, trying to fend off the nervous ache I feel. Then regret it as I wince with pain.

"Easy, Asia. I know Ford's entertaining, but try not to give yourself internal bleeding," Sonny jokes, lightening the mood with his humour. I appreciate it. I appreciate *him*.

"Ha bloody ha," I retort, feeling the pull of both Sonny and Ford, and not knowing what to do about it. We all fall silent as I remove my hand from Ford's check and rest it on my stomach. He places his warm hand over mine, his fingers curling around my knuckles carefully.

"I know you don't want a place in my crew, Asia. I respect your wishes. I respect you. But I will never coerce you into giving me information like that again. I want you to tell me stuff because you trust me enough with your pain. I'm sorry for what I did."

It's a heartfelt apology, and one that for some reason makes me well up. I blink back the tears. Why am I so emotional? I suddenly feel so exhausted that all I want to do now is sleep. He senses that and leans over pressing a delicate kiss against my forehead.

"Sleep, Asia. I've got you."

"Correction: whether you like it or not, Ford, and whether you feel comfortable or not, Asia. We've *both* got you," Sonny adds. He kisses my cheek. His lips lingering, and my body reacts instinctively as a rush of heat pools between my legs.

"He's right, we do," Ford agrees, settling himself into a comfortable position beside me. He's still holding my hand, and even though that simple gesture isn't supposed to turn me on, the fact that his thumb is rubbing gently over my skin, does.

"Sonny made a decision tonight. He's agreed to join No Name crew," he explains.

"You have?" I question, turning to look at Sonny.

"This might make Ford's ego grow to ridiculous proportions but he's a good guy. I might not agree with everything he's done or said, but I know that we're stronger together than apart. I get that now. Besides, who else is gonna keep that ego in check but me?" Sonny says, a wry grin pulling up his lips. The dimples are back; the dimples are doing something stupid to me right about now. Those bloody dimples. All these thoughts rush through my head, making it spin. Then Sonny runs his knuckles down my bare arm so lightly that I almost think I've imagined it and those thoughts spin to something elicit. My skin prickles under their touch. These two are killing me.

"There's no pressure on you. Whatever you decide, we've got your back, Asia."

"*Always*," Sonny adds.

"*Always*," Ford agrees.

And just like that Ford and Sonny shuffle closer, both of

them wrapping an arm over me, folding their bodies around mine. Neither push for more though I know they want to. But this whole thing... *us*, is confusing and new and exciting and terrifying. Right now, I need to wrap my head around whatever *this* is. As much as I want Ford's hand to slide lower and Sonny's lips to meet mine, I also need to be careful, certain, *sure* of my feelings. There's still Eastern who I can't stop worrying about, thinking about. I know there's more to us than just best friends and it isn't fair to dive headfirst into whatever this is with Ford and Sonny until I resolve those feelings for Eastern. I need to see him, speak to him first.

Then there's Camden and his strange on/off behaviour with me and the weird attraction I feel towards him, towards the guy who fucked things up for Eastern. I feel guilty about that attraction, that pull. Now certainly isn't the time to bring it up.

"Rest, Asia..." Ford whispers. His voice soft, cajoling.

"We've got you," Sonny reminds me. The warmth of his breath sliding over my skin.

"Thank you," I murmur, not able to find the words I need to express how I truly feel.

I'm not just thanking them for tonight, or for how they've stuck up for me and had my back since I've been here. I'm thanking them for so much more than that.

For the first time in a very long time, I allow myself to trust in someone other than Eastern. I allow myself to be held by both of them. Ford and Sonny might not understand the significance of this moment, but I do. *I do.* Maybe joining Ford's crew isn't such a bad idea after all?

33

Almost another week passes and on Friday afternoon, I find myself chilling out in the rec room waiting for Kate and Pink. Kiss FM is playing on the radio and my foot is tapping in time to the music. Kate is currently at her one-to-one therapy session with Mr Burnside and Pink has her extra-curricular class in mechanics. The girl is a walking talking contradiction. She loves it though and doesn't care that she gets her clothes covered in grease and oil on the regular. Not that it matters, the chick has a ridiculous amount of clothes. Likely all stolen. She's tried to give me a few, and I've happily taken a couple of tops and jeans off her hands, but some of her clothes are a bit out there, even for me. I'm kind of jealous that she's already got to start her extra-curricular class, my physiotherapy lessons aren't scheduled until after the Christmas break, which is why I have an extra couple of free periods this term.

Putting my feet up on the coffee table in front of me, I rest my head on the back of the sofa and close my eyes. I don't normally hang out here on my own, but I'm taking the risk today given Kate will be finishing in about half an hour and Monk is still in hospital. I managed to break his nose and shatter his cheekbone, not to mention split his lip and eyebrow. He might've got what he deserved but I still don't like it. The rest of the shitheads who jumped me aren't nearly as ballsy when he's not around and definitely not since I beat him in that fight.

Thoughts of Monk are quickly replaced with thoughts of Ford and Sonny, and before long my cheeks are flushing at the memory of their arms wrapped around me. Following that night and my fight with Monk, things have changed dramatically between us. I feel *safe* around them both. That's the only way I can describe it. Safe *and* attracted to them. It's the same kind of way I feel about Eastern, that I know they're going to be my friends for life and maybe, hopefully, something more. I can admit that now.

I can even admit that about Eastern, even though he isn't here to witness my 360-degree change of heart. Trouble is, that's three boys I'm attracted to. Four if I include Camden, which I won't. That's two too many, right? I don't even know what to do with that.

That night I'd slept solidly for eight hours in Ford and Sonny's arms and not once had either tried to take advantage of the situation. True to their word they just held me, and it had felt good.

So, so good.

Like I belonged.

My heart squeezes painfully. I really don't know how to handle these feelings for them all. For the past few days I've been avoiding any real kind of conversation with them under the pretence I'm healing, recovering from the ordeal of the fight, and whilst part of that is true, not all of it is. Pushing thoughts of Ford and Sonny firmly out of my head, I manage to get another five minutes of peace before the door swings open and two of my least favourite people walk into the room.

"Did you fucking see his face?" Red says, laughing loudly as she saunters into the room, Bram following her. I groan. Great, just what I need.

"Yeah, looks like things are going to hot up even more around here. I can't fucking wait," Bram responds gleefully. The second they spot me, their smiles turn to sneers.

"Well, well, if it ain't Ford's little obsession," Bram remarks, his gaze darkening with hate. I guess Ford hasn't managed to change their minds about me then. Not that I give a shit. I don't need their friendship or their respect.

"*Dick, Bitch,*" I smile at each of them in greeting.

"You've got some nerve," Red retorts, moving towards me. I stand, ready for her. Bram smirks, waiting for the fallout. I'm guessing he's going to let his girlfriend do the work this time. Too much of a pussy to do it himself.

"What the fuck is your problem with me?" I don't know why I ask Red that question, I'm not all that bothered about her response.

"My problem is that you think you're above us all. You think that your shit don't stink. You think just because you've got Ford and Sonny panting for you like dogs in heat that you're *safe*. You're not, *Skank*," she snaps, her eyes blazing with fury… well jealousy, actually.

"Oh, I get it. You're not the centre of attention anymore, is that it? Sonny got what he wanted the first day I arrived, and Ford's never given you what you really wanted, has he? Especially now that he chucked you out of his crew. So it looks like you're stuck with meathead here. Sucks playing second fiddle to someone who's a far better option."

"You lying little bitch," Red snarls. When I glance at Bram, I know he knows what went down between Red and Sonny that day, he's just too much of a coward to admit to it. His pride would be in tatters if he actually allowed himself to believe me. Instead he chooses to listen to the lies of his two-timing bitch of a girlfriend.

"We all know who the liar is here," I retort, getting in her face. I feel the familiar storm swirling in my chest at the thought of what she helped Monk and Bram do. I'll never get those sketches back. "The only *skank* who's standing in this room is you!"

Red lifts her fist, pulling back, ready to punch me. But Bram grabs hold of her arm and yanks her backwards. "Not here, not now. It's too hot. Mr Carmichael is watching us all way too closely at the moment. The guy's cooking up something, let's not get thrown in the mix, yeah?"

"I'm going to fucking kill her," Red screeches in my face.

"I'd like to see you try," I reply confidently, arching an eyebrow.

She spits in my face, the warmth of her spittle hitting my cheek, and even though I really want to fucking deck her right now, I don't because behind her Mr Burnside appears. Kate's standing beside him, her eyes wide. "You okay?" she mouths. I nod my head slightly to let her know I am.

"What appears to be the problem?" Mr Burnside asks, his gaze sliding between us both.

I wipe at the spit with the corner of my top, silently cussing Red. "Nothing, a misunderstanding. That's all," I lie.

"Red?" Mr Burnside asks.

"Yes, a misunderstanding," Red bites out, keeping her gaze fixed firmly on me.

"If you apologise to Asia now, I won't take it any further. But believe me, if I see behaviour like this between the two of you again, I won't be so lenient," Mr Burnside says.

Red grits her teeth, her mouth opening and closing like a fish out of water.

"Say it, Red," Bram mutters, his eyes narrowing at me.

Red snatches her arm from Bram's hold and leans in close. "This ain't over. You don't take Ford from us and get away with it," she whispers, before pulling back. "I apologise," she says loud enough for Mr Burnside to hear, but we both know that it isn't sincere.

"Good. Now you can go," Mr Burnside adds.

Red spins on her heel and storms out of the rec room. Bram grunts, then follows her. Kate rushes over. "You sure you're okay?"

"Never better," I respond with a reassuring smile. "Shall we head up to my room. I don't feel much like watching TV now."

"Sure."

"Actually, Mr Carmichael would like to speak with you, Asia," Mr Burnside says, his face a mask.

"Why?" I'm instantly in defence mode, suspicious.

"Come with me, please," he responds, not giving anything away.

"I'll see you later, yeah?" Kate asks, she squeezes my arm briefly, giving me a sympathetic look. I wonder if she knows what this is all about, but the concern on her face tells me she doesn't. Generally, when a student is called to Mr Carmichael's office it isn't for a nice chat about good behaviour. Fucking perfect.

"Asia, now if you wouldn't mind."

"I do actually," I mumble, but I follow Mr Burnside anyway.

Instead of taking me to Mr Carmichael's office like I thought he would, Mr Burnside walks me out the back of the main building and heads towards the car park behind the annex where Mr Carmichael is waiting for us.

"What's this about?" I ask.

Mr Carmichael points to the wall he's standing next to. On it is my name, my *tag* graffitied onto the wall in bright blue spray paint. What the actual fuck?

"Care to explain this?" he says.

"That piece of shit tag has nothing to do with me!" I exclaim. Whilst it's actually fucking amazingly good, it's about as far from my style as you can get and closer to someone else's I know so well.

"It's your name, and you're the only graffiti writer here, *Asia*," he insists.

"This is bullshit. Just because it's my name doesn't mean it's my work. A tag is like a fingerprint, it's unique. This wasn't me."

"Who then, if not you?" he looks at Mr Burnside, touching his arm gently. "I got this."

Mr Burnside looks at me with an almost apologetic smile. "Just be honest," he says, then leaves.

"I can't have my school falling into disrepute, Asia. There's been too much going on lately that needs addressing and for some reason it all seems to centre around you."

"This wasn't me!" I repeat. "Do you honestly think that I would do this knowing I could get thrown out of Oceanside and chucked into juvie for it? Despite what everyone seems to think, I'm not a complete fucking idiot."

"No, you're not an idiot. I actually think you're extremely bright."

"Then why accuse me of something that has nothing to do with me?"

"You want the truth?" he asks me.

"Yes, I want the truth." I fold my arms across my chest defensively. Here we go.

"I don't think *you* would, but I need to know *who* did and why."

"Take your fucking pick," I snap back. I know exactly who did this. This reeks of Camden, of *Bling*, but I don't give that away. I won't.

"What do you mean by that?"

"You said it yourself; all the shit that's going on here centres around me apparently. Hazard a guess. It could be any of the arseholes here." And it's true, even though I know who did this, bar a handful, any one of the people here could've been capable. Fuck knows what I did to deserve this... Oh, yeah, wait. Camden drew a line in the sand before I even arrived here.

"But you have an idea?" he presses.

"No. No, I don't have any idea," I lie. "So, if that's all?"

"Protecting people who've wronged you isn't brave, Asia, it's cowardly. Tell me who did this. Tell me who hit you," he says looking directly at my chin and the fading bruise that's clearly not as well covered as I'd thought.

"I fell out of bed," I shrug.

"Like Monk escaped Oceanside and got mugged?"

I don't answer. I've learnt that sometimes it's better that way.

Mr Carmichael sighs, then motions to someone behind me.

"This needs to be cleaned off. Bobby has the stuff you'll need to do that."

"Here we go," Bobby says, seemingly appearing out of nowhere. He dumps a bucket, a scrubbing brush, gloves and some cleaning solution by my feet then looks at me and winks. The filthy bastard.

"You want me to clean that off even though you and I both know I *didn't* do it? How the fuck is that fair?"

"It isn't," Mr Carmichael retorts. "But do you know what else isn't fair? My job, this *school* being on the line because not one person is brave enough to speak up." He's angry, real angry. I get it, but this is just the way it is. He, of all people, should know that.

"*No one* is going to talk. You know the score, Mr Carmichael. You know if you want retribution you have to deal with it yourself. That's the rule of the street. It won't change no matter how much you want it to. You took the law into your own hands. You understand how it works, don't you?"

"I want it to be different, Asia. I couldn't save my brother, but maybe I can help save some of you?"

"*Save* us? You know as well as I do, that's an impossibility. Wake the fuck up, Mr Carmichael."

He grits his teeth reigning in his anger before sighing heavily. "I'm not an idiot, Asia. I *see* what's happening and it *will* stop."

I bark out a laugh. "This is a school filled with criminals, *delinquents*," I spit that word out like the dirty thing it is. "You're going to have a battle on your hands trying to get this group of arseholes in line. Poke the lion and it'll rip you to shreds," I retort. Refusing to give him any more of my time, I bend down and pick up the rubber gloves, forcing them on my hands.

"Not on my watch, Asia. Things are going to change around here. I've been way too lenient," he mutters, almost to himself. Then to Bobby he says, "Once this is cleaned off, make sure you escort Miss Chen to my office. There's a few more things we need to discuss before the day is out."

"It would be my pleasure," Bobby responds. *I bet it would.*

"Fuck this shit," I grind out under my breath.

"Oh, and Bobby," Mr Carmichael says, stopping by his side.

"Yes?"

"When I'm done with Asia, you and I are going to need to have a discussion."

With that Mr Carmichael strides off leaving Bobby shitting a brick. Serves the fucker right. I don't like him. I hope he gets fired even if that does mean no more trips to the Tower.

For the next couple of hours, Bobby alternates between perving over me and pacing up and down whilst I scrub the wall clean. By the time I'm finished my arms are aching and my back is sore, any evidence of the tag all but gone.

"Good job, Asia. Scrubbing seems to be your forte," Bobby says, laughing, his gaze raking over me greedily. He steps towards me, leaning in a little too close as he bends down and picks up the bucket, spilling a little of the cleaning solution as he does so.

"Back off, perv," I snap, sidestepping him. "Haven't you got a story to put together so Mr Carmichael doesn't fire your arse for being an incompetent prick?"

He laughs again but with less bravado this time. "You just keep scrubbing and let me worry about that," he smirks, a puff of foul-smelling breath floating over me. I gag, pulling off my gloves before throwing them on the ground just as Camden rounds the corner. He's smoking a spliff like he hasn't got a care in the world. He looks between Bobby and me but doesn't even bother to hide the fact he's smoking a joint on school grounds.

Leaning against the far end of the wall he nods to Bobby.

"Put that out," Bobby grunts.

"Or what? You'll snitch on me?"

"Yes."

"Like fuck you will. Imagine what Mr Carmichael would have to say about how you've been turning a blind eye around here. Back off, old man," Camden retorts, scowling.

To my surprise, Bobby does just that. He backs up with the cleaning equipment.

"I thought you were supposed to be escorting me to Mr Carmichael's office?" I ask him, not particularly wanting to leave with him, but not willing to be left alone with Camden either. Lesser of two evils and all that.

"You're not quite done. Reckon you'll be finished in say... ten?" he asks, glancing at Camden for approval.

"That's about right," Camden agrees, pulling on the last dregs of his spliff before stomping it under foot. Bobby nods, gives me one last leery look, then walks off leaving me alone with the one person I really don't want to deal with today.

34

"I take it I have you to thank for this bullshit?" I say, scratching at my forearms. Some of the solution has splashed onto my skin and it itches like a whore with crabs.

Camden strolls towards me. He's got that spaced out look you get when you're high, and a lazy smile pulls up his lips. "Did you like it?" he asks.

"You're a dickhead! I thought you don't play games?"

"You moved the goalposts. Shit has changed." He shrugs, as though what he's done isn't a big. But he isn't fooling me, I saw the glimpse of regret in his eyes. Not that it matters now. His actions have a reaction, this anger is mine.

"What do you mean, *I've* moved the goalposts? I haven't done anything except try to keep my head down and survive this place!"

"You've been doing way more than just that." He barks out a laugh, too fucking high to keep his shit together. How much fucking Mary-J has he had? More to the point, why is he getting shitfaced during the middle of the day? He's normally so put together.

"You're fucking wasted. Go away," I say, giving him a look of disgust before turning on my heel.

"Don't you dare turn your back on me. I'm the fucking one you obey. *Me*, not *Ford*."

"Ford? I don't obey Ford and I sure as shit won't obey you. *Ever*," I growl, refusing to look at him.

"That's not what I heard. Pretty sure he fucking owns you now," Camden snaps back.

"What did you just say?"

"You heard me. The prick has you by the short and curlies, doesn't he? Quite literally. "

My face flushes red, heat prickling my skin and rising up my chest and neck as I spin on my feet. "Shut-up. You don't know shit," I retort angrily, shoving my fingers into his chest.

"I know enough. I have eyes everywhere, Asia. Every-fucking-where," he grinds out, his eyes narrowing at my hand pressed against his chest.

"What I choose to do and who I choose to do it with is up to me, Camden. Do I need to spell it out to you? I don't need your permission to do jack shit."

His head snaps up, the kind of languid heaviness in his limbs from the marijuana suddenly disappearing. "One of these days, you *will* be mine, Asia."

Something about the conviction of his words has me trembling but not with fear, with something far more unnerving. "Fuck you, Camden, or should I say *Bling*? You're all mouth. You don't rule me, and you *never* fucking will."

He steps closer, shaking his head. "Don't test me, Asia. *Don't*. I could hurt you." It's a warning, a threat even. The thing is, he doesn't seem happy about it. If anything, he looks resigned.

"Then do it! Fucking *do* it, Camden. Stop talking about it and get on with it. But let me tell you something, there is nothing, *nothing* that you can do to scare me. I can deal with your little lap dog Monk. I can deal with your little girls. I can deal with your *threats*. You cannot break me!"

"You don't fucking get it, do you?" He slams his fist into the brick wall. His fist splits, blood seeping from the wound.

"No. No, I don't get it." And I really don't. Why can't he just let it go?

"This is the law of the street, Asia. This is the law *we* live by. *Honour. Respect. Retribution.*"

"Not me. I've never lived by those rules," I lie.

"Yes, you do, and you know it. There are no white picket fences for the likes of us. This place here, it's a fucking pipe dream, papering up the cracks, trying to mould us into something we're not. You know as well as I do that it's too late for us. There's no changing even if we wanted to. We'll go back to Hackney and slide right back into the roles we left behind. Even here, we can't hide from them. *I* can't hide."

"You want to?" I ask, taken aback from his admission.

"Fuck!" he exclaims, running a hand over his face. "There's no hiding, no running. There's nothing good, not for the likes of me."

"You can make a different choice. It doesn't have to be that way." But even as I say the words, I know they're a lie. He's right. Of course, he's right. I might have told Mr Carmichael that I don't follow the rules on the street, but I've lived on the fringes of them my whole life. I have my position in the order of things, just like Camden does.

"The only choice I was able to give you was back in Hackney when I offered you a place in my crew. You turned me down, but worse than that, you made a fool of me in front of my people. Then I come here, reveal who I *really* am, and it still doesn't make a difference. You turned me down a second time." Genuine hurt passes over his features and it throws me. Why does he care so much? I shake my head, refusing to let him get to me.

"What the fuck else was I supposed to do? Roll over because you're someone I once admired? Thank you for setting Monk on me? Back down like a good little girl," I seethe. He winces, my words having the desired effect. Good.

"I told you I didn't have anything to do with his shit! Jesus, Asia, I knocked the prick out *for you*. I allowed you retribution, *payback* and now my crew is screwed up over it. Now my name is mud!"

"Why fucking bother if you dislike me so much?" I ask, but he talks over me, raging now.

"And after all that, you still chose *him*."

I laugh. I can't help it. I laugh so hard that tears of mirth, or maybe hysteria, spring from my eyes. "Really? I wouldn't have needed to seek Ford's help if you hadn't set Monk on me. He's had my back this whole time. Whilst you... you forced my hand. I had *no choice*. None."

"How many more times do I have to say it?"

"Stop with the bullshit, Camden. Admit it, you set Monk on me. *You* did all of that!"

"No."

"You're a liar!" I scream, not giving a shit now, as if I ever did before.

Camden flinches and despite the marijuana his body is

tense, wound tight. He's the complete opposite of relaxed now. Blowing out a long steady breath, Camden does something that surprises me. He reaches up and cups my cheek, brushing the pad of his thumb against my bottom lip. He's gentle, so very gentle and I don't know what to make of it.

"When I heard you were sent here, I contacted Monk. I might have told him to make sure you knew I was watching, even from afar." His topaz eyes flash with anger even though his touch remains gentle. "But I *swear* to you. Monk went rogue. What he did; hunting you down with his wolves, fucking with your art, that wasn't down to me." His hand drops away, his shoulders hunching over a little.

"And yet Monk's still a part of your crew. He's still gunning for me, despite everything. At least Ford had the courage to cut Red and Bram from his crew for what they did..." I breathe heavily, shaking with anger. "And fucking with my art? What have you *just* done, if not that? A tag is sacred. You know that better than anyone." I push against Camden's chest, forcing him backwards against the wall I've rubbed clean. He doesn't try to stop me. When his back hits the brick, I do something really fucking stupid, I press my body flush against his. Despite everything, my skin heats immediately, just the same as the spot on my face where he'd been touching me.

"I don't have a choice about any of this."

I bark out another hysterical laugh. "You're their leader. *You* have a damn choice even when *they* don't."

"You don't fucking get it," he retorts, both anger and regret lighting his topaz eyes. "It's not as simple as that. Not for me."

"Then explain it to me."

He presses his eyes shut, nostrils flaring. "I can't," he rushes out.

"I thought you were the leader of the gang? I thought you held all the fucking strings," I mock him, repeating the words he said to me all those weeks ago. "What fucking gives, Camden?"

"We're all owned, Asia. Including me."

There's a truth to his words and a part of me wants to delve deeper, to offer him the opportunity to open up and tell me what he meant by that. A bigger, angrier part wants to chew him out. That part wins.

"I don't fucking care! You took my best friend from me and you've destroyed a family. Tracy needs Eastern, Braydon needs him. You fucking ruined them, then you tried to ruin me with this bullshit tag because your jealous of my *friendship* with Ford." My nostrils flare, my hands reaching for his top as I scrunch up the material in my fists. Just like before, we are both caught in the moment. Neither of us backing down. Neither of us winning. This feeling I have inside expands and grows. I hate him, yet why do I suddenly want his lips on mine? *Why?* "Haven't you done enough?" I whisper.

One beat.

Two.

Three.

Four...

Our eyes meet, his gaze is just as ferocious as mine. We've been here before, he and I.

"It's enough," he concedes, his arm wrapping around me now, pulling me tighter against him. "For what it's worth, *I'm sorry.*"

"You admit responsibility?"

"I admit that I've not been the man I know I *should* be. I admit that it kills me to watch that prick Monk get away with what he's done and that I *can't* do more. I admit my poor imitation of your tag was a low fucking blow. I admit that my jealousy is making me insane..." He breathes out heavily. "I admit that I can't do a thing to change any of it."

I'm panting hard, my breath coming thick and heavy. My body trembles with the anger, from the feeling of his body flush against mine and his arm wrapped firmly around my back.

"But it won't stop..." I say, knowing it to be true.

"I *don't* want any of this, Asia," he sighs, not confirming or denying my point. Regardless, his response surprises me. So much so it takes me a while to respond.

"I can't forgive you. You could've made a dozen different choices but your actions, or lack of them, have shown me who you truly are. Just because you didn't give Monk the go ahead to chase me down like some rabbit and screw with the one possession I own that's truly mine, doesn't mean you're not responsible for them just as much as he is."

"It's complicated, Asia."

"That's not fucking good enough!" I shake my head, not willing to listen to any more crap.

"Asia..." he starts, then slams his mouth shut.

"Say it, Camden!"

He grits his jaw. I can see his internal struggle. "He has something on me," he finally admits.

"Who, Monk?"

Camden closes down, refusing to answer, but there is fear in his eyes that is undeniably real. What's going on here? What's he hiding? Or is this just another game he's playing to fuck with my head?

"How do I know that this isn't more bullshit? Just another way for you to get inside my head and screw with me, just like you screwed with Eastern."

"You don't."

"No fucking kidding. You were willing to let Monk have me if I lost the fight... You'd sell me out in an instant given half the chance. That much I do know."

"You're wrong. I knew you wouldn't lose."

"How? How could you possibly know that."

"Ford. I might dislike the fucker, but he knows how to fight. He taught you well. I also knew you wouldn't let Monk win. I see a lot of myself in you. You're a survivor and you protect the ones you love."

"Don't make me laugh, you don't belong to anyone, remember? I'm *nothing* like you," I spit, pushing away from him, disgusted that he'd even think we are similar in any way. I try to break free, but he grabs hold of my upper arms.

"You don't belong to anyone either, Asia, but that doesn't stop you from protecting the ones you care about. Trust me, we're alike," he insists, holding me as tightly as I'm holding onto him. I hadn't even noticed that my hands had found his chest once more.

"I belong to Eastern," I admit, knowing in that moment it's the truth. "He's my best friend. I *love* him. I tried to protect him. You could've asked someone else to do that job. You could've let him go."

"I know." Camden lifts his hands and rests them on my shoulders. "And now I'm giving him back... It's all I can do."

"What? What are you saying?" I ask, confused. "That's not fucking funny, Camden."

"Carmichael needs to see you. I suggest you go and find out why." He pulls himself upright, straightening his spine. With one last broken look, he pushes past me. I watch him walk away. After a few steps he pauses, then turns to face me.

"If you're smart, Asia, you'll make the right choice." With

that he walks away and disappears around the side of the building leaving me wondering what the hell he meant by that.

Turning on my heel, I run to Mr Carmichael's office hoping to God this isn't another one of Camden's games but knowing in my heart that it's probably going to be the start of many.

35

I hear talking from behind his closed door when I get to Mr Carmichael's office. The voices are low, muffled. Pressing my ear against the wood I try to listen but even then I can't make out what they're saying. Without even bothering to knock I open the door roughly. It slams against the wall.

Half a second later my heart crashes inside my chest, trying its best to break free from my ribcage.

"Eastern…?"

I have to blink a few times just to make sure I'm not hallucinating. When I'm certain that he's here, I rush forward ignoring the fact that Mr Carmichael and Mr Burnside are both watching me intently.

"What the fuck are you doing here?" I breathe out, as he stands holding his arms open. I run into them without hesitation, holding him against me tightly. His familiar smell of smoke and apples fills my senses as I breathe him in. "Eastern," I mutter curling my fingers into his top.

"Hey, Alicia," he murmurs. His voice is hoarse, full of emotion that I can't even begin to unravel right now.

"It's Asia, arsehole," I choke out, swallowing the sob behind a strangled chuckle. Easing back, I look up at his face, at his brown eyes flecked with amber. They're different, harrowed. I know instantly that shit went down at juvie, but now is neither the time nor the place to find out what.

"It's so good to see you, Eastern," I say, and I really, truly mean it even though I don't understand why he's here.

"It's good to see you too." He steps back then, easing me out of his hold before sitting down. I stare at him, frowning. What's going on? Only then do I notice another man standing in the corner of the room. He's looking at me with interest.

"What's happening here?" I ask Eastern, looking between him and the guy I don't recognise.

"Sit down, Asia," the man says.

"Don't tell me what to do," I retort automatically, drawing a raised eyebrow from him.

"Please," Mr Carmichael adds.

"Asia, do as he says," Eastern insists. The look on his face has my arse plonking on the seat.

"Why is Eastern here? Is he starting Oceanside too?"

"That depends," Mr Carmichael says, drawing up a chair beside me.

"On what?" I look at him suspiciously.

"On whether you and Eastern agree to some terms," the unnamed man adds.

Eastern's face pales. I know him, I know that something fucked-up is about to go down. I narrow my eyes, folding my arms across my chest. "What terms?"

"I'm Chief Inspector Crown," the man says, introducing himself properly.

"And?"

"And your friend here is in deep shit right now," he says, pulling no punches.

"Talk about stating the obvious," I retort sarcastically.

"He's looking at a long sentence, Asia. A sentence that could mean time in both juvie and adult prison once he hits eighteen. Drug running of Class B drugs is a serious criminal offense," Chief Inspector Crown continues without batting an eyelid at my sarcasm. "Eastern is looking at fourteen years in prison..." He lets that statement hang in the air for a moment so that we can all digest it. "But his sentence could be lessened to a stay at Oceanside on one condition and one condition only..."

"And what's that?" I don't trust this fucker, and I certainly don't trust the look on Eastern's face.

"It's simple. We need intel on the drug supplier, the real kingpin to the outfit Eastern has been drawn into. We want to take him down and obtaining information about the gang Eastern is now a member of is the start of that. So far, he's refusing to talk."

Shit. I glance at Eastern but he's refusing to look at me.

"Well, that's easy..." I begin. Eastern's head snaps up.

"Don't, Asia. *Don't,*" he warns.

"This is your life, Eastern. You've been given a second chance to live it. Don't do this to your mum, to Braydon, to *me,*" I beg.

"Eastern," Mr Burnside interrupts. "We don't know each other and you've no reason to listen to a word I have to say, but I will tell you this... Over the past couple of months, I've got to know Asia pretty well. She tries very hard to hide the fact that she cares about people, but she does. She's made friends here despite her instinct to push people away. Do you honestly think she'll want to see you in prison for fourteen years of your life? Do you think, given what appears to be a very strong bond, that she'll survive all that time without you?" Mr Burnside asks. He's using his therapist voice to try and get Eastern to talk, but like me, Eastern doesn't buy it.

"You're right there, *mate*," Eastern snaps. "You don't know a thing about me or my relationship with Asia. I *know* how much she'll hate seeing me in prison, but it doesn't change a thing. I won't talk. Not know, not ever. I did the crime. *I'm guilty*. It's all on me." He looks at me then, pain in his eyes. "I'm sorry, Asia," he whispers.

The thing is, he and I both know he did it for his mum, for Braydon. He might not have made the right choice, but he did it to help them. Inside I'm screaming at the unfairness of it all.

"Why bring him here? Why dangle the carrot when you know Eastern isn't going to change his mind?" I bite out, feeling both incredibly sad and angry all at the same time.

"We were hoping that you'd help us with that," Chief Inspector Crown says. "You could save your friend from a seriously long time in prison."

Fuck. Fuck.

Eastern glares at Crown, his eyes narrowing. I watch as his fingers curl around the seat rests. I know my best friend and I know that he's about to lose his shit. If he rips into Crown now I know that this offer will be taken away in an instant. "Give us a moment?" I ask, looking between the three adults in the room. "I need to have a conversation with Eastern."

"Five minutes. I suggest you make this good," Chief Inspector Crown says, before leaving the room.

"You too," I say to Mr Carmichael and Mr Burnside. "This is between us. Can you give us this at least?"

"Think about this very, *very* carefully," Mr Carmichael says looking at me and Eastern both. If I didn't know any better, he seems conflicted as though he's not happy with what's going down here today. "I understand what's at stake," he says, looking between us both, "but I also know how the system works. How it works on the street. I *get* it. Don't do anything unless you understand how both your lives, and those of the ones you love, will change."

I know what he's trying to say. I know what agreeing to Chief Inspector Crown's terms will mean for us, for Tracy and Braydon too. The repercussions are huge. We're not playing games here.

"We get it," I say. Once they both leave, pulling the door closed behind them to give us some privacy, I turn to Eastern. "You have to do this. You have to talk."

"No." He shakes his head, gritting his jaw and getting that determined, stubborn look I know so well.

"Listen, you heard what Chief Inspector Crown said. They're going to put you away for a long time, Eastern. I don't want that for you. Your mum and Braydon need you…"

Eastern glares at me. "And what about you, Asia? Do you need me?"

I swallow hard.

"Even now, you can't admit it, can you?"

"This isn't about me, Eastern. This is about you, about your family."

"*You're* my family. Fuck, don't you know how I feel about you? Do I need to spell it out to you?"

"Eastern, don't…" My heart squeezes with pain, with… love. I love him like a friend, I always have. But I do know that if given the chance it could develop into so much more. Seeing him here today, knowing what's at stake makes me realise that. Why is life so fucking cruel?

"Bollocks to it," he grunts, standing. "I'm going to say this because it might be the only chance I get." Eastern grabs my hands then pulls me upright. "You're stubborn, pig-headed, determined and so fucking strong, Asia. I don't know any other person who's been through what you have and survived it."

"Eastern, stop," I whisper. But he doesn't stop, and my heart fucking breaks.

"You make me laugh, and my shit days are more bearable when you're by my side. You're talented and feisty and fucking insanely beautiful even with all the colour." He smiles then, a genuine, heart-warming smile that turns me inside out. "You're my best friend, and ever since we kissed. No," he says, shaking his head. "*Before* we kissed I knew I loved you and it's because I love you, love mum and Braydon that I will not put you all in danger to get me out of prison. *I refuse.*

"Eastern, I don't know what to say..." I mumble, feeling helpless for the first time in a very long time.

"I'm about to go to prison for fourteen years. Maybe, for once, you could tell me how you really feel?" He rests his hands on my shoulders, his thumbs stroking against my collarbone. "Think of it as my final wish..."

"You're not dying, Eastern," I choke out, even though this feels much the same.

"I may as well be. When I'm out of prison I'll be fucking thirty and you'll be married with kids, some famous street artist as rich as Banksy."

"That *isn't* going to be your future, Eastern, and it won't be mine either. You're going to do as Crown says and you're going to tell him what he wants to know to save yourself."

"No, Asia! This shit I'm a part of goes way beyond Camden and Hackney's Hackers. They're just small-time criminals caught in a web of grown-up gangsters. The guy behind this outfit is not to be messed with. He owns half of fucking London. *He's* the man they're after. They call him the King and we are all his fucking servants. He's the latest ruler in a long line of them." He shakes his head, turning his back to me, but I scoot around him forcing him to look at me.

"I don't care who the fuck he is. You are going to tell Crown what he wants to know because you love your mum and Braydon, because you love me... You're going to do it, because I love you like a friend," he flinches at that, hurt chasing across his features. "And a promise of so much more," I add gently, my heart squeezing inside my chest.

"You mean...?" His eyes flash with surprise, then hope, then fear. Eastern drops his head, his shoulders go slack. "Fuck, Asia. Why didn't I listen to you? It could've been so different. This is all my fault. I let you down. I let everyone down," he mumbles, swiping at his eyes. Like me, Eastern rarely cries, he's always so strong. Not this time.

Gently I cup his face in my hands, wiping at his tears with the pads of my thumbs. "Look at me," I say. He lifts his head and for a moment I just look into his eyes. "This is going to be okay. *We* are going to be okay."

He shakes his head. "You can't know that. Nothing is ever okay for the likes of us."

"If you can't trust that, then trust *me*... Please?"

I can see him mentally pulling away, shutting down and building barriers to protect his heart and those of the ones he loves, and I can't let him. I won't. Making a decision, I do what I should've done a long time ago, I let him in.

I act.

Leaning in, I press my lips against his, curling my hands in his hair and tugging him closer. A small sound of surprise releases from his lips, before he opens his mouth to my searching tongue. He tastes of home, of years and years of friendship and laughter. He tastes of the first tendrils of real, life-changing love. Moulding myself in his arms, our kiss bonds us, draws us closer, stitching us together and reshaping us into something *more*, something everlasting, something *powerful*. Yearning and want, desire and hope, bleed between us, forging us together. Though I'm scared, I know this is right. We belong to each other.

When we part, I take his hand in mine, squeezing it gently. "Do you trust me, Eastern?"

"Yes," he says simply.

"Then this is the plan. You'll stay here at Oceanside. We'll make sure Tracy and Braydon are safe and we'll deal with this together, okay?"

"Okay," he murmurs.

Half a minute later Crown, Mr Carmichael and Mr Burnside enter the room. Crown doesn't waste any time. "What have you decided, prison or Oceanside?"

Squeezing his hand for moral support, we all wait. When Eastern fails to answer, flicking his gaze helplessly at me, I answer for him. "Oceanside. On one proviso."

"And what's that?" Crown asks, giving me an assessing look.

"You promise to move Tracy and Braydon into protective custody, you provide them with a home and enough money to live without Tracy having to worry how she's going to care for Bray. Otherwise you can forget about Eastern giving you any juicy information."

"Or, I can just throw Eastern into prison..." Crown retorts with a shrug that's way too affected to be sincere.

I bark out a laugh. "Oh, come on. We all know if that was the case you would've done it already. Instead you bring

Eastern here knowing full well what we mean to each other and hoping I would change his mind. I have, so agree to the deal or *no fucking information.*"

I catch the glimpse of a smile pulling up Mr Carmichael's lips and respect fill his gaze. He nods, mouthing 'good job' to me.

"Fine. You've got a deal..."

"You'll keep Braydon and Tracy safe?"

"Yes. We have a witness protection scheme. They'll be safe, I can assure you both of that. But in return, I have one condition of my own that applies to you, Asia."

"And what's that?"

"We need more information on Camden, the leader of Hackney's Hackers. Find out all you can about his involvement with the King. Get close to him, join his fucking crew if you have too, I really don't care but get us information and I will ensure that not only will Braydon and Tracy be safe with new identities and a home rather than that flea infested flat they live in, but you two get a new start in life when you leave here. Camden managed to wangle his way out of a very long prison sentence to a short stay here and we have every reason to believe he's very much in the King's pocket. Camden's the key to it all and you, Asia, are going to unlock his secrets."

"What the fuck? Asia is *not* joining Camden's crew. Over my fucking dead body," Eastern snarls. He crushes my hand and I wince with the pain, but I don't try to protest because... because... Because there are things I need to understand about Camden too, and despite everything that has happened these past few months he has hidden depths I need to explore. Secrets that I need to understand.

"Take the deal or everything is off the table," Crown growls.

"It's a deal," I state before Eastern can say otherwise.

"Asia... *please*."

"Nothing changes between us, *nothing*," I say fiercely.

"Camden won't let you go once he has you. I know that better than anyone."

"Then you don't know everything. He's let you go, *for me*."

Eastern's forehead creases on a frown. "What do you mean?"

"Trust me, okay?"

For a long drawn out moment, Eastern just stares at me. His fingers loosen from around mine, but I refuse to let him go. This will work out. It *has* to.

"I trust you. I don't trust him..."

"Then do as I say, *please*," I beg.

And that's how after a further hour of Eastern divulging everything he knows about the King's outfit, he walks out of Mr Carmichael's office as a fellow student of Oceanside Academy and the real storm, the one that changes my life forever, begins.

To be continued in Reject #2 Academy of Misfits...

Available for pre-order here now.

AUTHOR NOTE

Thank you for reading this story. I hope you fell in love with Asia just as much as I did whilst bringing her to life. She's tough, determined, strong and doesn't take any crap lying down. As for the boys, they're only just beginning to show their true strengths and their fierce loyalty. Things may go a little awry in *Reject*, but by the final book it will get better, I promise. I don't ever do a story without a HEA and these guys will get one. They sure deserve it.

If you read the Academy of Misfists Playlist page you'll know that this story was inspired by the song "Bad Guy" by Billie Eilish. I remember surfing You Tube and happening across the music video and immediately thinking *'that's Asia'*. I watched it on replay a few times over before the muse insisted I jot down some ideas that had already been brewing from the inspiration I get in my day job. That night, I wrote a line: *"I was the kid your parents warned you about…"* and the story of graffiti writer, Asia, stemmed from there.

In truth, this story was already percolating a lot longer

before this point. My own parents fostered young children when I was in my late teens and early twenties. Each and every one of their stories have stayed with me to this day. From drug addict parents, to abusive homes and abandonment. It was inconceivable to me that these beautiful, innocent children could have gone through so much heartache at such a young age. It opened my eyes to a world that isn't always full of light and happiness, that there is darkness and pain. Having only ever been brought up in an environment where I was loved and cherished it devastated me to hear their stories, and whilst all of them are teenagers / young adults now (and thankfully in a much better place with homes and families that adore them) their stories and tough start in life never left me. I think that's why most, if not all my stories have that thread of darkness and gritty realism. Like Camden said, not everyone gets to live a life behind white picket fences. We aren't all blessed with happy home lives. A sad but undeniable truth.

This series, therefore, is dedicated to those kids who didn't get the best start, and to the ones who are still fighting to survive. This series is for you. Keep strong and if you need to, reach out.

Much love, Bea xx

For anyone who may need help, here are a couple of incredible charities within the UK that will support and advise young people and children who may need it:

https://www.childline.org.uk/

https://www.nspcc.org.uk/preventing-abuse/our-services/childline/

Made in the USA
Monee, IL
20 November 2020